Immortal Water

Essential Prose Series 145

Canada Council   Conseil des Arts
for the Arts   du Canada

ONTARIO ARTS COUNCIL
CONSEIL DES ARTS DE L'ONTARIO
an Ontario government agency
un organisme du gouvernement de l'Ontario

Canada

Guernica Editions Inc. acknowledges the support of the Canada Council
for the Arts and the Ontario Arts Council. The Ontario Arts Council
is an agency of the Government of Ontario.

We acknowledge the financial support of the Government of Canada.

Immortal Water

∞

Brian Van Norman

**GUERNICA
EDITIONS**
TORONTO • BUFFALO • LANCASTER (U.K.)
2018

Michael Mirolla, editor
Interior and cover design: David Moratto
Guernica Editions Inc.
1569 Heritage Way, Oakville, (ON), Canada L6M 2Z7
2250 Military Road, Tonawanda, N.Y. 14150-6000 U.S.A.
www.guernicaeditions.com

Distributors:
University of Toronto Press Distribution,
5201 Dufferin Street, Toronto (ON), Canada M3H 5T8
Gazelle Book Services, White Cross Mills
High Town, Lancaster LA1 4XS U.K.

First edition.
Printed in Canada.

Legal Deposit — First Quarter
Library of Congress Catalog Card Number: 2017955487
Library and Archives Canada Cataloguing in Publication
Van Norman, Brian, author
Immortal water / Brian Van Norman. -- First edition.

(Essential prose series ; 145)
Issued in print and electronic formats.
ISBN 978-1-77183-243-4 (softcover).--ISBN 978-1-77183-244-1
(EPUB).--ISBN 978-1-77183-245-8 (Kindle)

I. Title. II. Series: Essential prose series ; 145

PS8643.A555I46 2018   C813'.6   C2017-906458-4   C2017-906459-2

For Susan

Your old men shall dream dreams,
your young men shall see visions.

—JOEL 2:28

Spring—The Past

It is a hard thing to grow old. It is not easy as one's limbs grow stiffer, each function less exact, when each thought is more memory than hope. Yet so go the days that are the ghosts of what was, with the dull recollection of a change that came, and we were suddenly no longer young.

The old do not view the world from a height, softened by mellow sunset, bathed in streams of prophetic light. That is for the dead perhaps; away from the prison of a gnarled body and aged mind, freed from the narrow sickbed and the awful pangs for the past. For that is the worst of it—remembrance—of sinews that furled like waves in a storm, that muscled through the day's toil and barged like a bull through tavern doors; of legs that were fearless of the long travel and loins that were fearless of night; of hands that grasped what the eyes desired, of eyes that were clear and bloodless and peered bravely into the passionate distance. Our ignorance was our comfort.

Immortality, or its illusion, is the greatest gift of youth.

∞

These were the thoughts of Juan Ponce de Leon as he wrote them in his private journal. His calloused hands were accustomed to the toil: practiced from writing ships' logs, colonial reports, military commands — the bureaucratia of governing. Yet their thick fingers threatened to strangle the quill as it dipped from ink pot to parchment. He had never liked writing, finding it drudgery. Still, he'd discovered himself more often these days seeking solace in the measure of words; making some sense of this quixotic voyage upon which he was now embarked as its captain-general, and chief dreamer.

For an instant he glanced up from his chronicle through the leaded mullions of the ship cabin's transom. Outside he glimpsed birds in flight, a flock of gulls flashing white against a hammered grey sky. They moved west, the birds; flying so quickly. If only his ship could find some air and race after them with the speed of their flight. Then he might reach his dream in time; just, in time. It would all be so simple then.

He felt a sensation of apprehension. With his advancing age he knew this voyage must find success or he would be reduced to nothing; a mere old man unheard and undone. And he, who had once held so much power, would have only the spectre of that power to haunt him for what remained of his life.

His thoughts delved briefly into the past. They settled

on that bitter day of the trial at Santo Domingo, when his powers had been stolen from him, when he had been humiliated. It was that day which had birthed this voyage, those motives which drove him now. They would only resolve themselves when he had accomplished his vision. There was urgency in the scratch of his quill as he put it to parchment recording his past. At the moment it was all he could do.

∞

The years passed more quickly as we grew used to them. Yet we were too busy to notice. The wine warmed in our mouths and began to leave a stale taste, for we were changed: still strong, still ferocious ... but seasoned. We travelled then the tracks to our dreams. And other roads, smoother, enticed us along their elusive paths. The highwayman of dreams is necessity, however, and most of us fell prey to him. There was wood to be cut and water to be drawn and a man must somehow make his living. The settled life is the hardest of all: knowing you've stopped by the roadside, knowing your journey is done. Still, even among old men there are dreamers.

And that is why I followed Columbus.

He was a dreamer, yet his feet were solidly on the road. Each step was measured, each league planned. Even when his dream was ridiculed, when he was called a fraud; even when we lesser men who had followed him were near to mutiny when the food had run out and the water was brackish and scurvy gnawed at our mouths and his road seemed empty and endless; still, he was sure.

The sea, he said, is the road to the new. The sea is not endless. The sea must have shores. And so he carefully crafted his dream. From the tomes of Galileo he sought knowledge. From the tales of Galician fishermen he learned the way. Even from the earth's curve he determined the distance. And then he made others believe in his dream and hauled us up from our cozy ditches and took us again to the travel.

∞

It had taken the remains of his treasury to outfit this voyage and two months to attract the best men to carry it through. Even more time was lost in the blizzard of paperwork necessary in order to leave behind the known world when one embarked on an exploration. These were normal events and he was accustomed to them. But his deception had caused yet more delay as he'd shaped the required ruses to dupe the Viceroy's officials. He had made them believe that what he was doing was not actually what he intended at all.

He now lived that lie to attain the truth.

So he watched carefully as the ships were loaded: first with stone ballast supposedly to furnish the foundations of a colony, then with huge barrels of fresh water and salted meats to see them through the voyage and supply the burgeoning settlement, and finally the armaments required to protect them. He knew from past experience the weapons would surely be needed to fight those guardians of the secret he sought. They were fearless warriors; a threat even to the accomplished *conquistadors* he had brought with him on these ships.

Then the zealot was brought aboard. For each voyage of discovery, each conquering of indigenous tribes, occurred only through the benefaction of Holy Mother Church along with her crusading minions, of which the friar was so insistent a part. Juan Ponce had tried to block his inclusion but to the powers of the Inquisition there could be no argument, no matter how distant the old world from this one. The monk's purpose was to spiritually support the new colonists in their creation of a community and to evangelize the natives. In his mind Juan Ponce knew there would be no community and the Calusa would never submit to the Church. They were the killer pagans he knew he would meet when they landed. They were what stood between him and his mystic goal; they and this sacrosanct zealot.

But another, more exotic creature soon caught his attention. Following the cleric from the dock up the ship's plank came the oddest yet most significant of this journey's elements: a single woman. She wore the accoutrements of a servant: a loose fitting gown over kirtle and petticoat, the gown dyed black in Spanish fashion, matching the river of her hair. Her eyes were the colour of submerged stone. Those eyes could blaze up to burnt umber with anger or passion, but otherwise they remained dark and impenetrable.

She was Calusa: an offering given him when he'd first found their land. After the battle with the Calusa, a slaughter on both sides, the natives driven off, she had mysteriously appeared. He'd thought she'd been sent as a kind of ambassador. He'd wanted to learn from her of her land but she would not tell him. Those onyx eyes remained adamant, her voice stayed silent. So he'd given her a Christian name, unable to pronounce her native one, and placed her in his household as a servant. Yet now she mounted the ship with her head raised like a noble, disdaining all those who watched her come aboard.

After nine years of servitude she had come to him surreptitiously. Even then she had claimed to be a witch. It was she who had planted the seed of this voyage but he could not be sure, even now, if she had been telling the truth; could not be certain if her tale came from something deeper, darker, no less than retribution. But she was an animal, without a soul according to the Church, thus incapable of intricate motives. He could only trust his judgement, not knowing what the future would hold, or the extent of her part in it.

With the loading done, cargo stored, the tide correct, the men set to cast off, he had come aboard last of all. This was his expedition. Because it was his, the others had joined for their various reasons ... greed mostly. They thought Juan Ponce de Leon a good bet: tough and experienced, a man who would lead them to treasures such as Cortez had done, or to found a new outpost as had Balboa; or become wealthy by enslaving natives in the way of Velasquez. They could not have known then how much he had changed, and he could not tell them for fear they would think him insane.

His goal was more precious than gold or power. But he could not share it. Only the witch, who was there to guide him, only she knew. And he thought the zealot suspected something. So he slept with the witch and prayed with the zealot in the hope that one or the other would bring him success.

∞

That voyage accompanying Columbus had brought us to a New World, a magical place of jewelled lagoons, of warm beaches and emerald mountains which rose so suddenly from the sea. And the Genoese became a sea-god: Viceroy of those new Indies; a pale Neptune to the naked brown bodies which gathered about him in welcoming swells as his booted foot found first purchase on sand.

One cannot know what occurs to a man when he has discovered the crown of his dreams. But if God's light ever shone in a human face it did on that day in the smile of Columbus. His vision is mine now, the sea my road too. I search for a virgin water so sweet it will bring me youth again. Would old Columbus have believed this?

I hardly believe it myself.

∞

They had come prepared. He had seen to that. This was his second voyage to *la Florida*. The first had been much different from this: into the void of the undiscovered, a search west with no thought beyond finding currents, wind patterns and new territory. He'd had no idea then of the land he would come upon and claim; no dream beyond mapping. A practical exploration back then; not like this one at all.

His ships were stout Galician caravels: sturdy, dependable vessels built to roll with the ocean yet cross the sudden shoals of a reef. They were sixty tuns, square-masted, with lateen rigged mizzens which could sail them within ten points of the wind. Juan Ponce de Leon was proud of them. It is best, he thought, to have practical ships when embarked on a voyage of dreams. But now they were be-calmed three days out from Hispaniola. There was nothing anyone could do. The ships' passengers were left to private device. They came up on deck for the air and the sun. Each engaged in their own interests while their captain-general sat below in his cramped cabin, staining his hands with indigo ink, adrift on a sapphire sea.

A knock on his door disturbed him.

"Enter," he murmured half to himself.

The door swung open. On the threshold stood Alonzo Sotil, ship's pilot and navigator. He was a young man but had been taught his trade by the master, Anton de Alaminos, and was truly skilled. He wore a short, close fitting doublet and hose with slashed breeches, affecting the latest fashion even aboard ship. Juan Ponce was often amused by his youthful foibles but just now the interruption rankled.

"Well?" he muttered.

"Captain-general, the second watch has been ordered to stand to," Sotil replied.

"That is why you disturbed me?" Juan Ponce returned in rougher tones.

"Sir, we are drifting. There is no wind and we are still moving north-east in some current."

"That is to be expected. You studied the ship's log from my last voyage, did you not?"

"I did, sir, but you indicated that particular current ran just off the coast of Florida. My calculations put us far from there."

"Perhaps the current has shifted, perhaps it is another current."

"Whether or not that is so, the fact remains we are off our course."

"You expected to reach Florida so easily? Sotil, these are mostly uncharted waters. Be patient!" Juan Ponce replied harshly. He had waited a long time for this; no man wanted more to reach landfall than he and time ticked inexorably on; but he had schooled himself to waiting. The pilot had yet to learn that skill.

"It is my duty to report my concerns," Sotil said stiffly. "I can see you are busy. I'll be on the aft castle if you require me."

"One moment, pilot," Juan Ponce softened his voice to halt Sotil's exit. He was too old a sea hand to let the matter drop. Sotil would depart and then fume to himself at his post. Juan Ponce did not want his pilot frustrated. He placed a hand on the younger man's shoulder. "You have done your duty, and I appreciate it. This calm has had its effect on me, too. But I have been through this before, with Columbus. It lasted for days. It seemed as though it would never end."

"You were with Admiral Colon?" Sotil murmured in wonderment. "I never knew."

"On his second voyage out," Juan Ponce replied. "He never liked the Spanish form of his name. He was Genoese by birth."

"But his son, the Viceroy, he uses that name ..."

"The son is not the father," Juan Ponce retorted bitterly.

Sotil was not a stupid man. He heard the antipathy in his captain-general's voice. He knew some of the history behind that hatred. It would not be healthy to prick such a delicate matter.

"I fear heavy weather, sir."

"Then we must meet it," the older man replied. "What choice have we? Whatever the weather you will deal with it but now I have other matters to attend. The colony must be planned for the day when you bring us to our destination."

The praise had mollified the young man's pique. He departed smiling and thoughtful. His captain-general was a gruff, sometimes difficult leader but he was Juan Ponce de Leon, one of the last of the *conquistadors*. He had once been powerful. He would be again when they birthed this new colony. And Alonzo Sotil would be there from the beginning, to become rich and important. He was impatient for it.

But the older man was lost in contemplation. Already he had returned to his desk and retrieved the quill from the ink pot. For a moment he stared just above the desk at his family coat-of-arms, the shield of Leon. It stood for something: his history. Not just his own life but those of his ancestors and his progeny, too. It set pen to parchment again.

∞

Those early years I recall so clearly: the winding streets of San Servas, the hot, light azure of the sky and the brown-shouldered mountains surrounding my home are the clearest of my memories. Home was always a place of flowers. They bloomed on vines and in window boxes. Their brilliant hues lit the household in rainbows. For my mother possessed a love of flowers surpassed only by that for her children. She treated both with such gentle nurture that, if the flowers were pretty my sisters outdid them, and my brothers and I grew like strong mountain pines. She was the gardener of us all.

And over us all, like the weather in his distant moods, ruled my father. I have no doubt he loved his family though he was a man more to learn from than love. I have absorbed his lessons, I think, too well. My son, too, is as distant from me as was I from my father.

Perhaps it was he who actually began this. I can recall that exact moment when my childhood ended. It was a warm morning. I was ten years old. I played with some village lads after prayers and we were joined by an older boy. He was the smithy's son, big, like his father. There was an argument over coloured stones, a game we played then, and I decided to prove the lout wrong. We fought my first battle and I, the novice, was beaten. In tears I ran home to my mother. Usually she would dry my tears and comfort me with willing arms. But on this day news of the fight had somehow reached my father. He took me from my mother and led me to his chamber. He sat me before him on a stool. I still remember his words.

"It is time to understand just who you are." His voice was like ice. "It seems I have left you too long with your mother. You cling to your tears like a woman. You are Juan Hernando Ponce de Leon, son to the Lord of Villagarcia, nephew to Rodrigo the Marquis of Cadiz. You are a noble of ancient lineage. Certain behaviour is expected of us. Do you understand what I am telling you?"

I nodded, my trepidation stopping my tears.

"Good then. Now, from this shameful incident I shall teach you two lessons. First, you must never again accept a peasant's challenge. He is beneath you as dust to your feet. And second, tears are not for gentlemen. Peasants may bawl and women weep and children may howl to their hearts' content, but you are none of these. Your tears are a sign of weakness, Juan. Guard your emotions. Be the private man. No one respects the fool who renders his feelings public. Soon you will be leaving this house to take your place at court. You must learn from your errors and never repeat them. You may go now, but not to your mother. You are a Castilian lord; seek strength in yourself."

At the time these were only words and I too young to comprehend them. Yet after this my mother changed. I do not know whether my father had spoken to her or if it was I who had transformed, but things were no longer as they had been. The flowers were only flowers, my sisters merely women and my mother ... well, suffice to say, my father replaced her. I followed his code. And so I missed something in life.

Unless ...

Unless I find the end of my dream, this voyage's far destination, and begin again.

To learn the things I was not taught.

2

For Age, with stealing steps,
Hath clawed me with his clutch.
—THOMAS, LORD VAUX

Autumn—*The Present*

Mountains of ocean *rolled around him beneath a lurid sky.*
The horizon crackled with forks of lightning, thunder boomed
above roaring waves. Each great wave was a green undula-
tion, a moving aqua emerald mass combed with hoary white
spume, the spume in streaks along its surface, sometimes
leaping in silver geysers like reaching hands.

He was on a ship, but no modern vessel. The ship heaved
and bucked beneath his feet and when he looked round he
felt even more distressed for this was a single hulled, weirdly
shaped vessel. He navigated from an aft-castle. He guessed it
might be some kind of ancient caravel. It was frightening for
him to be aboard a ship as small as the one he piloted now
particularly in such a powerful sea.

And he saw down the deck odd, powerful men, all wearing
red caps, climbing rope netting up to wooden crosstrees high
above him. They desperately took in sail up there, their bare
feet seated in hempen loops while he steered with a simple

rudder arm. The ship ascended water cliffs: climbing up, up the steep sweeping sides, then would slip out of control down the backsides of rollers at speeds which would soon take her straight to the bottom.

Lightning again split the skies. The sea rushed beneath him, climbing the flanks of the ship, spewing great waves across its decks. He could taste the tang of salt. The ship turned and turned like a spinning top between cliff crests of ocean. He felt himself dizzy with the ship's motion. He did not understand it; could not comprehend its whirling speed. It seemed set upon drowning him, horribly, within the green hands of a spectral sea. The hands weaved up through white spume to take him.

And then he awakens.

His head still spins. The taste of salt is in his mouth. His body is sheened in sweat.

Daylight shows through a crack in the curtains. It is a Sunday morning, he becomes aware; the day after his retirement party. Ross Porter wakes too suddenly from his sleep. It has been a fractional sleep filled with frightening, twisting dreams. He cannot recall much of them but the last one, the ocean. Before there had been another dream: some sort of foot-sucking quagmire through which he had slogged, a half-submerged meandering swamp trail lined with bearded trees whose branches interlaced above him. The dreams have been recurring a while now; months actually. They trouble him deeply.

He awakens with the unfamiliar pangs of a hangover: the kind brought on by cognac and cigars yet also by those unknown depths he has only just now in his dreams confronted. This hangover has brought much more than a queasy stomach and headache; it is the kind which displaces his mind.

Emily is dying.

His first truly conscious thought rattles him. His Emily: his partner, friend, lover, his wife is going to die and there is nothing at all he can do to save her. This is no dream. His awful thoughts stay with him as sunlight seeps through a chink in the bedroom drapes. It illuminates a shard of the room in hard gloss. His eyes follow the light. He glances toward the gifts from last night: the golf bag he will never use lying by the door and eleven volumes of Durant's *History of Civilization* still in their packing on the floor. He glimpses his rumpled suit hung over a chair with a rose in its lapel. The rose has withered.

His gaze lifts past the chair to the wall above the dresser. A portrait of the family hangs there: Emily before her illness, himself with a hand on her shoulder standing beside his son Robert. His grandson Justin, blond curls and impish round face, is tucked in the lap of Robert's wife, Anne, seated seamlessly beside Emily. He is more proud of that picture than any baubles of retirement. It represents something intimate, lasting.

He'd thought.

He reaches for water on the night table and misjudges the distance. The glass falls with a wet thud, staining the grey broadloom black. He swings his legs over the side of the bed and leans down to pick up the glass. Suddenly the room spins. A fluttering in his chest frightens him. He keeps his head down and tastes once again the burn of cognac. He gives himself a few moments, then slowly rises, testing himself, and goes into the bathroom.

Ross Porter is not accustomed to this. He is fifty-nine

years old. Things should not end at fifty-nine. And then, perhaps because of the hangover, or perhaps because of the withered rose and spilled water glass, Ross Porter apprehends that he will die; get old, and die. But first he must watch his wife perish before him; end hard in the grip of her disease.

He cannot know her death will also create a beginning. No one can read the uncertain future; particularly one's own.

He glares into the mirror at what he sees glaring back: touches of grey in his chestnut hair, lines on his narrow face, his pale blue eyes now steely in the mirror's harsh light. He must shake away the shadow and go downstairs to Emily. He must find a way to keep up appearances, bolster the spirit within her wasting body. He takes a hot shower scrubbing off the hangover, feeling the scald of the water wash away his perplexing tremors and gradually he becomes what she needs. She does not need the remains of last night: the self-indulgent husband drinking his way through a celebration of himself. He must think only of her today.

She is with me today. That is the true celebration.

∞

Emily is in the kitchen. She is humming some tune from the seventies, some love song he hardly remembers: the Bee Gees, before disco. She smiles at him.

"Well, you finally got up!"

She hurts him with that. She sees something in his face and swiftly changes topic.

"It was a wonderful party last night. How do you feel?"

"How do you think?"

"Are you alright, Ross?"

"Just leave it, will you?"

"I'm sorry."

Her apology distresses him even more. He is the one who should be sorry. He tries to lighten the mood.

"Hope I didn't make a fool of myself."

"Of course, you didn't. Want some coffee?"

"Please."

"I'll make you some toast."

"Just the coffee, thanks."

"The house should be quiet today; no little Justin running around." She smiles again and hands him the coffee. Their fingers touch purposefully. Her fingers are warm from holding the cup but warm in another way, too. They heal him a little.

"When did they leave?"

"Early this morning. Robert talked about you over breakfast. He was so proud of you. They've gone to Anne's mother's. He'll be back tomorrow to help us pack."

"I told him he shouldn't take days off work."

"Oh Ross, he's an executive."

"Still, you never saw me ..."

He stops as he sees her grasp the counter. She turns away from him, sure sign of her pain. He waits an instant, giving her time to adapt, then goes to her his hands on her shoulders, feeling her quiver. Her face has tightened into a mask; her eyes are opaque. The flesh at her temples is nearly transparent.

"Come and sit down," he murmurs.

He leads her to a kitchen chair, white wicker rustling as she sits. He stands over her looking into her face but she is not with him. She looks so frail he fears she will shatter.

"Can I get you something? Some water? Your pills?"

"No. It's gone now," she responds quietly.

For a while they sit, each observing the other, searching for something to say; just the proffering of conversation again. In the end he cannot stand the silence, the deep search of her eyes, and so speaks before he thinks.

"Maybe we should reconsider this trip. It might be too hard."

Her face hardens as she fights the pain, and his ruminations.

"Don't say that, Ross. I want to go."

Her voice is flat, soft ... frightening.

"We could postpone it until you're stronger," he murmurs.

"We both know that isn't going to happen. And I want to be with them when Robert and Anne take Justin to Disneyworld."

She is pleading now. Not overtly, but he senses it.

She should not have to plead.

"Okay, just a thought."

"Let me warm up your coffee."

She struggles to rise but is weak from the pain. She sinks back into the wicker chair. He can see she has exhausted herself, preparing his party when she should have been resting.

"You just take it easy. I think I'll go for a run. Clear my head."

"Are you sure you should?"

Her caution eggs him on in ways she could not understand.

"Hey, I might be retired but I'm not finished yet."

Even as it comes out he can see how his words affect

her. It is something only two people who have shared years together can sense. He's sorry he's said it. Prevaricating will just make it worse. Instead, he kisses her cheek. Warm porcelain on his lips.

"I'll just jog. If I feel anything I'll stop and walk. I'll be alright, Em."

"I know you will."

It has not been a good morning for either of them.

∞

He starts out slowly, warming into his pace. It has snowed in the night. A wind frosts the trees around him; all silver. The air is fresh and very cold. The hangover makes breathing hard. As he runs he thinks, delving into himself. Immersed in quiet intensity, he misses a corner he'd planned on turning. When he runs he can take stock of things; flow with his thoughts inside solitude. He can run through the pain, through those other thoughts trying to catch him.

If only I could keep running.

His route takes him along a railroad line flanked by maple bush. The wind makes the trees creak. There is a pond to his right, iced over now. He glimpses a fox lapping at its edge where the ice has not yet sealed in the water. Normally he would stop to watch but today the scene is lost on him. Already he is turning inward.

He recalls little Robert in the sand at the beach so long ago. A small, tanned Robbie with a pail and toy shovel laughing, tossing sand over his shoulder with Emily smiling behind him. He takes his son up in his arms and dips him into the waves near the shore. Robbie giggles as each wave brushes him. Water hisses upon the shore.

Then Robert last night, in his Armani suit, laughing with men so much his senior, comfortable with them; his father can no longer lift him.

Where has the time gone?

Ross descends an embankment. He slips on the snow, loses his balance and hits the ground hard. He'd promised to be careful. He rises slowly; testing himself. His right hip is numb. It will ache later in the day. He starts out again. The road is wet. A car passes throwing up slush. Grey dribble on his black sweats. He glares at the car. The driver ignores him.

He turns another corner, his body on automatic. The street here is not so frequently travelled and still snow covered. The houses have a sleepiness inside their cozy white blankets. He hesitates. This street has only one exit and he is not sure he wants that today. Then he mutters a challenge to himself, running harder, passing through the gate at the end of the street.

Polished granite gravestones stretch away over rolling acres. The wind taunts him: snow now in ghostly swirls on the hillsides. There is only the sound of the crunch of his sneakers on snow. He follows his route past the graves of his parents. He stops, not something he has done often, and returns to the plot. The headstone wears a mantle of snow. Engraved on its granite are the names of his mother and father. They are the long dead. Twelve years now. He recalls with a kind of loathing how cautious they had become in their age.

At his dad's funeral his mother had cried until he'd taken her into an alcove away from the embarrassed glances of other mourners. She'd looked to her son, her eyes pleading for answers. He'd comforted her, the son supposed to help his mother through her grief while not comprehending her grief at all. She'd been so desperate about how she would have to live alone.

She'd never really ever recovered. She moved into an apartment. She took up quilting. Still, she was not the same. Even her smile was wan and weak. He visited her often, he and Emily. Emily and she would talk together. He did not know how to talk to his mother, or rather, did not know quite what to say. Just two years later she too had died. The hospital had called it pulmonary embolism. Ross had called it what it was ... a broken heart.

∞

When he arrives home he finds Emily asleep on the couch in the family room. She is beautiful, the signs of her illness vanished in the softness of her sleeping face. She has lit a fire. The room smells of wood smoke and potpourri. He reads the paper in the chair beside her. Occasionally he glances at her, remembering how she had been: the strangely conservative teenager, yet with a streak of saucy sexiness so attractive to him. That unique girl appears in brief flashes: the smile which would light her face, her hair tumbling in auburn waves, the way her eyes widened faintly, just a little more blue, when he'd told her he loved her. Even as she became older she'd retained her vitality. He had always thought of her as healthy, always thought somehow he would be the first to go. And now this terrible thing has come and he will be left without her.

He thinks of her smiling in pictures. She'd kept the photos and scrapbooks of their life together. Ross was the history teacher, Emily the historian. Even when it had been hard, when the money was tight and Robert had come unexpectedly; still she'd made things seem easy. And now when again they will not be easy, he thinks, it will be my turn: an old man with his strength gone.

Why do I think of this now?

He cannot fathom a future beyond Emily. It is too dreadful to contemplate. He finally comprehends his mother; after twelve years he shares something with her he had not known before. He is just a little amazed at how life repeats in very small ways. He reads the quote of the day in the paper. He has read it each day for years, often writing it on the blackboard at school for his students to ponder. They'd made fun of him, but he'd kept it up. He felt it built character.

This day it reads:

> "For Age, with stealing steps,
> Hath clawed me with his clutch."

And he knew it was the truth.

3

*Old men have more regard for expediency
than for honour.*
—**ARISTOTLE**

Spring—The Past

Start of the night watch. Sailors in their red caps had gathered for supper, their wooden bowls filled with *caldareta*, fish stew. They ate heartily and watched as the boatswain doused the hot coals in the pewter brazier. Steam rose about them in clouds turned tangerine by the last rays of the sun. The hammocks where they would sleep were scattered about the deck, not hung up yet for the night. They took their meals to their mats as dusk loomed about them. On the after deck an apprentice turned the sand glass, calling the hour.

Juan Ponce de Leon looked over his ship from high in the stern castle. At first his gaze fell on the mainmast: its great sail spread, hanging limp in the breezeless dusk. Down the deck crowded with bales and barrels and men, twilight thickened. Amidships where the bombards rested some sailors had gathered. He heard the strains of a lute and considered the irony of such soft music amidst iron cannon. Even now he was losing sight of them. It always amazed him how quickly it grew dark in this new world. Behind him the watch leader lit the signal lantern. He noticed across the darkening sea a pinpoint of light where the lantern of his ship's sister glowed. And then came the watch leader's deep-throated shout.

"Good watch, starboard lookout!"

"Bright green!" came the reply.

"Port lookout, good watch!"

"Bright red, sir!"

In a moment the bow announced: "Bright top!" and the routine was completed. It would continue like this all night at each turn of the glass. It did not disturb the other sailors. Rather it comforted them hearing the ancient chorus, knowing their comrades kept the good watch. The hard voices of men can sometimes seem soothing, Juan Ponce contemplated. This is a good ship, he thought, and good men I have chosen.

He was the metaphor of his ships. Though of noble blood he did not, somehow, fit the part. Rather, he was the weathered lines of a seaman, the brazed skin of the labourer, the soldier's sinews and grim scars, the grey close-cropped hair of a monk. His clothing was practical. In the evening warmth he'd discarded his doublet leaving only a linen shirt, unlaced at the neck, and economic buckskin hose. Round his right shoulder was slung a thick leather belt and from it, at his left hip, hung the tool of his trade. In an age of earrings and jewelled fingers this man wore only a silver cross and Toledo steel at his side.

He was fifty-two years of age. Thirty-five of them had been spent fighting: against the Moors in Isabella's great *Reconquista* in Spain, then under Ferdinand among these islands against the native Taino and Carib. Now he knew he would fight again: the Calusa. He had a new king now, Charles. He had lived through three rulers, fought for them, conquered new lands for them, and in return they had given him—nothing.

The time had come for himself.

Age had wearied but not weakened him. Men still feared him. He found fear a useful tool but there were cracks in his armour now. He could feel them in the aches which had never been there before, in the shortness of days which had once seemed so long. His power waned as an outgoing tide. It was inexorable. Now was his final chance, he knew. There would be none after this. He stiffened a little at the thought. The helmsman beside him, thinking he had made some error, straightened as well and paid careful attention to his work. But his captain-general made no remonstrance. Instead he climbed down from the deck and went below.

The cabin was dark. He crossed to his desk to light the lantern which hung from a beam above it. Even in the dark he knew the witch was there. He could hear her breathing from the narrow bed. When the lantern was lit she continued sleeping, the long ropes of her hair coiling about her, her body dark brown and undulant. He studied her for a while: a beautiful, savage face. Then he turned to his desk.

∞

This woman with me, this Calusa witch, does not fear me as others do. She never has. Even when I beat her for her insolence she did not cry out, taking the slaps with hard silence. And when I had finished, panting from my anger, she would gaze through me with those obsidian eyes. Pain does not reach her. Love cannot touch her. The only thing she shows is passion. In that she is unlike any woman I have known.

I found her on that first voyage to Florida, or rather, she seemed to have found me. It was after the skirmish with the Calusa at the place I call Mantanca. It is not so strange to have named the place 'Slaughter'. The battle had been a costly one. The Calusa had no fear of us. We had lost men and they had lost even more. Only after they had surrounded my ships, their poisoned atlatls piercing the air, killing my men with their accuracy, only then did I order the bombards to open up. The natives retreated then, the guns' thunder terrifying them as their canoes cut away for the shore.

We had not been ready for their savagery. My exploration was merely to have been a voyage of discovery, not conquest. We had neither the tools nor the men to fight properly. We were preparing to depart when a strange thing happened. A single canoe appeared from the shore and came toward us. She was in it, alone.

My men in their rage had wanted to abuse her; send her back to her people as a sign of what was to come. But something about her prevented them; that fierce fearlessness I now know so well. Instead, they conveyed her to me.

I took her back to San Juan de Puerto Rico as a slave: to learn my language and tell me about her people. She revealed nothing to me but disdain, as if somehow her heritage was beyond mine. She was hiding something, I knew, but I could not discern it. After that, for a long time she became insignificant, submerged in my household as a menial. I'd forgotten her once I discovered I had other enemies far more treacherous than the Calusa. And when those enemies had overcome me, taken my titles and lands and power, when my wife had left and my children were estranged, when I felt old and cheated and insignificant, it was then she'd contrived to reappear before me. She spoke a guttural Spanish by then, her native tongue unable to lisp out Castilian purity; but what she said to me was stunning.

I had ordered wine. I sat on a balcony facing west. She brought me the chalice. Its silver chasing sparkled in the rays of the setting sun. The wine was rich and cool.

"Where is my steward?" I asked, surprised to see her, yet at that moment realizing that somehow the years had not seemed to age her.

"I told him I would bring this. I wanted to speak with you."

"And he allowed it?"

"He was persuaded," she said, smiling. It was not a smile but more a sneer, curling her full lips as she handed me the cup.

"Your place is below in the servants' hall. You dare come to me with ..."

"My place is with you. You are troubled."

"You know nothing of me."

"I know enough. Drink your wine."

"You risk speaking to me thus?"

"There is something beyond this wine you drink. Something secret and sacred. Something I know which will end your troubles."

"What can you possibly mean?"

"Water."

"You are a foolish woman, get out of here."

"Sacred water. I was sent to tell you this."

"You were cast out by your tribe."

"No. I was an offering. When Calos, my king, knew he would not destroy you, he sent me to you. But you would not listen."

"You would not talk."

"Not as a slave. That is how you treated me."

"Then what are you now?"

"A messenger. I have knowledge for you. I have watched you carefully. You were too proud in your past. You are not so proud now."

In that moment I was ready to strike her, beat her for her insolence. I stood. I towered above her yet she did not shrink from me. She even offered her face to receive the slaps. Then I found myself suddenly intrigued, as though she had cast a spell upon me. In that moment I changed. To this day I have no knowledge why. I have found she possesses an unusual power to confound the weak and unready. I thought I was neither but, in reflection, I was at my ebb when she chose to appear.

"Alright, I'm listening. Have your say."

"In my land, deep inside my country, far into the quagmires where men do not go, is a water so pure it brings youth to those who drink of it."

"I've heard this rumour before. It's mere fiction."

"I tell you it is real! I tell you now Calos is willing to share a part of his land where you can regain the power you've lost. You are an old man, broken by your troubles. I have something for you: this water, this chance to regain your vigour, to make of you what you once were."

"Why should I believe this ... what ... fortune telling?"

"Because I tell it. Because Calos is willing. Because

now I will be your woman and be your guide. And after all, now, what have you to lose?"

So she set me upon this strange voyage. She has promised me confirmation. She has promised to lead me to that sacred water. Oh, there is more to this than the telling. It is something in her beyond all telling. I felt it that day. I feel it now. I do not love her. She is too primitive. She is useful for only two things: as a release with her body and as a guide with her knowledge. I cultivate one to reap the other.

The sailors call her la Vieja, the old woman. They fear her. She has an old soul. Yet she has no idea what age she is. It seems unimportant to her. But then she is a witch. And there is the water.

∞

The scratch of his pen had awakened her. She muttered something, her eyes glittering in the lamplight. He knew what she wanted.

"Not tonight, woman," he muttered, "I have work to do."

"Making marks in that book," she said, smirking. "It takes your manhood from you."

The men despised her. They thought her merely an old man's senile whim. There had been trouble about it the first day out. But though she did not fear Juan Ponce, his crew most certainly did. He quelled their impertinence with harsh commands and a flogging for one of the ringleaders. Yet he knew there was talk. And the zealot, protected from punishment by his position, still stirred the men against her.

Despite his convictions, the monk hated her. She was all he stood for yet she had betrayed him by not accepting his faith. She had laughed at him and for a zealot that is the worst of responses. Even Juan Ponce did not dare do that, though he felt much the same. The monk had come on this voyage with a mission. Juan Ponce had taken him only because he was sanctioned by the Inquisition. So Juan Ponce used the zealot, as he used this woman, for his own design. He prayed and confessed and attended mass, though he secretly believed none of it.

"Go back to sleep," he muttered. She did not respond and within a few minutes she was again sleeping. He envied that in her. Once he had had that ability. Now age had stolen it from him as he found himself awakening too many times through the nights ... an old man's fragility.

He continued writing on the parchment before him. The ship's log lay beside it, untouched. He let it remain: plenty of time for that later. Right now he charted a different voyage.

∞

The day I first met him, Don Pedro Nunez de Guzman, Knight Commander of the Order of Calatrava, replaced my father. I was presented to him as his page, a position my father had secured for me. And as the great man shook my hand and my father humbled himself in the background, I was aware I stood in the presence of power.

He was a diminutive man barely taller than me, though I had only thirteen years and he was at the peak of his abilities. Unlike my father he was never officious. He would go about his affairs in an offhand manner with pleasant words for even the lowest of stable boys. Yet when he appeared at court, I strutting like a peacock behind him, the waves would part as he approached the throne. And King Ferdinand would invite my master to conversation, less the king and more the equal of Pedro Nunez de Guzman.

Those were fruitful years in the house of Guzman. For a lad who had known only harsh northern climes, the April freshness of Andalusia and the gentle moods of my new master were a far cry from childhood. Though I was but one of several pages, Don Pedro paid me special notice. A master swordsman and tactician, in his training yard I learned the things which sustain me now.

And then, of course, there was Seville. Seville too was a wondrous teacher. For the young rustic its streets were classrooms. The world came to the city up the muddy Rio Guadalquivir. Along its docks and in its markets one's senses were taxed to their full. I followed mine without hesitation. On long summer days I would wander until, footsore and weary, I would find a stool in some exotic tavern and the sights and smells of my lessons would mingle in a cup of sangria at the end of the day.

Yet despite the intentions of Don Pedro, I was not a prime student. By my seventeenth year I had mastered the arts of weapons and war and that strength had evolved for which now I am noted. But I lacked the finer touch. For music I had no ear and for the dance, no feet. When the ladies gathered on warm spring evenings around the fountains of Don Pedro's domain, I became stiff and formal. In the diversions of courtship I was lost. And that which gave me grace in the training yard turned me clumsy and bearish amid polished manners. My colleagues grew distant. None took the pains to discover that beneath such proper armour lay the pounding heart of a frightened boy.

In the training yard I became merciless, numbing those witty tongues with terror. I hurt them, every one, as I exacted my revenge. Thus my notoriety began almost without my knowing. Worse was the realization that now I would never be what I wished. I would not become Don Pedro. I would be my father instead.

∞

It was late when Juan Ponce extinguished the lantern. The dog watch had been called and taken its place. He was weary. He undressed and went to bed. But the witch awakened and with her passion aroused him despite himself. And the wind came up.

4

Wandering between two worlds, one dead,
The other powerless to be born.

—**ARNOLD**

Autumn—*The Present*

They drive south. *Snowbirds* now, Emily jokes. They follow a thousand mile asphalt route migrating south like the birds they glimpse high above in flying wedges. They speak of the birds, of their long flight and wonder how it is birds know their way. Mozart plays on the car stereo, 'Eine kleine nachtmusic' like flight, accompanied by the hum of tires.

They've prepared for this journey: through years of work and savings, of plans and dreams and annuities. Ross has spent a great deal of time on this, to get it just right, to ensure their crossing into the U.S. will be a secure one, to confirm their Florida ports-of-call will be ready and waiting. He has ensured Emily's medications are sufficient. He has had their car tuned and examined, filled with the necessary fluids, given new tires. He has supervised the car's packing just as a seaman would oversee cargo loading into his ship. On a journey of uncertainty it is best to be prepared.

Emily has packed carefully. She has arranged their

summer clothes in neat bundles: folding the bright colours of golf shirts and sundresses into their suitcases. The cases clicked shut with an air of finality. Robert and Anne had helped them. Justin had wanted to go along. He'd sat in the driver's seat and cried when they bid each other goodbye. Robert looked long and lovingly at Emily.

"So, I guess we'll see you at Christmas, mom," he said softly. "You take care."

It was all he could say.

"Don't worry, Robbie. The sun will be good for me."

Then they left the solid brick house which had been their home. It had somehow grown bigger as they had grown older and Robert had moved away. They had rented it now to a French teacher, a new girl hired by Ross' former school. She had loved its 'quaintness' as she called it, all the old things that were not old to them, the antiques which had never been called so before. Her freshness had bothered Ross, her thinking beneath her young woman smile that he was old and sexless.

As they left their town behind and the car crested a hill, Emily glanced back. Their town disappeared in the earth's curvature as one would see from a ship leaving shore. They both felt a twinge of regret. They were leaving all the familiar things which had made their lives full. The hills were covered with trees, bare now in November, old trees now. He had seen them younger. There were still patches of snow from that first early snowfall.

He recalled tying young Robbie's skates by the pond near the back of their house; remembering Robbie on the ice with his hockey stick. Ross would pass the puck and the boy would swing with his stick and plop to the ice: Robbie's face ruddy red from the cold, the pond ice like glass.

The pond is gone now, filled in and paved over, all part of the new town growing around him through the years. Robert's house is built where the pond was. He doesn't remember the pond. Ross does. He has grown old with the town. He is its metaphor. The lines on his face match the lines of streets on the town map he keeps in his workshop.

Perhaps it's just as well we're leaving.

"Ross! Watch those cars."

"Huh?"

"They're slowing down for Customs. Are you alright?"

He doesn't wish to be caught in daydreams. He answers back gruffly.

"I see them."

She turns her head away knowing it's not worth the argument.

They cross the bridge at Detroit and answer the usual questions: anything to declare, how long they'll be here ... edgy about Homeland Security; but the man in the booth is not what they expected.

"Where ya goin'?"

"Florida," Ross says. "We're retired. Spending the winter down south."

The Agent is a big man. He leans with difficulty out of his booth handing them their passports. He is a cheerful, compliant type; not at all the look Ross conjures of muscular Homeland Security. Still, the man has a gun holstered to his belt.

"You two don't look old enough. I got six years left, then I'll see ya down there! Have a safe drive."

Through the long flat of Ohio they travel. Late in the day they pass through Cincinnati and into Kentucky. They stay the night at a Days Inn. Their room has beige walls and two economical prints hung above the bed. It is clean, though. It smells of Febreze. Emily is tired from the drive. After dinner she goes to bed. Ross watches the news on television keeping the sound low. He doesn't feel like sleeping.

It is Monday night. He is not marking papers. He thinks about Andy Taylor, his assistant department head, his friend from his years of school. Andy would be working tonight. He was always diligent. Andy and his wife, Carol, had planned on joining Ross and Emily in some Florida Shangri-la. Emily gets on well with Carol. It would have been fine.

But then, last year, Emily had felt something wrong. She'd hidden it from him, making secret trips to the doctor so she would be strong when she told him. The dreaded word. The tears were his. She had done her crying elsewhere. Then came the operation and months of treatments. Emily with a scarf on her head; she would not wear a wig. She was always that way. He was the one denying.

Robert had called it unfair.

Was I so different? Bitter. Bitter.

"Are you coming to bed, dear?" Emily's voice comes past the blue light of the television.

"In a minute," he responds, trying to shut down the sound of his mind. "I just have to brush my teeth."

"We've got an early start tomorrow."

"I know. I'm coming."

What is her secret?

∞

The next day takes them up into the Appalachians. The hills are aflame with colour. Walls of russet and translucent yellow glow down the valleys, the sun like brass; far off they glimpse wood smoke curling up from a hilltop. Emily plans their stay on Sanibel Island. Ross will run in the mornings and they will have breakfast and swim. In the afternoons when the sun is too hot they will read. Ross can get started on Durant's volumes. Some days they'll take side trips to Naples or Sarasota or down to the Everglades. Evenings they'll walk the shore, walk for miles. They will have late dinners. They will go to bed early.

"That's just the first week," he reminds her. "Then we've got the mobile home park."

"Oh, I wish we could stay on Sanibel."

"We haven't got the money for that."

"Ever practical Ross. What would I do without you?"

"Likely have more fun," he says, smiling, for a moment forgetting his troubles.

∞

They drive through southern Georgia and begin to see Spanish moss. It beards the trees. They look like old men. Emily's metaphor. Emily says the trees look wise. She says it to make him feel better. The moss reminds Ross of his nightmares.

They stop for the night near Ocala. After dinner Ross jogs down a dirt road that runs through orange groves. The run loosens up his aches from the drive. When he arrives back he is pleasantly tired. He has not ruminated this time at all. The terrain so new and the trees aromatic, he has been able to put things aside. Emily phoned home to Robert while he was out. It is snowing that night in Ontario. It makes her feel strange to know she's in Florida.

They turn in early and Ross, despite his fatigue, dreams again.

It is not the dream of before, not the sea. This one is jungle-like. This one has visited him several times. Familiar. Muck, lacing tree branches, deep greens and black water. He does not know yet that this dream will obsess him, shake his life as no other thing has. Eventually it will become the *dreaded dream*: the dream that returns time and again while he searches for its meaning.

∞

He is driving a car; driving down a dirt lane under mammoth trees smothered in Spanish moss that sways as if it were conscious. He is on a quest with some unnamed goal. There is someone else in the car with him: a woman—some ethereal presence. Yet he can't take his eyes off the corridor running between the trees to see who it is. The track is precarious. It is rutted and narrow and overhung with branches like fingers which scrape on the roof of the car. He worries about his car's paint. He keeps to the narrow trail. The person with him is some kind of guide. She is not Emily. He does not know her, does not even attempt a look at her. The path narrows further. Danger on either side. Then the trees form a wall in front of them: a green leafy mass. The car can go no further.

He stops the car and gets out. The air about him is thick and hot. It stinks of mould. He can feel sweat trickle down his back. He spies an opening, an aperture through the branches, forbidding and shadowed. He sees his hand in front of him pointing down that dark tunnel.

"Don't go in there, Ross," the woman's voice utters. Not Emily's. "You'll be alone."

"I am alone," he says back.

A hand on his shoulder. Cold hand. He shrugs it off but it returns; on his shoulder like ice. She is trying to stop him from following his path.

"Ross. Ross?"

A woman's voice; this one familiar.

He comes heavily back to consciousness.

Emily shakes him gently, a silhouette in the darkened room.

"Are you alright, Ross? You're sweating buckets."

"I was ... dreaming."

His heart is beating too fast, pounding. He is drenched in salt sweat. Emily turns on the light. The light snaps off the final fragments of the dream.

"Are you sick?" she asks quietly.

"No. No, I'm alright, Em. Just a nightmare. I've never ... it felt so real."

Somewhere in the back of his mind: old, bearded trees. Spanish moss.

A guide?

"It's passed now?" she says.

"What?"

"Your dream?" Her voice is filled with dread. She is frightened.

"What time is it?" he asks.

"Nearly five. What was it about?"

"What?"

"Your dream."

"I can't remember," he says, lying.

"Do you want to get up?"

Anything not to think of trees.

"Might as well"—he tries to sound calm—"get an early start. Beat the traffic."

"Are you sure you're alright?"

"I'm fine." He hears himself sounding stronger.

Yet the dream recurs in flickering traces as he drives. The yawn of the passage winks in and out of his mind. The voice warning him. Ross finds it hard to concentrate. Who was it with him? Who told him not to enter the passage? Emily discerns something is wrong. She knows better than to say anything.

When the rainstorm hits it comes with a fury. The rain pelts against the windshield, so hard and heavy the car's wipers have trouble keeping up. Neither of them can speak now as Ross concentrates on the road and Emily marvels at the force of the storm. There are purpling clouds and splits of forked lightning and always the incessant downpour. From beneath the car waves seem to wash up from the road. It is hard for Ross to hold the car straight.

There is a truck ahead. It is splashing up water, along with the rain pouring down, making it nearly impossible to see. Ross considers pulling onto the shoulder but if he does, he thinks, he will become an obstruction. A vehicle might clip his rear left. He cannot stop. Road travel is really a matter of inches. Too far to one side or the other and vehicles collide. He cannot pull off. He grips the wheel tightly, Emily notices and gasps as he pulls into the passing lane. For a moment the liquid spatter conceals everything. For a moment he must drive on faith: that the truck driver knows he is there, that no one comes up behind him, that he will not hit what might be ahead. It is a very long, dangerous moment. Then suddenly he is past the truck's splash and, despite the rain, can see again with his car's wipers smacking back and forth at full tilt.

He relaxes slightly yet remains alert. The storm lasts twenty minutes. It is twenty minutes of tension which exhausts them both. And suddenly, the sun reappears, as though nothing had happened. The rain has soaked into the ground or drained efficiently from I-75. Only the trees droop lower, their grey beards weighing them down.

They drive in silence until they reach Tampa. The road becomes choked with traffic. It seems the storm has had its effect here. There has been an accident. They pass the scene of the mishap: a transport truck has run over a car. The car is crushed, the truck still on top of it leaning at a precarious angle. There are firefighters desperately trying to free the people trapped inside. Ross does not think they will be alive. The storm takes certain travellers for its own. They are thankful it is not them. Emily talks about tricks of fate, how someone could simply be out for a drive and suddenly life would change, or end, meaninglessly.

Cancer is like a car accident.

∞

On the night of her birthday she told him everything. The cancer not cured: the tortures of surgery, chemo and radiation all for nothing except they have given her a little more time; Ross, a little more time. He had no idea what to say to her, how to comfort her through his own shock. He could only embrace her wordlessly. The candles on the birthday cake remained lit as the two held each other. She'd been making a birthday wish when she'd told him, knowing her wish would never come true. It was simply a matter of time.

"How much time?" Ross asked, desperation in his voice. "Did they say anything at all?"

"It could be a year. I don't know."

"Surely they must have a better idea than that?"

And with that declaration of his despair, Emily seemed to have gathered her power around her. She pushed him away just enough to gain an objective distance, impatient with his lack of thought.

"All I know is I'm not going to let it tear at me. I've had a good life and I don't want it ending in bitterness. We have time left to do things together and with the kids. I don't want you to tell them. Eventually they'll have to know, but not now. I don't want this to be the only thing in our lives."

"Em, don't say that." But she was swathed in determination.

"It has to be said. I'm not giving in to it and I don't want you to either. That would destroy me."

"I'll do whatever you want. I promise."

By the time they'd returned to the table, the candles had melted, their flame gone, wax smothering the cake's icing. Each ate a slice without the icing. Emily had insisted.

A highway patrolman waves them around the accident. Ross resolves to pay more attention to the road. Accidents will do that.

Bitter. Bitter.

∞

At Fort Myers they cross the bridge that soars over the Caloosahatchee River and then leave behind I-75 for the first time in twelve hundred miles. They turn onto a little highway that follows the river and leads to the causeway for Sanibel Island. Over a bridge it's as though they've journeyed back in time. The road is a narrow, slow two-lane with its blacktop cracking. It is called Periwinkle Way. Many homes along it are old and comfortable looking. It is not as it was, but close enough.

"Oh Ross," Emily says, smiling, "thank God we came back here."

"I was worried you'd be disappointed."

"I expected more development."

"It's nice they left some of it."

"We're going to have a lovely time."

"It's still different. Older," he murmurs.

"So are we," she responds cautiously.

It comes to him abruptly then that they have arrived here together, yet somehow separately. This is the last time she will see this place. She has come here to end. He has come, he knows now, for some kind of beginning. Just what it might be he has no idea. The dreams are its harbinger; the dreaded, frightening dreams which will not go away.

"It's going to be fine," he says with another lie. "I can feel it."

"Now we just have to find the cottage."

"It's up near the north end by Wulfert ... take a while."

"Ross, we've got all the time in the world."

He wishes he could believe her.

... and he smelleth the battle afar off,
the thunder of the captains,
and the shouting.

—JOB 39:25

Spring—The Past

The wind howled him awake: wrenching him from a night-mare of Moors advancing in a wild attack, their women ululating behind them the way they did when they sensed victory, the way it was when he first knew war. It was the wind that had made this dream, that and the hard roll of the ship. For a few seconds he was stunned. Accustomed to war's nightmares he had no time now to analyse this one. Another battle was taking place.

His ship shuddered around him. From above he heard the loud snap of sail as it filled with a gust and then pounding feet running along the deck. He was up quickly and dressing, grasping at handholds to steady himself. The cabin pitched and rolled throwing him off balance. He sat on the bunk pulling on his boots. The witch was awake. Her hand grabbed his wrist tightly.

"What is wrong?" she asked, her voice matching the grasp of her hand.

"Storm," he answered shortly. "Sotil was right. It feels bad."

"You are worried."

"Feel the ship."

"What will you do?"

"What I can."

"I will come with you."

"Don't be a fool. Stay here. You're safer below."

"Your sailors will blame me for this," she said.

"That's ridiculous."

"That priest will blame me," she said louder, but he was already gone. The cabin door slammed. She was left alone in the moving dark.

∞

Sheets, cascades of rain met him on the deck driving pellets into his face. Veins of lightning shot the sky turning the night into weird, flashing colours and bursts of thunder cracked with a supernatural violence. Then the ship rolled again and he felt the sea rising up to drown the deck. He grabbed a railing as spume washed over him, tugging at him, wanting to sweep him into its maw. When it passed he climbed quickly up a stern ladder.

Sotil was on the after deck. In the illuminations of lightning Juan Ponce caught a glimpse of his pilot's face, tight with tension. The boatswain was beside him ready for his commands. Their captain-general greeted them harshly.

"Why was I not awakened?"

"It came upon us but a while ago!" Sotil had to shout to be heard. "It wasn't so bad until now. I'm sending the helmsman below. The whip staff will do us no good in this. He must be at the rudder."

"Are all hands stood to?"

"They are, your honour!" the boatswain replied. He was a tough old sea-dog named Fernando Medel, built square and strong and with nerves of iron. He actually smiled as he answered. The boatswain was in his element.

"We must tree the sails!" Sotil ordered. "If it isn't done quickly, we'll lose some of them. Have men ready to haul in immediately!"

"Aye, sir!" The boatswain smiled more grimly this time and left for the main deck already relaying orders. His voice was nearly as loud as the thunder.

"Have you any orders, captain-general?" Sotil turned to Juan Ponce.

"It's your command, pilot. Do what you must but do it quickly. This will get worse."

"We'll have to come about and close haul. If it does get worse, it's our only chance!"

In the lightning bursts Juan Ponce watched his sailors climb the rat lines up to the yards while others stood to at the clew lines ready to release them. He knew how dangerous this was and cursed himself for not listening to his pilot and reefing the sails in the evening calm. Now it was too late and men might die for his error. Glancing across at Sotil he saw the same emotions. But there was no time for recrimination. The pilot stepped up to the railing to shout commands.

At his word men hauled down on the clew lines drawing the main course up into itself. The men on the yard, holding desperately to it with their legs, hauled in and slowly the great sail, fighting them for its freedom, began to furl. Other parties worked the foresail. It was like watching men in a madhouse, the sweeps of rain and waves and wind adding to the illusion as they buffeted the ship. Men clawed at the rigging and shrieked to each other to be heard above the howl. Big breakers lashed at the ship, their tips as high as the freeboard, their spray as they broke upon the deck, iridescent.

There was trouble on the foresail. The hemp had swollen with the wet and the men could not cast loose the lines. Sailors feverishly pulled at the thick ropes. Then the boatswain, cursing fearfully above the wind, took an axe to the lines, cutting them, letting them fly loose writhing like beheaded snakes. The sail, flapping wildly, began to furl. The canvas snapped in the wind like gunfire until the crew gained control of it. Finally, after what seemed hours, the martinets were secured on the yard and the sails were held close to their crosstrees. Immediately, Sotil shouted down the hatch for the helmsman below to come about. He used the wind in the mizzen to push the ship round and for a moment the sturdy caravel seemed to roll almost onto its side. Juan Ponce heard a man scream. He knew what it meant. Someone had lost his hold and been swept overboard. There would be no chance for him. The storm had claimed him for its own.

This is like my dream, thought Juan Ponce. *This is like war.*

The ship righted itself and faced into the storm, its lateen rigged mizzen holding it there, the helmsman below fighting the rudder to help it. A second helmsman was placed on the rudder as well to help the struggling sailor there who, each time the ship crested a wave and fell back into a trough, was tossed about like a doll on a puppeteer's stick. Sotil ordered parties amidships to man the pumps. Other men lashed down cargo which had broken loose. The animals, kept below, had panicked. Word came up that two men had been trampled while trying to calm the horses. Mayhem. The storm's fury increased.

It bent its full force on the caravel. All night it tried and tried again to capsize the ship. It laid traps, ambuscades of deep troughs and wind shifts and huge breakers which would come at the vessel from two sides, choosing courses at random, turning and turning about in a maelstrom of seething water. Dawn came but few noticed, so deep and thick and low were the storm clouds. The air became lion coloured, then almost green.

Below decks, the passenger-colonists fouled the air with sea sickness and the stench of terror. The master-at-arms was sent to prevent their attempts to come up to the deck. Once loyal soldiers now seethed toward the hatches stopped by mariners locking the iron grates, imprisoning them in their roiling dungeon. Finally, it became necessary for Juan Ponce himself to confront them.

At the head of the mutineers was the zealot.

∞

Bartolome de las Casas had come to the New World as a soldier. And while most mercenaries had arrived anticipating wealth and glory, the young Bartolome was different. He was an idealist. He had dreamed of the Indies as Columbus once had: a place for a new order and ultimately, a better humanity. What he'd found was not his dream. His employment, he'd discovered, was slaughter. He had served under Juan Ponce de Leon in the past: in the campaign to subjugate that part of the island of Hispaniola which the natives called Higuey. He had looked on as the hunting dogs routed out natives and the Spanish fell upon them with the

fury of their arrogance: murdering, burning, turning innocents into slaves, all in the name of God and Mammon.

It had sickened him.

Juan Ponce de Leon had become the island's governor
as a result. Bartolome de las Casas had followed a different
route. He'd joined the ranks of Dominican friars, renoun-
cing all worldly possessions, steeping in asceticism and
swearing upon his new-found, personal God to defend those
hapless natives crushed under the boots of the *conquistadors*.

He had chosen a very hard life.

It showed in his face. It showed in the pinched flesh
and harsh lines of malice, in the bitter, iron eyes which had
lost their compassion, in the mouth that so quickly uttered
curses upon those who stood against him. For the love
which had at first guided him had twisted itself into hatred.
The cause had become a crusade. His ideals turned to fan-
aticism and he, in the end, came to believe himself more
important than his faith. He saw himself now as a symbol,
a misunderstood Christ to these ignorant savages who so
often would not heed his call. As for those Spaniards who
scoffed at his evangelism, they would go to hell.

That antipathy was focused now on the man he knew
was a hypocrite. He was not fooled by Juan Ponce de Leon's
false prayers or noble status. Even his own inclusion on
this damned voyage, forced by the Inquisition, was a sham.
For Don Juan was a madman. Las Casas knew this. The old
veteran had lost his faith and now made bargains with witch-
es. The fury with which las Casas faced Ponce de Leon was
as harsh as the storm above them.

"Open this grate in the name of God!" he screamed
through the iron lattice. The captain-general's weathered
face stared balefully back at him.

"You are stirring up trouble again, *fray* Bartolome," the old man replied evenly.

"You deny these men freedom?"

"I deny them the deck. We are busy up here."

"They are not animals to be kept below! Should the ship founder they deserve a chance to save themselves!"

"The ship will not founder. It's in good hands."

"It is in the hands of God!"

"As I said. And in those of pilot Sotil."

"Remove the grate! What right have you to imprison us?"

"The right of my rank," Juan Ponce replied then raising his voice so the men below could hear, continued. "And should any man disobey my commands he will pay the penalty which is my right to deliver! Return to your quarters! You will only be in the way up here!"

"The men wish to hold prayers for our safety," las Casas said.

"That can be done just as well below deck. They have you to lead them, friar. Make your church down there."

"They are in terror!"

"Then soothe them. That is your duty. I go to mine. Master-at-arms, under no circumstance is the grate to be removed. Any attempt to dislodge it is to be met with force. Do you understand, *Senor* Alvarez?"

"Aye, your honour."

Juan Ponce leaned close to the grate, face to face with las Casas.

"The difference between us, friar, is that my powers are temporal, yours spiritual. Do not try again to usurp me."

"God commands all."

"Just now he's seen fit to have me command. Mutiny has a harsh penalty."

"You wouldn't dare ..."
"Try me, friar."

∞

The storm raged through that day and into the night. No
one slept. No one ate. The only nourishment came from the
pounding rain to which men would open their mouths and
drink. Late that night Sotil and Juan Ponce noticed some
abatement. The swells still rolled and the rain continued yet
they had become somehow softened, their violence spent.
But the pilot and his commander felt no sense of victory. As
in war nothing had been settled. They had merely survived.
The enemies once again became allies. The storm passed.

In the fragrant cool air of daybreak, a false dawn shoot-
ing up into clearing skies, the wind became constant from
the southeast quarter. It was a strong, fine wind. In the pal-
ing stars of morning the pilot and his navigators bustled
about taking sightings with their astrolabes trying to discover where the storm had blown them. Rosy light touched
the clouds in the east. An exhausted crew heard the commands of the boatswain and climbed again to the yard-
arms. The sails, flapping and crackling as they muscled into
a twenty knot wind, filled out, and with the wind abeam
the caravel scudded in search of its sister separated from it
during the storm. The sea was friendly again.

Las Casas led the men up from below and there celebrated three masses: the prayers for Lauds, those for thanks-
giving and finally, the sun turning grey sails to russet as
they caught shafts of light, the funeral mass for the dead.
All men, even exhausted sailors, took part. Las Casas revelled in the power denied him previously. He glanced up and

saw Sotil leaning on the after deck rail. Nowhere, however, could he find Juan Ponce de Leon.

Having posted lookouts for the second ship along with the day's first watch, the captain-general had gone below. As the prayers were spoken he was at his desk, once again quill in hand. This battle had brought on others within him.

∞

There is no storm so violent as that made by men. I know this now. I was born into war, trained to wage war, cultured in its ways and means. We lived for one purpose then: to take back holy Spain from the infidel Moors. I was at Ronda and then at Malaga when the Reconquista began to bear fruit; when Isabella and Ferdinand allied themselves in marriage and joined together the realms of Castile and Aragon and we began to defeat the Africans. It was, I think now, the last true Crusade and I am still proud to have been part of it.

It was Don Pedro who sent me to my destiny. I went willingly. I had grown tired of the indolence at court and, having failed there, I dreamed of what I thought was a warrior's glory. My armour shone, my horse pranced as I joined the column of men who set out to fight the holy war. Don Pedro had given me his own sword and I planned to make it more famous.

My first battle was a skirmish, a minuscule gust in the great winds of war. I captained a supply troop then, too young to be trusted on the battle lines. We were ambushed by a squadron of Moors. They rode down on us from a rocky ridge. There was no time for fear. They were upon us and we fought them. I killed a man then;

my first. Since then I have killed a hundred men and ordered the deaths of hundreds more but this one I remember the most.

He had dark skin and sleek, long hair. I will always remember his hair flying in the wind as he galloped toward me. He charged his mount into mine trying to bowl us over. His scimitar cut at my head. But my horse had stumbled drawing me out of harm's way. He charged again. We parried and parted then his horse turned away from mine and in that instant I reached out and thrust my blade into his back. I pulled on my sword and the Moor came with it off his horse to the ground. As he struggled to rise I plunged my mount over him, the hooves battering him. I had no time then to observe the result. I fought on against others and dust rose around us. After a time, I don't know how long, the Moors retreated. We did not give chase.

When we had cared for our wounded and drunk thirstily from the wineskin of victory, I went back to the place where I had killed a man. He lay there, broken like a child's doll; his hair caked with dirt and dried blood, his dark skin paled by the yellow dust. I did not grieve for him. He was my enemy. But neither did I rejoice. All I felt was a kind of relief. I had proved myself as a soldier.

Ten years of war followed. I will not recount them. War is like a sea voyage: days of boredom broken by moments of terror. That is all war is. Oh, I advanced through the ranks and brought notoriety upon myself. It was that public repute which gave me a wife I would not otherwise have had. War was good to me. And there were glorious moments, as we called them, as well.

Near the end I was at the great siege of Granada,

when Isabella had built the huge camp called Santa Fe, surrounding the Moorish city with a hundred thousand men. In battle our troops were magnificent: not beautiful by any means, but fearsome and well ordered. By then we were good at the business of war. The flags, the horses, the glitter of armour, the noise like a constant rolling thunder, and finally the turmoil of dust rising up to bury the battle within its shadow, beneath which runs every human emotion—this is war in its storm-glory. It is only afterward, in that strange peace which follows a battle ... it is afterward when the flies come and the stench of death hangs in the air that one recognizes the cost.

All battles leave scars: those on the body, and those unseen others. I have my share. Wounds are not victories. They are the ravages of the storm. And that which is termed glorious, is not. There is only courage and fear and love ... and war diminishes each one until the word glory becomes their replacement; a word made by desperate men to somehow contrive to make sense of a storm.

I was there at the surrender of the Alhambra. We entered a place which had known only peace for hundreds of years. We entered with arrogance. In those wondrous palaces of delicate arches and perfect gardens and fountains which spilled scented water, our war ended, and we were somehow diminished.

But we could not accept that.

The end of war brings an odd emptiness. To men who have lived close to death for so long, peace is a weak substitution. And so we replaced our peace with another kind of war. Inquisition.

It was that very year when the *Genoese* first found this new world; bad timing for him, good for us. There were thousands of us then, adventurers with no taste for peace, wandering from one place to another fretting over an Inquisition which persecuted and taxed us. Columbus beckoned. And we came.

We came as conquerors. We had taken back our old world and now wanted this new one. We knew only one way to do it. That is why the world calls us conquistadors. That is why the world fears us. We—I, could not forget war.

6

So here has been dawning
Another blue day.
Think, wilt thou let it
Slip useless away?

—CARLYLE

Autumn — *The Present*

Emily, the bride out of high school. They can't afford marriage but she isn't worried. She has wanted this, she's said, since their first dance in the gym in ninth grade. How hard it had been, he thinks, to have asked her: to cross the floor in front of his friends and ask the cute girl with the orange sweater to dance. The music was Elton John, "Your Song". Strange to remember a song and a place and a time, and emotions, so clearly.

After the dance, after their first walk home and first kiss goodnight, they began to date: movies on Friday nights and parties in friends' houses usually in rec rooms or basements. He found himself more and more enraptured by this girl so quiet and conservative. She played the piano, her lessons each week a chance for him to meet her and walk her home. At those times she would speak of Beethoven or Bach; how she loved the music he'd never heard.

He felt she was far too close to her father. That man

was the reason for her conventional ways. He would take her to concerts or museums, just the two of them wrapped in a culture they'd shared since she was old enough to appreciate it. When her father had discovered Ross' interest in history, he began every once in a while to include him on their outings. Those times had not been the most comfortable with Ross on the outside listening in. Once in a while Emily would touch his hand surreptitiously, wanting to include him, hesitant with her father around.

She possessed a mildness which concealed her intelligence, her bright spirit, and a subtle need to differentiate from her father. But she would not succumb to that need. She was loyal. Ross wanted to see more of her, be exclusive, the custom back in those days when you found someone special. But despite his presence at their family dinners, once each month, Ross could never break the shell of fidelity Emily and her father shared.

So he left her. He joined the track team and spent hours training, working off his frustration. He won a few races. He enjoyed the company of his team mates. There were other girls. He was young and needed to explore. But always, always, she was at the back of his mind as the presence to whom he compared all the others. He'd eventually spent a miserable summer trying to be like everyone else, trying to fit into the adolescent world which constantly changed around him, trying to draw him away from the beacon that was Emily.

At the start of the next school year, unforeseen by him on one ordinary day, she did something completely unanticipated and socially supernatural. She simply walked up to him in the school hallway. His head was inside his locker so he hadn't seen her coming. When he heard her voice, he was so shocked he banged his head on the locker's upper shelf.

"Oh God, are you alright?" she exclaimed apologetically.

"Yeah, uh, yeah I'm ..."

"Let me see. You might have a cut."

"No, it's alright. Why're you here?"

"I want to talk to you."

"Yeah?"

"I'd like to know why you stopped seeing me."

He had not expected that kind of directness, that *steel* in a girl of fifteen. Then again, knowing Emily, he should have. He found it difficult to find the right words to explain his feelings. In the end she found them for him with an honesty which was always the most wondrous part of her.

"I, uh, I just thought we should take a break. It was getting too serious," he mumbled.

"I thought you were the one who gave me a ring."

"You wouldn't take it."

"Because of my dad ..."

"What's with him anyway?"

"He wants to protect me. He thinks I'm too young. I love him, Ross, but not the way I love you."

"What? You ... love me?"

"There, I've said it. So now you can do what you want with it." Tears glistened the hazel of her eyes as she stood there trying to be brave. Within that moment in a school hallway he knew he'd never again give her up.

"You love me?" he uttered again, loving the sound of the words.

"I had a talk with my dad. He can't change, but he's okay with us seeing each other."

"You'll wear my ring?" He tried to make it hard for her, his boy's pride exerting itself.

"On a chain round my neck. I can't flaunt this in front of dad. Is that so important?"

"This isn't easy ..."

"You think I don't know that? I'm sure it's already around the whole school I've come here to see you."

"Forget the ring. You're right. I'm sorry. You really love me?"

∞

The Sanibel cottage is a clapboard affair with a veranda looking out over the beach to the west. The beach is a glistening stretch of shells, billions of them washed in by the tide, running for miles along the Gulf side. The place is not much for what it cost. Still, it is perfect for them. It is far enough up the coast to be isolated, yet near enough to stores for amenities. They spend their first day grocery shopping and unpacking the car. It is not long before they have settled in.

They share a bottle of wine that night. They sit on the veranda in bleached wicker chairs and watch sunset turn the Gulf waters golden. Pelicans sail by in low, gliding silhouettes inches above the waves, searching the sea for their supper. They seem so primordial in their shapes. The light diffuses and as the sun sinks below the horizon it glows magenta across the sky. Then only a few low-slung clouds in the west hold their colour. A breathless pink twilight replaces them as dusk closes in.

Emily's hand finds his.

"There must be a God," she says solemnly, "to make this kind of beauty."

"There must," he answers.

"You're very quiet."

"I was thinking I might go in and read."

"Can't you stay here for a little while? It's so peaceful. Just relax, Ross. You've been working all day."

"I want to get started on Durant. We brought all those books. I should read them."

"I'd appreciate it if you stayed," she says softly, her voice breaks a little. "I don't want to be alone right now."

He squeezes her hand reassuringly. He has caught the sound of her desperation. No one wants to die. No one wants to leave ocean breezes or sunsets or even the dark of the night. She cannot be strong all the time. It is his turn now. He is thankful for the dark. She cannot see his face.

"One condition." He affects a bantering tone; his way of lightening the mood.

"And what might that be?" she replies, strong enough still to respond in kind.

"The price of a kiss. You haven't kissed me in three days!"

She leans over to meet him, their lips touch softly. He still feels electricity in her kisses.

He finishes the last of the wine.

"So, what's on the schedule for tomorrow?" he says.

"I haven't thought of a thing. If it's sunny I'd like to lie on the beach."

"What? No plans?"

"Well, we could ask the pelicans over for lunch," she says, laughing. He has helped her. He has done something right.

"I thought maybe we could drive up to Captiva," he says. "The guy at the store says it's hardly changed."

"I don't know how I kept up with you," she says, chuckling.

"If I recall you were always a little ahead of me ..."

"Up at six every morning." She makes her list tapping his hand with her finger each time. "Off for a run, then to school, teaching, marking, your research, coaching ..."

"... Grooming the garden, cutting the grass, shovelling snow, doing odd jobs for the wife ..."

"I wasn't that bad, was I?" she responds quietly. He has forgotten her mood.

"Of course not, I loved every second."

"Of every minute of every hour of every day of every year?" she retorts in their personal patois; the mood passing like an ill wind.

"From the start to the ..." He stumbles.

"... Finish." She speaks softly the word he cannot.

"I'm a clumsy ass," he says. He has reminded her, he knows, of the end.

"It's getting chilly. Let's go in. You can read."

"Alright. About tomorrow ..."

"Couldn't we put off Captiva? I really would like to get some sun."

"Of course we can."

"I'll make you a sandwich," she says, the moment forgotten.

As she enters the cottage Ross stays in his chair. The sunset has caused a reflection within him. He and Emily were married still young with their lives ahead. He remembers her in the garden pruning rose bushes. So tan. Her hair shining auburn with golden streaks catching sunlight. The garden had taken years to create but she'd always found ways to improve it. Ross was installing a fountain for her, a kind of grotto amid the rose bushes where the water was to run over rocks and ripple the surface of a small pond. He would place the rocks where Emily had planned. They were heavy and he was sweating. Emily came to help. Together, young and strong, they lifted and set. Ross mortared the stone but as he finished he felt Emily's hands on his back under his shirt, caressing.

"I take it we've finished for the day," he said, turning and smiling, holding her. Her eyes had already gone smoky.

"What time does Robbie get back from his practice?"

"Not until five."

"Is the gate locked?"

"Yeah, we haven't been round front all day."

"Make love to me. Here. Right now."

"Are you crazy? It's daylight!"

"No one can see in."

Already she was touching him, arousing him with her lips whispering in his ear her hands stroking the back of his neck. Risky love by the fountain; the aroma of roses mixed with their breathing and the sounds of a Saturday: lawn sprinklers hissing, the buzz of a mower, children at play on the street. They shared that sweet danger together.

∞

The next morning they lie on the beach. Ross begins reading the first of Durant, ancient pre-history, and finds it hard going. He chafes at the inactivity. It is almost six months since he has stopped teaching but there were still things to do. He'd set his affairs in order buying annuities and medical plans, organizing the trip, puttering around the house at the few jobs remaining unfinished. He and Emily had looked after Justin while Robert and Anne went to Spain. He had kept himself busy.

Now simply sitting troubles him. It has no purpose. On

holidays he could relax with the knowledge that he would return to work. But now there is only a long, leisurely stretch into the distance. It feels like a vacuum.

He leaves Emily and jogs on the beach: the casuarina trees waving like wind wands in the breeze, the wild sea oats clustered at the edge of the sand, the different hues of the sea. Once he stops to watch a sandpiper strutting along the shoreline. It is looking for food where the waves rush up. Each time a wave comes the little bird runs from the water, fretful of wetting its tiny feet. He laughs at it. He breathes in the sea air and feels the sun warm on his back. Simple things. *They should be enough.*

When he returns he swims, showers and fixes lunch. After eating Emily wants to read. Ross tries Durant again. Nothing. He putters around looking for something to fix in the cottage but he has no tools. Emily glances up from her book. She looks disgruntled.

"Ross, what's the matter with you? You haven't sat still for five minutes."

"That damn faucet needs tightening."

"We can live with it for a week."

"Maybe you can. The dripping last night drove me crazy!"

"Well, right now you're driving me crazy."

"What does that mean?" he mutters.

"It means," she says sharply, "we've been here one day and already you're pacing about."

"Is that so?" He is not ready to back down on this. He doesn't know why.

"Look," Emily says, sighing, "if you want to fix the faucet go into town and buy a wrench."

"What about you?"

"I'll be perfectly fine."

"Don't you want to come?"

"No, Ross, I don't. But I think you should go out for a while. I'm really not up to having a fight. You seem to need to have one."

"I just want to fix the faucet!" he says, raising his voice, not meaning to.

"I don't think that's all there is to it."

"What?"

"You're bored."

"I'm not bored!"

"You wanted to go to Captiva today."

"I suggested it. That's all. Don't make me feel guilty."

"I'm not trying to make you feel guilty," she says in the soft, even voice she uses to show disgust. "This discussion is going nowhere."

"I'll go into town," he replies, knowing she is right.

He drives much further than he had intended, going nowhere in particular. He is angry with himself for being so foolish with Emily. She does not need his tantrums. But he is angry with her as well for having seen so easily through him. His nagging doubts have reduced him to glass, transparent to all but himself.

What turns a man to glass?

Everyone said he was lucky: the right time, the right place, the right age, that revered golden handshake—the wrong man to retire. And thoughts of retirement evoke Arthur Felder: long hair, jean jacket with 'Suck!' scrawled across the back and what do you do when you're fifty-two and an eighteen-year-old tells you to fuck off? Ross did not hate him then, but he feared him. There were strategies for that kind of boy: guidance counsellors, a vice principal visit, just talking with him trying to gain his confidence. Ross couldn't think of one that would work. He simply watched the boy self-destruct.

People thought him to have been a good teacher, he knew, but they had known nothing of Arthur Felder. Ross told no one about him, not even Emily. And finally when Arthur was expelled for some offence against some other teacher ... that was the beginning ... when Ross first thought of leaving teaching. And while he remained he protected himself. The closeness he'd once shared with his students vanished. The History Club was disbanded. Those precious after class conferences dried up as Ross lost touch with young minds and their culture. His classes became dry affairs. He covered curriculum; nothing more. He seemed to be losing his powers. He seemed more insignificant every day.

Five years later, just before he retired, Ross met Arthur in a grocery store. He was the meat manager. He had a wife and a little boy. He said the boy was a hellion. Ross hoped it was true; hoped the boy would do to his father what the father had done to him.

And then Arthur told him he'd been his favourite teacher. Arthur was studying night school history. He needed a high school diploma to be promoted to store manager. But the history, he said, was for fun; from what Ross had given him.

Ross recalled giving him nothing.

Arthur was young and had a small future. It was enough for him. It was only just then that Ross came to hate Arthur Felder; because it had never really been his fault at all.

∞

He finds himself entering Sanibel village. He does not remember how he arrived or what he came for. The car clock
tells him two hours have passed. Emily will be worried. He
decides he'd better return to the cottage. He wheels into a
parking lot to turn around. Across the street is a small, white
house with a sign in front and a huge live oak in the yard.
The big tree dapples the walls of the building. The sign tells
him it is a library.

A library will offer some peace.

It is only two rooms, their walls lined with shelves. It
is quiet, musty and empty but for a studious looking young
woman with long, honey blonde hair and horn-rimmed
glasses. She glances up from her desk.

"Good afternoon, sir."

"Hello," Ross says, smiling to match her smile.

"Can I help you with something?"

"No, just browsing," he answers, shambling toward the
stacks. Already he feels calmer.

His eyes search the book spines with practised skill.
His fingers touch titles softly. He moves quickly away from
the fiction section. He has never liked fiction, never understood Emily's need for novels.

His preference is history: mapping humanity. It had led
him into his own research. He remembers fondly the proud
moment of the letter: a missive from the Quebec Historical
Society; a promise to publish his work on early French
Canada. They'd offered money. The money was unimportant. But when the article had come out there were telephone
calls from professors. They were surprised Ross was merely a teacher. *Merely* a teacher. They'd laughed about that in
the history office. Still, he was proud. He'd tried not to show
it but it was there. He'd felt significant then.

"Excuse me, sir," the librarian's voice intrudes. "I'll have to close soon."

He has stayed too long. She does not know him. There is a wariness in her eyes.

"Good Lord," he says, smiling, trying to put her at ease, "what time is it?"

"Nearly five o'clock. I really have to close up."

"I'm sorry. I just ..." He does not want this young woman to distrust him.

"Are you sure there's nothing I can help you with?" Her voice is uneasy.

He is in the history section. Strange what habit can do. It gives him an idea, something to dispel her worry.

"You see I'm a teacher, I mean a retired teacher, and I'm interested in local history."

"Oh?" she says. "On vacation?"

"Kind of. Would you have something about the island itself?"

"Of course. But you're in the wrong section. We keep local history over here by the desk. We get quite a few requests for it."

"I'll only be here a week. Perhaps something brief?"

"Would you be interested in the original natives? There's quite a lot on them: the Calusa. They even say Ponce de Leon landed here. Pine Island, I think. And if you have time there's lots to see."

Durant is too distant; too obvious a retirement task. He needs something closer to his current circumstance.

"Really? Sounds intriguing miss ..."

"My name's Angela."

"And I'm Ross Porter. Nice to meet you, Angela."

"I just love local history." She smiles again, her fears assuaged. "This book has maps of the area. You can actually go and see some of the things they mention."

"Where?"

"Oh, there's Mound Key just south on the mainland and the Ding Darling Wildlife Preserve, right here on Sanibel. You can rent a canoe and go into the mangrove canals. I've done it myself. It's quite safe. There are ancient shell mounds built by the Calusa hundreds of years ago and who knows"—she grins impishly—"you might even locate the fountain of youth old Ponce was supposed to be looking for."

"Angela," he says, ignoring the little joke on his age, "you've just saved my marriage. I think this should do the trick perfectly."

"That's wonderful, Mr. Porter."

"I'm looking forward to this," he says.

He hurries home. He examines himself more objectively and finds Ross Porter a happier man. Angela has given him books; enough for a solid beginning. They sit on the front seat beside him. He pats them with that touch which others reserve for their pets. Still, he does not recognize their import, the new direction they have offered him or the places to which they will eventually guide him.

This is a step, he tells himself.

He does not feel so empty.

∞

When he returns he sees Emily on the veranda. She appears tense but as she watches him exit the car and walk spryly toward her, she smiles. She meets him halfway, as she always has.

"Ross Porter, where in heaven's name have you been?"

She puts her hands on his shoulders and shakes them. "I've been sitting here hours! What are you laughing about?"

"Oh, nothing much," he says, "I just found the tools to fix that faucet."

"Oh," she replies with a twinge of disappointment.

"These!" He proffers the books.

"How can you fix a faucet with those?"

"By doing what you said. Ignore it," he says, smiling. "I'm sorry, Em. I did all this planning for the trip and forgot myself. Oh, I thought the Durant would keep me occupied, but I felt kind of duty bound to read them."

"So what have you got?"

"Histories."

"Naturally." She pats his arm.

"Local histories. I talked to a young woman in the Sanibel library ..."

"Oh really?" She chuckles sardonically.

"And she told me about some places to see. Remember when we went to Quebec ..."

"Of course ..."

"... To finish my research?"

"It was wonderful."

"Well, we can do the same here! Oh, I won't drag you along if you don't want to go. But I'd love to share this. Look, I know it sounds foolish but I needed something."

She pauses a moment, then as they walk back to the cottage she puts her arm through his.

"While you were gone I had time to think. I know all of this has been hard on you, Ross. I'm sorry I was so unpleasant before."

"No, it was me. The faucet thing was stupid."

"No, it wasn't. It opened up things we hadn't talked over."

"We will," he says, not wanting to think of that now. "Would you like to read these books with me?"

"Any novels on the subject?" she replies lightly, knowing him; his signals.

"Well there might be. We could ask Angela."

"From the library?"

"Yeah. This could be fun!"

"It's good to see you happy."

7

*This is now bone of my bones,
and flesh of my flesh.*

—**GENESIS 2:23**

Spring—The Past

For two days they followed a zigzag pattern in search of their lost sister ship, commanded by Cristoval de Sotomayor. The weather was kind and the winds kept up steadily from the southeast. Lookouts were posted and each night they hung lighted lamps from the crosstrees. At each turn of the glass they would fire a bombard, its thunder echoing across the waves, and listen for a return. There was none.

The third day in the morning a school of dolphins joined them. The big fish frolicked around the ship leaping in mottled grey arcs, sometimes crossing its bow, sometimes cruising beside it. The ship's company lined the decks to watch their strange sea dance. The dolphins sang to each other in a weird, clicking chatter which seemed to welcome the ship to their realm. They stayed an hour. When they veered away, Sotil was almost inclined to follow them in the hope they would lead him to his sister ship. One could never tell with dolphins. He smiled as he suggested this new course to his captain-general. The old man's reply was curt.

"Superstition. These fish are as likely to bring you over a reef as they are to lead you to Sotomayor. We have an agreement if you recall: a two-day search then return to San Salvador for rendezvous. Damn this storm! It's brought another delay."

"We could stretch the search to three days, Don Juan," the pilot said, surprised at his commander's frustration. This was the man, after all, who taught patience. "Surely his pilot Miruelo might think the same. San Salvador is a long way back."

"Sotomayor will follow his orders to the letter. Now, set your course for San Salvador. We must wait a little longer, it seems, for our landfall. And as for these fish and your superstition, you should know better."

Strange words from a man who believes in a witch, Juan Ponce thought grimly of himself. Even as he spoke he noticed her on the after deck. She had come up to view the dolphins. She was of them, of all primitive nature, as wild and untamed and singular. He watched her closely for a moment, this woman so impervious to him. She sat in the sun, her hair tumbling over bare brown shoulders, she no longer deigned to wear Spanish clothing, as the wind tousled her tresses. Her dark eyes swept the sea. She smiled for some reason.

∞

Her name was Mayaimi, from the union of Calos and her mother. Her mother had been of the Timucua tribe, the Mayaimi clan, noble, though not royal as Calos of the Calusa.

The Spaniard called her by another name, a name without grace or meaning, a name befitting the slave they had tried to make her. She never used it for, in her own mind, she was never a slave.

The dolphins recalled her home. As she sat in the sun she remembered, for the first time in a very long time, the things she had put aside for Calos. At first it was small memories: weaving nets for fishing, gathering berries and roots from the land, collecting the shellfish which would become both food and lodging. After their insides were eaten the shells were piled and moulded to become the base for the tribe's dwellings in the mangrove swamps. And then she recalled the house of Calos, big enough for a hundred to gather to hold the sacred ceremonies of the three souls. Men and women together: the women singing, the men wearing masks of beasts and birds to which all souls belonged, to which she would belong eventually after passing through water. All that she had given up. Then there were the things she had forced away.

As if she would ever succumb to the foolish mumblings of the stinking monk who was always trying to persuade her to believe in a nothing; a common man ridiculed and slaughtered at the hands of his enemies on a wooden cross. That could not be a god. Even when the stinking monk spoke of threes: of father and son and spirit, they were not the right threes, they were nothing at all like the three who ruled all things. The monk had no notion that she was a sorceress: holy in her own way, noble in her birth, a woman who could commune with spirits, a sacrifice by Calos and a spy as well sent to discover the ways of the stinking Spanish.

They did stink. They smelled of the animal meat they consumed so voraciously. Even before she had reached the huge cloud canoe they inhabited she had nearly retched from the stench. And when they had stripped her and begun to abuse her, those things had bothered her less than their breath in her face.

Then their chief, the big Spaniard she called him, had claimed her and taken her far across the sea to his home on the island of the slave people who served every Spanish whim: their pride wiped from them, their customs destroyed, their worth as a people reduced to nothing. When they tried to befriend her, she rebuffed them. When she was taken into those dank stone dwellings the Spanish seemed to prefer and forced into the confines of clothing which rubbed rough against the body, so different from the soft moss she had worn at home, she had not succumbed. When they had made her servile: scrubbing stone floors, sweeping stone walkways, laundering their stinking clothes, she had borne it all for Calos.

As instructed, she had learned their stuttering language and eaten their cooked, tasteless vegetables and worn their stinking clothes and become a slave in their presence. But on her own she had kept certain things. She would find shellfish at the shoreline; she would gather new kinds of fruits and eat them; she would commune with the spirits who called faintly for her. Fortunately there was always plenty of fish for the servants who were seldom allowed any meat. Good. She affirmed to herself that she would not stink, not become one of them; not be their minion. And she held this all close to herself as she watched and waited and read the signs of the man who thought he owned her until she knew it was time to strike. It took years, but she was not a daughter of Calos for nothing. She had not been chosen by him for no reason. When the time came she had stalked the big Spaniard as she would a lizard within the swamp.

As his situation diminished the Spaniard had become worn and tired despite his ridiculous pride. She had used that to her advantage. Her first real chance was to serve him his wine. A muttered threat to a dogsbody servant had allowed her access and then she'd told the big Spaniard the tale of the water. She could see in his slate grey eyes—eyes like a lizard—that at first he did not believe her but she had entranced him, becoming more familiar each day as his powers waned and his children grew sullen; until his wife was gone forever and then Mayaimi had gone to his bed and given him something his wife never had. And all the while she'd whispered: "Water." And eventually he'd believed her, or at least his desperate pride had.

And now she was going home to her rightful place and a welcomed tribal marriage and the freedom to live as a true human should. Just now the dolphins had presaged her return, greeting her homecoming as dolphins will do. She smiled at them as they whirled away from this stinking Spanish ship.

∞

Observing her, Juan Ponce could not help but recall wistfully another moment when, long ago, he had first seen his wife. A much different portrait, far removed from this dusky woman. There had been promise then, so long ago.

"What is this creature doing up here?" A harsh, high-pitched voice interrupted his reverie. He turned to face the feverish eyes of las Casas.

"What is she doing here?" the Dominican repeated.

"Watching dolphins."

"The men can see her. She troubles the men."

"She troubles you, friar, and you in turn trouble the men."

"She is a witch!"

"Because she does not submit to your calling?" Juan Ponce could feel his anger rising.

"You know what she is. When this voyage is done she shall suffer the question."

"Inquisition for a native? Not even the Church will agree to that."

"She must undergo salvation."

"According to the Church she has no soul. She is an animal."

"Then you sleep with beasts! When will you answer for your sin?"

"Enough! You are the one who believes they are human. That is why you're here, is it not? To convert them? That is why your Inquisition has forced you upon me."

"You dare speak to me in this manner?"

His temper had carried Juan Ponce into a dangerous realm. Like it or not, this monk had the power to harm him. Words whispered in the wrong ears and all he possessed, all he dreamed of, would end. The Inquisition would descend upon him even here, half a world away. Juan Ponce had no desire to be caught in that web. Age is good for one thing, he decided: it brings the wisdom to retreat without shame.

"Of course I am wrong, *fray* Bartolome," he said quietly. "Until the Church decides on this question, neither one of us knows the state of this woman. Suffice to say, friar, that she cannot be a witch if she is animal, and if she is human, in living with me she might find the right path with your gentle persuasion to guide her."

"If these Calusa you speak of are to be converted, then she must be first to seek salvation."

"Together we'll see to that. Will you hear my confession this evening? Obviously it's long past time."

"Of course, my son," las Casas said, smiling his triumph. "Now remove the woman. I shall speak with her again and perhaps she will come to know God."

Juan Ponce gave the order. The witch retreated. Las Casas was pleased.

Beneath it all he was a simple man.

∞

The following day offered the best weather they had yet seen. The thought that it took him away from his destination irritated Juan Ponce. Once or twice he nearly ordered Sotil to begin again the search for Sotomayor. He knew it would be useless but the urge to move forward was powerful and it played on him like a melody stuck in his mind. He tried to keep busy, even inscribing in his ship's log the details required by the government; but when the wind is fair and the ocean easy there is little for a commander to do. Sotil took care of the ship's daily workings. For Juan Ponce all that was left was his cabin and his other, internal voyage. He had trouble writing. His obsession to push back the curtain of the future, now that he was so close, rejuvenated his impatience. There are times in men's lives when age matters little. Sometimes it is the moment which counts, not the years.

The witch was impatient, too. She demanded to know why they had turned back. She was angry about it. Not overtly, she would never show him that, but his own frustration allowed him a glimpse of hers. Then again, she was ageing, and if there were truth to her stories, it might be that she too sought what he did. But was she so devious? Could she, a simple Calusa woman, possess that kind of subterfuge? He laughed at the notion. More likely she was upset having been denied the deck, having lost to las Casas, whom she considered a fool. And yet, strangely enough, she seemed to like Sotomayor. Juan Ponce found this peculiar. For if Juan Ponce de Leon had gained a reputation for dealing roughly with natives, then Cristoval de Sotomayor, his lieutenant of so many years, was infamous.

He was a huge man, blessed with prodigious strength. Younger than Juan Ponce, he had arrived with Ovando when that nobleman had been sent as Viceroy after Columbus had been arrested and forever refused ownership of the lands he'd discovered. Sotomayor knew little of this. He had simply signed on to make his fortune. Many men came with the same reasons. But there were not many like Sotomayor.

He was assigned to Juan Ponce's squadron at the beginning of Ovando's terror. The Viceroy's plan was simple: end the anarchy in Hispaniola with an iron fist. If a tribe would not submit, eliminate it: men, women, children, animals, houses, crops. Leave nothing but ash. Juan Ponce de Leon became Ovando's most trusted captain in this. He followed the orders because he saw their sense. And Sotomayor followed Juan Ponce. Absolutely. Perfectly. Without mercy. Neither man was troubled by slaughter. It was merely the business of war.

Juan Ponce treated Sotomayor as the son he wished he had had. And Sotomayor returned that favour with complete loyalty. He had profited, but he found his love

for battle far outweighed that for gold. Juan Ponce de Leon
gave him both. It was a bonding of minds. Even in the bad
days, when his mentor had been outmanoeuvred and forced
to give up his positions, the fiery lieutenant had stayed with
him.

And finally, when Juan Ponce de Leon had decided to
claim again what was rightfully his, to muster this voyage,
his obvious second was Sotomayor. Even the witch had
smiled when she heard his lieutenant was to join them. Juan
Ponce did not try to understand why. Perhaps Sotomayor
reminded her of her own tribe's warriors: tall, fearless, and
deadly. Juan Ponce might be the brain of the expedition
but Sotomayor was its sword. They would have need of that
sword, he knew. The last time had been hard. A pine forest
island called *Slaughter*. That had been mere exploration.
This time they had come to claim.

Thoughts of Sotomayor cheered him. Their marriage of
arms had been more complete, more honest and forthright,
more filled with joy than his actual marriage. Leonor had
hated Sotomayor. She had called him common, bloodthirsty,
ambitious. Sotomayor had accepted her insults passively.
And when she died he'd attended her memorial and comforted the family as best he knew how. His loyalty shone.

It was after that when Juan Ponce, for the first time,
had lied to him. It was not difficult. Sotomayor was not an
intricate man. He believed without question the tale of
founding a new colony. And so he too had been deceived.
Thinking these things brought the old man to his parchment again. The past was his only solace now with the future held in abeyance.

∞

It was during the wars in Spain that I married. My mother had died while I was away and so I was unable to bid her goodbye. It created a kind of emptiness in me. I began to feel a need for permanence, for a woman to somehow fill that chasm for which I have so little understanding. Children were a part of it. Each man wishes his name carried on. But it was more than that. It was time, for some reason, to marry. There was no rationality to it; only a strange new mood.

I left it to my father to arrange it, knowing he would choose wisely and well. It would be a union of houses, the business of marriage. My reputation, solid by then, and my maturity made the matchmaking easier. I was past marital age. Not old, but certainly no young man either. And by this time I considered myself more adept socially. I had made the acquaintance of ladies at court as well as that of the camp prostitutes. In my arrogance, I thought I knew women.

Leonor was of noble birth, of course; her family of like circumstance to mine. Her father was an honourable man. He provided a dowry of twenty five hundred escudos. Not a great sum, but reasonable. She was sixteen when I first met her. I had no idea what to expect as I presented myself to the family. I remember it was early evening, the sun cool and low in the sky.

Her father was just a little older than me: a plain man, rather bookish and dour, and I think slightly in awe of this rough captain who had entered his house to claim his daughter. We took wine together. He asked about the war. There was no talk of the daughter until his wife appeared to take me to meet her. His wife was a plain woman, very shy. I began to despair of my father's choice. In his dreams each man wishes a beautiful wife, one of whom he can be proud, one who pleases his senses as well as his house.

I prepared myself for the worst.

She was in the garden. She sat on a bench in a bower of orange trees, their blossoms pungent; their webbed branches holding the twilight magically. I felt in that instant like a boy, giddy with anticipation, an odd mixture of fear and hope mingling and making the heart beat just a little faster, making my senses alert and crisp, so that when she stepped out of that dappled grove in a glance I was able to see everything and remember it, perfectly, to this day.

She took my breath away.

This all happened in seconds, yet I recall it seeming to last much longer. When she stepped into view she had covered her face with a fan and so, quickly, I studied the rest of her. Her gown was of green moiré silk. It rustled like restless leaves. The fastenings down the front were embroidered in silver which sparkled like early stars in the twilight. They raised to a low cut bodice and beneath the dress a lace chemise. The fan itself was organza inset with pearls. It concealed all of her face but her eyes. And it was her eyes which took me.

Her eyes were green. They were cool. Lagoons of sea green, touched with sparkle, just like the sea if the sea were perfect. Her hair was shot through with auburn, her flesh pale and almost porcelain. I have seen its like only in those delicate figures which arrive sometimes from Cathay. She seemed so fragile, so feminine, I feared one touch would shatter her.

And then she lowered the fan. She smiled. This will stay in my memory forever. It was not just her mouth that smiled, her lips full and curved like scallops of sand on a shore, but the coolness of her eyes changed to that emerald flash one glimpses, if he is watchful, as the sun sets upon the New World's sea. Her flesh dimpled a little at the corners of her mouth, and within her smile there seemed a quick flame that glowed and reached out to touch me so I was infected and smiled as well, just to keep the warmth, hold the rose in her cheeks. She smiled as if she smiled only for me.

She was beautiful.

I thought then that beauty meant something. I thought it meant sensitivity, a softness of soul not to be found in harsh features like my own. It was hard to think otherwise in the face of such symmetry, such radiance as lived in the smile of Leonor. The sea has great beauty, yet it is capable of other things: of storms, of rip tides, of hidden shoals. The sky is vast, and yet one lives beneath but a small part of it. How was I to know then that Leonor was merely beautiful flesh, that within lay a soul like bitter herbs and a mind obsessed with smallness. I did not realise she could call up that smile when it suited her, only when it suited her, and the rest of the time she used her cool eyes to hide her feelings just as the sea conceals its dangers beneath placid waves.

In time we married. In bed that first night there was nothing. She lay still and silent while I raged on top of her trying to make it love. I thought it was merely the loss of virginity. But it kept on. She would submit but it was only that: submission, duty, disdain. It was not long before I went back to the war.

War loves me.

While I was gone my son was born. I did not see him until he was three. She named him Luis. He had eyes like hers. The first time I saw him he shook my hand. I have never kissed my son.

With time her obsessions grew. She had married a man from whom she'd expected great things. She wanted the best of Venetian glass, silver from Milan, plate from Cathay, Antwerp tapestries and Rhenish chalices. She wanted each thing about her to be as beautiful as she. I was a soldier. A very good soldier. I had my share of booty. But it was never enough. And when she discovered my ineptitude at court her disappointment in me was complete. The business of her marriage was bankrupt.

She told me that, many times.

Only once was she happy. It was when I had earned the governorship of the island of San Juan Bautista. Only then did she deign to come here to the Indies to share life with me. She was the one who demanded a capitol at San Juan de Puerto Rico. She wanted a house like those she had known in Spain. I built it. It cost many natives their lives. It cost me financial damage. But I saw her smile again. Once.

And when I lost my position as governor, she left for home. I lost it through intrigue at court, through Diego Colon, the son of Columbus my friend, through snivelling men a thousand leagues distant who plotted without my knowing. Yet Leonor blamed me. She had raised my son and my daughters to loathe me. She had taught them gentility and intrigue, the things at which she was so adept. Oh, it was my fault as well. I was absent too often. I never knew them. I was too busy fighting my wars. And when I was home I could not find the way to show them how much I had missed them. I fell into the only method I knew. I became like my own father. My children grew distant as I had done.

I have never been one to express emotion. I thought, when we married, Leonor would change that: make me more human, give me the softness I have always felt but not shown. How was I to know, on that quiet evening in a twilit garden, there are those in this world who do not even feel?

And yet each time I break open an orange to drink of its juices and eat its sweet meat, its pungency reminds me of her; of that first evening before I knew her when, for a moment, I was in love.

∞

The boom of a ship's gun curtailed his writing. He heard shouting from the deck. Another problem, he thought, sighing as he rose from the table. It was time to return to command. He had just reached the door when it flew open. A young sailor stood there, flushed and breathless, his red sock cap awry on his head. Quickly he removed it.

"Your honour!" he said.

"What is it, boy?"

"Pilot Sotil sent me to get you!"

"I can see that. What is the trouble?"

"No trouble, your honour. He wishes you on deck."

"Why was that bombard set off?"

"A ship, your honour. The lookouts have seen a ship!"

"What ship?"

"I don't know, sir. I was sent to find you."

"And you have."

"Yes, sir."

"One thing, young man ..."

"Sir?"

"If you are called again to seek me out, knock on my door and wait to enter."

"Yes, captain-general, I'm sorry. It's just ..."

"Never mind now, but remember."

"Yes sir."

"And boy ..."

"You're honour?"

"Would you mind removing yourself from the passage so I might get to the deck?"

With the ship's boy at his heels Juan Ponce climbed the gangway. As he reached the deck a second gun fired: its concussion splitting the air, smoke billowing from its mouth and drifting away in a ghostly whiteness. He climbed to the after deck. Sotil was there, smiling. He pointed into the starboard distance handing Juan Ponce a telescope. A soft boom reached across the waves answering their signal. Juan Ponce trained the glass on the horizon and glimpsed a brief whiteness against the sky. Sails.

"Sotomayor?"

"Who else could it be, captain-general?"

"Who else indeed. We'll wait a little to be sure."

"Of course."

"Some luck finally, eh Sotil?"

"I have no doubt, Don Juan."

"And now you'll tell me the dolphins have brought him," Juan Ponce said, smiling.

"Superstition, sir. Superstition." Sotil's eyes twinkled.

"I bow to your knowledge," Juan Ponce said. "Alaminos was right about you."

But he was thinking of dolphins. If dolphins could do this then so might the witch bring him rendezvous with his destiny. At last he dared to hope. The witch did not have cool, sea green eyes hiding every emotion.

Hers were as black as pitch.

8

*Not to know what happened before
one was born is to remain a child.*

—CICERO

Autumn—*The Present*

In the lethargy of a hot afternoon Ross Porter sits in the veranda's shade. The Florida books have whetted his appetite. Not everyone takes an interest in history. But for some, like Ross, there is a joy to envisioning the past. He knows he is only beginning, a rank amateur in this new world he has discovered, but he has that gift which allows him glimpses of lives which to others are merely dust. He has read all morning. He has even joined Emily on the beach soaking up some sun, enjoying himself.

That evening they eat at a seafood place nearby. The decor isn't much, a touch too trendy for them, but the crab legs and swordfish steaks are superb. The room's openness creates a soft cacophony of diners conversing, silverware clinking, and occasionally some laughter. In the midst of the restaurant Ross and Emily have made a separate solitude. Ross is talkative, alive with what he has learned.

"A shell culture, Em, these Calusa didn't have pottery.

They lived in the coastal swamps on shell mounds. Apparently they built whole towns on them. Their weapons, their plate ware, tools, jewellery; everything made from shells, wood or bone."

"They must have been quite primitive."

"Well, just building those mounds indicates they were fairly sophisticated."

Emily's interest is piqued. She leans closer to the table.

"What kind of social structure did they have?"

"They had what the Spanish called a *cacique*, obviously a chief. Hereditary position as far as I can make out. Only allowed to marry his sisters or cousins."

"Like the pharaohs."

"Something like that."

"Did they have a similar religion?"

"They were animists. I'll show you the pictures of masks they made; wooden masks representing spirits."

"But how did they live?"

"Hunter-gatherers: lived off the land and sea. No agriculture other than harvesting what grew wild. There's no mention yet but I'm sure they must have traded with other tribes."

"They must have been ripe picking for the Spanish."

"From what I've read they caused the first explorers real trouble."

"And the library girl said we could see where they lived?"

"Some remains. There's a place called Mound Key and apparently some kind of bird sanctuary near here. You can canoe through the swamps and come across ancient mounds they built from shells. I'd like to go."

"What about mosquitoes? It *is* a swamp."

"This is winter. There won't be any mosquitoes."

"I'll take some repellent anyway."

"You mean you'll go?"

"Of course. I'd like to see the birds. This Ding Darling reserve has quite a reputation."

"How do you know?"

"I did a little reading myself."

"Always ahead of me, aren't you," he says, chuckling, feeling a touch foolish.

"More coffee?" Emily smiles demurely.

As he drinks his coffee Ross ruminates for an instant on the two of them shopping at the supermarket not far from their house. Emily would have her list and send him to gather a dozen eggs, some milk, and some cheese while she shopped the produce department. This was not drudgery, not when they did it together. It was one of those little things so insignificant at the time, so important in retrospect. It was the way two people, in a long love, lived together.

At the cash register they would wait in line and look over the covers of fan magazines with their escapades of celebrities behaving badly. Emily would assume a quiet innocence, all starry eyed and blinking as she played at believing their silliness. Ross has always loved her sarcasm: funny and ever so slightly cunning yet gentle enough to laugh off.

She is not a mean spirit. She could never be.

∞

The canoe is yellow fibreglass. Ross takes the stern, Emily the bow as they cast off from the little dock set within the green of the mangrove. They round a point and steer southwest down a wide channel. They paddle slowly and easily, knowing they will be out all day. Not far down the channel

Emily sights an anhinga balancing on a mangrove branch, its wings spread at odd angles out from its black body, open to the air. It is a strange, beautiful bird. It peers past them from its delicate perch as if they were not even there. The wings flutter a little then expand again like a cape. It notices them, offers up a bewildering call to the air, then settles back as they pass.

"Why does it do that, spread its wings?" Ross asks. Emily has her ornithological book in her lap, binoculars on a cord around her neck.

"It says here"—she lowers the binoculars—"anhinga swim underwater to feed so they have no oil glands like other birds; it would increase their buoyancy, so they have to dry their feathers before they can fly."

"Odd bird," he says.

"Like you," she says, laughing.

It has been like this always, this sharing. With three of us then.

On canoe trips in Algonquin Park young Robbie squirming amidships, constantly questioning. Emily answering. Ross, in the stern steering their course through the cold, clear waters. Robbie was always searching for bears on the rocks at the water's edge. At night in the tent he would sleep between his parents and worry about a bear attack. Emily would soothe him to sleep with stories of gentle animals in the forest.

Now there are only the two of them. Ross wonders what it will be like when he is alone. Has Emily presaged the future with her humour? Will he talk to himself, be one of those strange mutterers avoided by others? Will he become like that rare bird perched precariously in a world which does not comprehend? People will pass him by. He will be something for table talk later on in their evenings. They will not understand.

"Oh Ross," Emily exclaims, "look out at the water!"

Her voice brings him out of his sad reverie. He did not think it would happen again so soon. The history was to have smothered those doubts.

"Why can't it?" he mutters, too loud.

"What? I didn't hear you." Emily turns back toward him.

"Nothing," he says.

"Out there. The water. See the way it ripples!"

The channel has widened to form a big bay. In the distance are low lying islands. The morning sun reflects off the water. In some places it is placid and smooth as a mirror. In others the wind has caught it and wavelets tremble and dance making quick sparkles of the sun's rays. It constantly changes.

This is one thing, Ross knows, which is ageless. A Calusa warrior might have looked on this scene five hundred years past. He would have gazed out across the bay and seen the same backdrop of mangrove and sky. Would he have considered things changing? Only the water transforming in wind, only that changed, and then only fleetingly. The sea makes Ross feel insignificant. It makes even history seem small.

And yet, that same Calusa might have been the first of his people to glimpse Spanish ships drifting in from the open sea with their big white sails; floating islands to the native, moving clouds across the water. The water might ever remain the same, but never those things upon its surface. Ross cannot imagine what a primitive man would have thought. For that man life would have changed abruptly.

All he knew would have altered with that first glimpse of a civilization he'd never conceived or even dreamed of.

Further down they find a direction buoy bobbing just off the coast of the island. They paddle into a tidal canal and suddenly are submerged in silence. The breeze cannot reach through the thickness of mangrove. They find themselves in a leafy tunnel with grey branches interlacing above them. The water beneath is motionless. The air around them is tinged with green. The stillness is petrifying. There is only the sound of their paddles dipping softly into the water. The mangrove hangs lower as they float further in. They duck their heads as they pass beneath weaved branches. There is an odour of decay. This is the primordial. This is a place where even history is a child.

The nightmare enters his mind for an instant. This mangrove canal possesses that same feeling, that same green silence and ominous monotony as the spectral dream path. He wants to know what it means and why it recurs and seems so real and who was with him if not Emily. The mangrove seems to close in on him making him feel claustrophobic. They round a bend then and he glimpses the end of the passage; beckoning sunlight a hundred yards down. He paddles more quickly, surprising Emily. She gasps at the sudden push of the canoe. When she turns to glance back at him, he forces a smile. It is like baring his teeth but she accepts it. Through the arch they come into a saltwater lake.

Ross slows his pace welcoming the sunlight. It is very hot here, and humid, and there are mosquitoes. Emily produces the insect repellent. They spread it on their hands and faces. It has a rancid, chemical stench. Still, he is glad she has thought to bring it.

∞

Emily serving drinks; Jack and Alice Voight were over for supper. Jack was in the math department. He said he'd found some interesting stocks and was sure they would appreciate. He said the product was the coming thing. He wanted to know if Ross was interested. Emily was. They talked for an hour together while Ross sat with Alice and watched television.

When they went home he and Emily had had a fight.

"I think we can handle it financially." Emily was excited.

"What about the mortgage, and Robbie's education? We need our money for that."

"This investment really looks good. Jack seems to know something about it."

"He's a mathematician for heaven's sake. What does he know about business?"

"Just think, Ross, that's all I'm asking. We have money in the bank ..."

"We get interest from it, and it's safe."

"But Jack thinks we could make more on this."

"Look, I work for that money. I'm not about to throw it away on some math teacher's concept of the future. What if it doesn't pan out? What then? If Jack Voight had studied a little more history he might recall 1929."

"My ever conservative Ross ..."

"That's right! And we're doing alright despite it, aren't we? The answer is no. Let Jack Voight take his flying leap. I'm not interested."

Jack bought the stock and made enough money to leave teaching and set up a business of his own. The stock was for a company called Research In Motion. Emily never said anything.

Perhaps history isn't always the answer.

∞

The memory has driven away the dream. He is thankful for that. Now he stays in the present, foregoing the past and the murky future. And then they are deeper into the swamp. A water snake passes ahead of them. The snake is jet black. It weaves through the water leaving a silky ripple in its wake. There are yellow leaves dotted here and there on the mangrove and fallen leaves grown old and brown floating on the water, and always the monotonous stillness of air.

At first they do not recognise the mound. It is so old it is part of the landscape. Perhaps it has lain here five hundred years, perhaps longer. They see it first as a strange paleness in the vegetation. Then, in the flatness of swamp the chalky rise begins to stand out. In another environment it would be a mere nothing but here it possesses significance beyond its meagre size. It might be four feet tall but if one came across an oasis in the desert, or a lush valley between mountains, or a high rise in the midst of a small town ... it would be like that ... a marked difference from everything else around it.

There is a break in the mangrove as they pass it, a kind of landing which marks its edge. People have been here before to see it. They have left their marks where they pushed their canoe prows upon it. It is mottled and opalescent with age. It is almost holy. For a long while they study it from the canoe, lying just far enough off the landing to observe its entirety. Finally, Emily speaks. Her voice is the lowest of whispers but seems to shatter the silence.

"My God ..."

"I know."

"Here. In this place."

"It's a burial mound. The guidebook says ..."

"Don't tell me," she murmurs.

"No. Later."

When they leave, Ross takes a photo, feeling guilty about doing so, but wanting the memento. Emily remains quiet. She does not turn around. Her paddling is lethargic. Ross begins to think it was a mistake to have brought her here.

I did not mean to test her.

∞

She says nothing on the way home. They have dinner at a small six table restaurant but Emily only picks at her food. When they get to the cottage, she goes to bed. For the first time since they have arrived she does not want to see the sunset.

For a while Ross leaves her alone, not knowing what to say. He reads again. There is nothing more on the Calusa among his few books, so he picks up an edition of the Florida Historical Quarterly. There is an article on the first European to meet them; the Spaniard, Juan Ponce de Leon. He knows the myth: the man who sought the fountain of youth. He tells himself the concept is ridiculous. But his mind cannot focus properly. His wife is alone in the bedroom in some awful solitude and he hasn't the strength to help her. Today he has witnessed timelessness. And Emily, the innocent bystander, has come face to face with death. It was all supposed to be so simple. History, his friend and companion, has turned on him just when he needed it most.

He closes the book.

Now I must try to do something well.

When he enters the bedroom, he sees she has been crying. She does not, this time, try to conceal it. She looks small and hollow and the tracks of her tears have stained her face. She lies on the bed, her head on a pillow. Ross sits and gently places his hand on her forehead. She feels cold. For an instant he fights the urge to retreat. But her eyes are pleading. More than anything now he knows she needs him. He must offer her more than his fear.

"Are you alright, Em?" he whispers, and instantly knows he has said the wrong thing.

"I ... I don't want to die."

Mutely, he takes her in his arms, hoping his closeness will make some difference.

"I'm frightened."

"We'll find something."

"There's nothing."

"There must be," he answers. Her head is on his shoulder. She cannot see the glitter of tears in his eyes.

Like glass. Like shattered glass.

9

Had I but died an hour before this chance,
I had liv'd a blessed time; for, from this instant,
There's nothing serious in mortality ...
—**SHAKESPEARE**

Spring—The Past

The caravels used sheet anchors while a yawl conveyed Sotomayor and Miruello, his pilot, across the sea to Juan Ponce de Leon. He squinted as he watched their approach, the strong sun making the water sparkle, the ship's boat riding the waves like a cork bouncing up and down as its sailors strained at their oars. Sotomayor clambered aboard ship, heaving his great body over the railing into the warm greeting of Juan Ponce. But Sotomayor had brought bad news.

"The mizzen has splintered, my captain," Sotomayor said, speaking as if he were personally at fault. "The lateen is nearly useless. Even now it barely holds in place. I must have my men rig a spar and replace it."

"And just now the wind favours us," Juan Ponce growled in return. "I wonder, Cristoval, if somehow I'm destined to failure on this voyage."

"You've seen worse circumstances, Don Juan."

"But none, it seems, as frustrating as this."

"Then, by God, you should go on without us! Miruello and Sotil could plot some course. We could meet again in a few days!"

"In uncharted waters with a vague destination?"

"Only a thought."

"It can't be helped. Until your men complete the repairs we must wait, my friend."

The two made their way down the crowded deck, past barrels and sacks lashed to the railings, around gangs of sailors mending hemp or scrambling to Medel's orders. They grinned when Sotomayor passed as they never would for their captain-general. Sotomayor was their familiar, Juan Ponce thought, as the hammer is to the nail. Still, the carpenter commands. He led his lieutenant up to the stern where the pilots were busy taking their sightings.

"At least the time will give Miruello and Sotil a chance to discover where this whore of a storm has blown us," Sotomayor muttered. "I gather we're far off our course."

"So it appears. Well, we'll have to make the best of it. This delay will affect the men. We must find some distraction for them."

"I have the very thing in mind," Sotomayor said, his big face spreading in a winsome grin.

"Let me guess," Juan Ponce said, smiling as well.

"If you like."

"You wish me to order the steward to break out the wine?"

"And what better time, my captain? Are we not, after all, delivered from that God-cursed storm? Safe? Whole? Filled with well-being? I'm sure the men would accept a cup in celebration, as would I. If I recall, Don Juan, you possess a wondrous *madeira*. A splash of that would do this sea dog some good. I have nothing on my barque but ship's stores wine. Disgusting, but it does in a pinch."

"Thus, you invite yourself to supper and make yourself popular with my men."

"The sign of an intelligent leader, my captain! Does your cook still prepare his excellent Galician pork pie? And perhaps stuffed peppers and *polvorones*!"

"Fish stew, my voracious friend, for you and the rest of us. When we reach landfall we'll fill ourselves full but until then, *caldereta* for all."

"You are a hard man."

"And you a glutton. I'll have the pilots join us. But now *fray* Bartolome will wish to conduct the mass."

"A pity he wasn't called directly to God in the storm," Sotomayor said, smiling.

"Well, he will not be called to supper, I can assure you."

After Vespers and at the change of the watch, Juan Ponce ordered wine for all hands off duty. Below, in his cabin, a table was set for four. He sent the witch, complaining, to visit las Casas, at once keeping his promise to the monk while ridding the men of her company. The superstitions of sailors are multitudinous and a leader must defer to them, as the carpenter must care for his tools.

The cabin was crowded with the four men. They hunched round a board and barrel table set for the occasion with earthenware goblets, wooden bowls and spoons and a leather flagon of the promised wine. There was hard biscuit to dip in the stew and olives and onions and salted beef. Evening light seeped through the transom panes as a dim, bronze ray catching dust motes floating in the air. The steward entered with candles and set them on the table. He served the stew from an iron pot. It steamed in their bowls and its fishy fragrance wafted into their nostrils. The only ceremony was concocted by Miruello who raised his goblet in a toast to their survival and to the wisdom of Anton de Alaminos, the great pilot who had taught both he and Alonzo Sotil.

"I take it you've solved the puzzle of our location." Juan Ponce smiled at the man. Quite unlike Sotil, Miruello was a studious individual who cared less for the worldly ambitions of his compatriot. Yet the two of them shared the knowledge. Without them even Juan Ponce, who had first sailed when these young men were but children, would have been helpless. These callow pups were his navigators, the best he could find, and worth their weight in gold.

"We have, captain-general," the young man responded earnestly. "We're two days at most off our course. Once the mizzen is mended we should have little trouble regaining our position, provided this breeze continues."

"And no calms and no storms and no sea sirens," Sotomayor said. "Well, perhaps one or two mermaids could prove pleasant."

"Let us eat, gentlemen"—Juan Ponce interrupted the big man's melodramatic sigh—"it seems the cook has been especially good to us tonight; no worms in the biscuit and this stew smells almost edible."

"A true feast," Sotomayor said, "when I remember those days in Higuey when all there was to eat was lizard meat. Bad enough without Indians hanging from the trees stinking up everything."

"Pleasant conversation for a meal," Sotil muttered.

"I recall when I first arrived in these Indies," Juan Ponce said, changing the topic, quaffing his wine, "and my first meal here was that breadroot of the natives."

"*Cassava!*" Miruello looked up from his stew.

"Indeed. This was a much different land then, full of promise. We all felt a sense of wonder. Columbus had affected us all."

"You came here with Admiral Colon?" Miruello's attention altered quickly from the stew to Juan Ponce. Until now he had known no one who had sailed with the legend.

"These gray hairs tell that tale," Juan Ponce responded. "But I wasn't part of the first voyage. I was at Granada then."

"You were there when it fell?" Miruello seemed not to believe his ears. Another legend.

"I was. And shortly after that, I was here." The old man's voice softened and he took some more wine. "Each island was a new discovery. I tell you Columbus kept us hopping. He could never get enough of it, roaming from place to place, always searching. At that time we were sure we had reached the east. Columbus refused to believe otherwise."

"It has always amazed me," Sotil said, "that the old Admiral would look at the evidence and still not see the truth."

"But that was before Balboa's Pacific and the map maker Vespucci," Miruello said. "There was no real proof until then."

"That's true," Juan Ponce answered. "Columbus was obsessed with Cathay and its riches. Suffice to say he died believing himself a failure."

"Had he lived six more years and seen Vespucci's maps he would not have thought so," Sotil said. He spoke with near devout fervour when he mentioned the name of yet a third legendary character.

"Ah, the Florentine," Juan Ponce muttered. "To be sure he wrote his letters and drew his maps for the *Casa de la Contratacion*; still, he worked for the Medicis. Then the German, Waldseemuller, got hold of them and put them together and named the continent *America*. No, Columbus would have mourned that effort."

"But that was the proof of his theory."

"Not at all, Sotil. His theory was Cathay, not America."

"Still, it could have placed him in power again."

"His theory did not lose him his powers. Bobadilla did that on orders from the Crown: shipped him home in chains. The Queen and the King and those bastard clerks of theirs in Spain ... it was they who continued demanding riches."

"But Diego Colon, his son, is now Viceroy," Miruello said, not heeding the warning glance from Sotil.

"That was not accomplished through Colon's worth or royal gratitude, my young friend." The old man's voice was rising, his words sharp and bitter. "But by conspiracy. His father was a much different man. Diego Colon is nothing in comparison: a cunning courtier, a dandy who has ruined men's lives by lifting his codpiece to the King's cousin, marrying her, then claiming his father's rights!"

His words boomed out flatly in the small chamber. For a moment there was silence. Miruello looked down at his stew; Sotil studied his goblet; only Sotomayor looked at Juan Ponce with the deep concern born of a knowledge the others could only guess.

"But we were talking of you, Don Juan, and your beginnings here," he said calmly.

"You know all that," the old man muttered.

"But I do not, sir," Sotil said, glancing toward Sotomayor for approval and, receiving his nod, he continued. "And neither does Diego. We have heard the stories, of course, your exploits are legend, but I would enjoy hearing the truth from its source."

"The truth is brutal," came the answer, again an introverted mutter. "I was a soldier. I did a soldier's work."

"You are too humble," Sotomayor said, trying to lighten the mood. He turned to face the young pilots. "I tell you, gentlemen, with you at this modest table sits a true *conquistador*! In those days rebellion was rampant on Hispaniola. That bastard Bobadilla was Viceroy then, but his rule was corrupt. Colonists murdered, natives refusing to work ... finally Ovando was sent to replace him. Now there was a man who knew what he was about! I came over with his fleet. Oh, I was but a green boy then, and fortunate to be assigned to Santo Domingo under Don Juan. I tell you, gentlemen, it was the best thing that could have happened to me, for it was Don Juan who ended the native rebellion in a single campaign. Ovando's gratitude was such he awarded the province to our captain, and double shares to each of his men."

"Sotomayor embellishes, gentlemen, just like all the others," Juan Ponce said, but his mood had lifted a little in amusement.

"Not so, my captain, not so!" Sotomayor insisted.

"But how did you manage to end the rebellion in just one campaign?" Miruello asked.

"The Viceroy's orders were specific," Juan Ponce responded. "The natives were to be given the chance to recant. I visited their chief's village to negotiate this. Of course they refused. But unknown to them I'd placed a cavalry troop at the ready just outside their encampment. It was Sotomayor's gunshot, I believe, which was the signal to advance."

"It was indeed!" Sotomayor said. "Even then Don Juan recognised talent!"

"What happened?" Miruello questioned.

"Quite simply," Juan Ponce answered evenly, "the natives were taken by surprise. The men with me in the village formed a phalanx withstanding them while our cavalry swooped in. When we finished there were no survivors."

"A brilliant tactic, wouldn't you say?" Sotomayor said.

"You mean you killed everyone?" Sotil asked.

"Every native within a league," Sotomayor responded. "We set the war dogs loose to track them and at the end there was not one left."

"Women and children, too?"

"Everyone," Sotomayor said boastfully.

"*Jesu,*" Miruello whispered.

"Exterminated, as Viceroy Ovando had directed," Juan Ponce said flatly. He dipped a biscuit into his stew and took a bite.

"Please excuse me." Miruello rose from the table unsteadily, his voice tremulous, and left the cabin. Sotomayor watched him then turned to the others and chuckled.

"It seems our young pilot has no stomach for good *caldereta*. See, he has hardly touched his food!"

"This kind of thing," Sotil spoke softly, "was common?"

"It still is," Juan Ponce answered. "Your hero, Cortez, slaughtered thousands in that Aztec city. I take it you don't approve."

"No sir, it isn't that." The young man groped for words. "It just seems excessive."

"It is war, Alonzo," Juan Ponce placed a hand on the young man's shoulder. "To conquer you must use the means to conquer. At times those means are terrible, but necessary. I would rather have my enemy capitulate. But if he fights he accepts the consequence."

"Did the natives know that?"

"When I became governor what was left of the other tribes worked for me. I treated them well. Ensured they had food and lodging. I allowed no landowner to mistreat them. They never rebelled again."

"And Don Juan went on to conquer the entire island of San Juan Bautista!" Sotomayor boomed proudly.

"Did you use the same methods?" Sotil asked.

"It was called Boriquen then, the name given it by the natives. Had I been given the proper chance I would have settled that island peacefully."

"What prevented you?"

"Colon! Diego Colon. His machinations at court in Spain, in addition to his marriage, had secured for him the appointment as Viceroy. He'd claimed it was his right, given him by his father, Columbus. Diego Colon had Ovando removed. And when he arrived he replaced the good men who had fought for this land with his own lackeys. And without those experienced men we lost order. Nearly a hundred Spaniards were killed that year. Even Sotomayor almost died."

"How?" Sotil said, staring at the giant across the table.

"I was cocky," Sotomayor muttered. "We were tracking natives. I came to a stream and rather than let the dogs go first, I waded through to the other side; got an arrow in my neck for my stupidity. Were it not for blessed Becerillo protecting me, those warriors would have had me too. But he crossed the stream and stood over me until I could be rescued."

"Becerillo?"

"My hound," Juan Ponce answered, and to Sotil's surprise the old man's voice seemed to catch with emotion. He lifted the tumbler of wine to his lips and took a long swallow.

"A wondrous animal," Sotomayor said softly.

"In two years my colony on San Juan was secure," Juan Ponce said. "In two more I'd amassed a fortune. Gone now. Swindled from me. For you see I'd fought the wrong enemy. The Boriquenos were nothing compared to Diego Colon."

The door opening interrupted them. It was the woman back from her visit with friar Bartolome. She was silent as she entered. She had bruises on her face and a little blood dribbled from her mouth. She took her place on the bunk, curled her legs to her chin and stared at the men.

Thoughts of further conversation ended.

∞

Mayaimi was furious. The stinking monk had harangued her since she'd been sent to him by the big Spaniard. At first the monk had been kindly, telling her little stories from the black book of scribbles he carried; little parables of meekness and mercy, stories of the nobody he called god. She had followed her usual pretence of listening but allowed her thoughts to take her outward, beyond the dusky deck where the monk had met her, above the sailors swilling their wine, into that world she knew she was ever closer to reaching.

And with that proximity she had begun to doubt herself. She wondered if, after so long, she would be accepted. She thought longingly of a boy she'd known, a boy with whom she'd explored their bodies, that boy a noble and a good match who'd told her he'd cared for her and would ask for her as a wife. But would he now? Too much time had passed. He would have found another by now. Even with her return she could never re-capture that careless liberty she had once known with a boy, with her tribe, with the other girls among whom she'd been considered most beautiful and accomplished.

For despite her recalcitrance toward the Spanish she knew she had changed. She was no longer a fresh, nubile being laughing easily, or running like a deer through the pathways between villages. She was a woman now, an old woman in so many ways, far past marital age, despoiled by the Spaniard, tainted from her long banishment which had seemed so important to Calos at the time.

She recalled, as she glanced past the monk and over the water, other dusky evenings returning home from the sea aboard the huge log canoe of Calos, often in his arms at the prow as they approached the shore. She had loved those voyages with her father as he'd travelled the coast maintaining his realm, each village or town dressed up to meet him with feasts and tribute and fealty. She'd had no idea why he took her along with her brothers, yet without her sisters, on those wonderful excursions. Perhaps her father had truly loved her. But why then send her away? Why did it have to be her? What had been in his mind to tell her to do this, how to do this, knowing he was ruining a life he'd spent so much time cultivating?

Then the stinking monk was shaking her, hands on her shoulders, pulling her back to his sermon. Angry now, he shouted she must seek salvation; that she was the one to make her tribe placid and pliable for him to preach. But how do you tell a god about god? Calos was a god. And how could anyone think the Calusa pliable?

She decided then she would lead this priest into Calos' hands and the priest would be stripped, skinned and roasted. What would his nobody god do then? And Calusa warriors would gather from all across Calos' realm and become the claws which would tear at these Spanish until they were ripped to shreds. They had fought before, that first time when Calos had sent her on her mission. But that time there had been only one tribe, not the host from across his realm which could be brought to war by her father.

These thoughts comforted her and she allowed herself a dream for a while of the tribe called Timucua, of the lake called Mayaimi, from which her name had been derived. A peaceful tribe, they'd lived deep in the interior of her land, the fresh water lake by their village so clear it shimmered like crystals. She would spend time there when she was a child, enfolded within the warm clasp of her mother, learning the ways of the inland people so distinct from the Calusa.

The Timucua, unlike the Calusa, farmed their land; grew gourds which they traded for shell instruments. She had worked those little glades where cultivation was possible, learning the patience which farming can bring, learning that time could bring forth achievement. It was a lesson which had stood her well during the long years of her exile. She had grown up headstrong. It had been allowed by Calos until one day she had been returned to her mother. Calos had said she needed further instruction if she was to become his best daughter. Then her mother had taught her the meaning of prudence, to conceal her unruliness beneath discretion, to learn female ways of empowerment. She was a quick study. She had returned to Calos after a time with apologies. He had smiled as he'd accepted her. She was to have made a good marriage but during her time with her mother something had happened. So Calos had told her what she must do for him.

Be a spy. Live with the stinking Spanish.

She so missed her mother's embrace. Missed a boy. Missed royal Calos. Her life.

Then the monk grabbed her once again snapping her from her reverie to focus upon his ugly face. And the anger aroused by the stinking monk's treatment burst to the surface. Despite herself she could not hold back and she spit on him. He slapped her, several times, shouting while he beat her. She took it as she had with the big Spaniard when he'd thought he was gaining control of her: without a response, with that restraint taught her by her mother, with the strength that came from Calos. For to kill this monk, which she could easily do, meant she would in turn be murdered by the Spaniards. The stinking monk was inviolate. So she held her temper yet again as the monk sent her back to the cabin where she found the three men in conversation, and overheard as she entered the big Spaniard's words: "The Boriquenos were nothing compared to Diego Colon."

He might have known the Boriquenos of whom he'd made slaves but he knew nothing of the Calusa. They would never submit. And this Diego Colon who had ruined him did not possess the incredible powers of Calos, the god.

And none had the power of water.

She knew then she would take the big Spaniard through water.

10

I heard the old men say,
"All that's beautiful drifts away
Like the waters."
—**YEATS**

Autumn—*The Present*

At the end of the week they leave Sanibel. They drive north to Tampa through its outskirts taking Route 60 going east to a suburb called Brandon. After the island's beauty the interior is a disappointment. It is a long strip of plazas, malls and franchise restaurants. They come to the place where Ross has arranged their rental.

Happy Hills Retirement Community.

It is pleasant enough. It has palm trees along its roadways and quaint streetlights outside each mobile home. It has a pool and shuffleboard courts and a large hall for entertainments. The mobile homes seem well kept and have signs on their lawns, little wooden signs with names burnt into them: The Watson's, Marg and Bill's, Shangri-La. People wave or nod as they drive by. Old people. Wrinkled flesh. Grey thatch. Bifocals. Bandy legs. No one is young here. Ross Porter stares straight ahead as he drives; his thoughts a mayhem of confusions.

What am I doing in this place? I am not old. I am not old!

In this place they carefully cut their lawns and hang out wind chimes on their carports. They have cocktail hours where they reminisce about the old days when things were better. They take long, slow walks in the mornings. They go to bed after the nightly news. They arise with the birds. They sleep little. Sleep is too close to death. They are waiting for death; putting it off day by day, never sure if the next will be their last. People die here often. They get suntans and then they die.

Purgatory.

Emily looks at him. She is smiling. She says something about such sweet people. He marvels that she cannot see they are walking ghosts.

I forget. She is too.

They park at a building marked "Office". It is attached to the manager's home. The office and the home form an L shape of beige stucco. At the corner of the L stands a little garden with a fountain in its midst. It is a plaster, Italianate thing with cherubs pissing into a pool. They walk around it to get to the office door.

"My Lord, that's ugly," Emily says.

Ross does not answer.

"The neighbourhood's nice though, isn't it ...?"

"What's the address of our place?" he asks.

"You should remember," Emily says, smiling. "Fifty nine."

Ironic.

"The street name," he says too harshly.

"What's the matter, Ross?"

"Nothing."

"Something is."

"I just need to know the name so we can get the key."

"Hibiscus Way. Fifty nine Hibiscus Way."

The cold breath of air-conditioning greets them as they enter, and a mass of beige carpet. A desk squats at one end of the room and behind it an old style monitor and computer. There are two brown faux-leather easy chairs and a glass coffee table with a fern squatting upon it. On the walls are three framed pictures. One is a blond, blue-eyed Christ on dark velvet. The second is a needle point linen saying: "Jesus Loves You," and the third, behind the desk, a poster with a shining cross and spread across its glowing expanse:

PREPARE TO MEET THY GOD,
BE REBORN IN CHRIST.

The girl at the desk glances up. She is slovenly. Perhaps twenty-five, her hair is straight and bleached and cut blunt to her shoulders. She is wearing a tank top which partly exposes her breasts. Her makeup is far too thick.

"How y'all doin' today?" she says lazily.

"Fine," Ross says. "And you?"

"Bored silly." Her voice drawls out the words as if just saying them was an effort. "Can I do somethin' for y'all?"

"We're here to pick up the key for fifty nine Hibiscus Way. We're renting the place for the next few months. The owner's name is Tremblett; mine is Porter. Ross Porter."

"Don't know 'bout that. I'll have to check the computer."

"Fine."

She turns her back on them to work the keyboard. She types with one finger, slowly. It takes a few minutes to find what she wants. Ross and Emily glance at each other. Emily lifts her eyes into her lids. For the first time since arriving, Ross smiles.

"Yeah. I got it now. Porter. Fifty nine Hibiscus Way. Y'all Canadians?"

"Yes, we are."

"Well you're gonna find yourself right at home here. We got a park full of Canadians."

She rifles through a desk drawer and withdraws a key.

"This is it. Now it's back down this street here, turn left and go half a block, then a right. Place is down at the edge of the park. You got an orange tree in your yard. Right pretty when the blossoms are out."

"Thank you, miss ..."

"My name's Darlene."

"And I'm Ross. This is my wife, Emily."

"How do, ma'am."

"Quite well, thank you."

"And are you the owner, miss ... Darlene?"

"Lord, no. My daddy's the manager. Willis Skanes. He'll be down to meet you; let you know the rules and such. I better tell you now though, bein' it's Saturday. There ain't no swimmin' in the pool on Sundays. My daddy's kinda religious. He's got a committee makin' the rules."

"I thought that," Ross replies, covering a smile.

"Stupid, really." Her voice turns bitter. "He gets it from up home. We're from Tennessee. Been here a while though."

"I see. Thank you, Miss Skanes."

"Y'all just call me Darlene."

"Thank you, Darlene."

"We got a bingo tonight in the hall. Might wanna come up and meet some people."

"We're pretty tired from the drive. I think we'll just settle in."

"Suit yourself. Have a nice day now."

Have a nice day.

Greetings from limbo.

As they drive to their new home, Ross finds himself enmeshed in a strange reflection. In Falmouth, one vacation, he and Emily had stayed at an inn. The inn had looked out over the sea and so one evening, when they had finished dinner and were walking the beach, they had watched the tide recede. The sea left the beach rocks reluctantly, lapping in among them then suddenly gone, leaving them dry. It seemed to Ross everything had stopped, been suspended. Even the weather stood still. A line of clear sky stood out to sea with another line of clouds over the land. It seemed as if the Earth had stopped its rotation.

Emily found a nest of rocks. The two sat amidst them, leaning back, his arm draped around her shoulders. He had no idea how long they were there. But he found in that interlude a feeling of peace which settled upon him like dust with the unusual thought that time is elastic. It is measured for us in minutes and seconds, in days and years, in the span of a life. But time lives somehow independent of us. It can stretch and contract and curl back on itself. Who has not felt minutes fly by like seconds or waited impatiently, studying the tick of a clock as it marks time but does not truly measure it? Of course, there *was* time. But it felt timeless. He wonders now if there is a way to find one of those moments and stay in it; leave time behind.

He recalls then when Robert told him about taking the drug Ecstasy. He'd told him long after he'd done it. Ross couldn't be angry. He'd asked him about it. Robert had said the strangest thing about the experience was not so much hallucinations but, more startling to him, he had lost all sense of time; at one point he felt he'd never come down from his high. It had frightened him. He'd never taken the drug again. But for a while he'd lost time. Ross wondered if there might be some other potion which might do that. Extend time? Then he quickly discarded the thought as desperate; driven by this weird introduction to Happy Hills.

Yet there is timelessness. I've felt it.

Why can't I be like the sea?

∞

The place is sufficient. It has two bedrooms, a kitchen and living room and a glassed in Florida room with yellow tubular furniture. There is a bar at one end of that room. Ross searches inside and finds a half bottle of bourbon. Strong drink. He takes it anyway straight from the bottle. The room is hot without the air conditioning. He can feel sweat on his back. Through the windows he sees an old man in the carport next door. He is rail thin. He wears a pair of Bermuda shorts and a straw hat. His glasses have slipped down his nose. He lights a cigarette. A beer can lifts slowly to his lips. He just sits there, staring.

Emily calls from the kitchen. Her voice is terse. The place must be made liveable; there are things to be done: fuse box, water, unpack the car. Ross takes one last glance at the smoking man, solitude in a carport, another generation so different from his, and goes to work. The air conditioner will not function. It hums but does not kick in. He is studying the unit when a voice startles him.

"How you doin' today!"

He turns and sees the man from the carport. He has added a loose Hawaiian shirt to the shorts and straw hat. He is smoking another cigarette. His voice has that rasp of too many cigarettes. His fingers are nicotine stained.

"Pretty well," Ross responds, "except for this air conditioner. I can't seem to get it started."

"Figured that. Not pushin' air, eh?"

"That's right. How'd you know?"

"Tommy Tremblett's been my neighbour here the past few years. Too bad about him."

"Oh? Why's that?"

"Died this past spring. Didn't you know?"

"I'm a friend of his son. We've just rented the place."

"Name's Jim White. Just call me Jimmy."

"Ross Porter. My wife Emily's inside."

"Think I can fix this for you. I'll just get a couple of tools."

"It's alright. We can get a repairman Monday."

"Round here you'd be lucky to get one at all. Not like up home. Too busy here."

"You're Canadian?"

"Down from Peterborough. The wife and me stay the winter here; got a cottage for summers in the Kawarthas, north of Peterborough."

"Sounds nice."

"Not bad. The wife ain't too well. We get on though. I'll just go get them tools and be back in a jiffy."

"You're sure it's not too much trouble?"

"What're neighbours for?"

"Maybe you and your wife could come for supper. Only hamburgers but ..."

"That's nice. Sure. I better warn you 'bout the old gal though. She forgets things."

"I'm sure it'll be fine."

Jimmy fixes the air conditioner. He was a mechanic, he says, for trains. He is seventy-four, has four children and seven grandchildren, worked for the CPR all this life, hates politicians, and is worried that if he gets ill his wife, Maggie, will have to go into a home. All this Ross discovers in the time it takes Jimmy to complete the repair and have two bourbons on ice. Jimmy likes to talk. He says it's all he does well any more. Not like the old days. His glasses slip down his nose as he speaks. He keeps pushing them back. He is formal when he meets Emily. He calls her Mrs. Porter despite her protestations. While he returns home to wash and bring Maggie over, Ross starts the barbecue. Emily makes a salad, fussing a little at the suddenness of company but grateful for the air conditioning.

Maggie is a big, robust woman who laughs easily and, though nervous initially, is quite friendly. At first glance there seems nothing wrong with her but soon it becomes apparent she is struggling. She repeats everything Jimmy says. He is her safe haven. If she follows his lead she will not be embarrassed. This much she knows. Her character still remains but self-assurance has left her. She knows what is happening to her. She struggles against it. But it is inexorable. At dinner Jimmy fills her plate for her. Once she takes Emily's drink by mistake. Everyone ignores it. The table talk turns to economics.

"Down here everything's cheaper," Jimmy says, "dependin' on the exchange rate, of course."

"Cheaper ..." Maggie echoes.

"But you gotta look in the newspaper ads to see when things are on sale."

"On sale ..."

"Me and another fella get up early Wednesday mornings. Go over the ads then drive down the strip so's we can have our pick. If you don't go early everything's gone. Why just last week, where was it, dear, one of the groceries ..."

"Groceries ... I don't know."

"Just let me think now."

"Yes," Maggie says softly.

"Damn, what was the name of that place?" It is important to Jimmy that he remember.

"The place ... yes ..."

"Wynn Dixie! Sure."

"Wynn Dixie," Maggie echoes triumphantly.

"Why they had corned beef on there so cheap you'd think you were stealin' it! Me and this fella got there late. His car wouldn't start."

"Wouldn't start," Maggie says, sadly.

"Well by the time we fixed it and got there the corned beef was gone; every last ounce of it, by God. And it was only nine thirty in the morning!"

"Isn't that awful," Maggie ventures. She looks over at Jimmy to be sure she is right.

"I'd say so," Jimmy says, patting her hand. He is proud of her.

Jimmy gets a bit drunk after that and tells stories from the old days. He tells them well, anecdotes of a life, but they go on a little long. Maggie listens blissfully. These are memories she vaguely recalls. It is as if her old life is new again.

This is timelessness too.

∞

When he married her, Ross married Emily's family as well and the bond which Emily continued with her father. When her mother died, Emily was with her, by her bedside, feeling her leave; Ross in a corner of the hospital room watching her father hold one hand, Emily the other until her mother had passed. And when she was gone Emily had folded her mother's arms and closed her eyes and then went to her father and held him. She'd accepted that death and lived with the loss.

That same year her father had died of a brain aneurysm. The man had had a good life and in the end he went quickly, without suffering; healthy until the moment of collapse. Yet Ross had never seen Emily so traumatized, so different from her response to her mother's death. After the funeral she would not be comforted. There were silent tears in the night as she would turn away from him in their bed, or long silences when there should have been talk. It went on for months. Ross worried she'd never recover. He tried suggesting counselling. She looked at him as if he were from another planet. He had tried in his way to comfort her but found, to his consternation, he was jealous of a dead man, knowing he'd never replace him. He was angry at Emily for her intemperate grief.

He'd just wanted her to get past it.

Yet he comprehends it now as he faces the inevitable. She'd lost a man she loved dearly, a soul mate who happened to have been her father. It took time and patience and love but he'd seen her through it and in turn had become, not her father's replacement, but more intimate than ever before in their marriage. He'd felt the full depth of her passion and partnership. And now, facing the inevitable, Ross understands what his mother had meant all those years ago when his own father had passed; her fear of living alone. As with Emily and her father, with Ross' own mother and father, so with Emily and him; there is a bond, but always an end.

I fear for my soul, so knowing the one departing.

∞

Emily goes to bed. Jimmy takes Maggie home. Ross has followed them outside. The night is humid. The sound of cicadas fills the stillness. Jimmy asks Ross over and gives him a drink while he puts Maggie to bed. Ross sits in the carport on the lawn chair Jimmy was using that afternoon. He looks across at his new home. The lights are on. They comfort him. They are warm amber in the dark.

Their bedroom window, however, is dark. Emily will be sleeping now. She had looked so pale when she went to bed.

Jimmy joins him. He has a drink and lights another cigarette. A night breeze comes rustling through palm leaves.

"Your wife's feelin' poor tonight, eh?" Jimmy says quietly.

"She has cancer."

"Sorry to hear it. Mighty nice lady."

Perhaps it is his manner mixed with the strain of arrival and the amber window twilight where his cigarette glows red and reassuring, or perhaps it was seeing him with his own wife, helping her through the evening, knowing they are companions in this, that lets Ross open up to Jimmy White. As the two men speak, there is a pause between each sentence, as though every word must be considered before it is uttered.

"I'm going to lose her, Jimmy."

"You certain?"

"Yes."

"Well then, enjoy her while you can. Make it good for her."

"I don't know if I'm strong enough."

"You are. Might not seem so right now, but you will be. You got no other choice."

"Sometimes I think I'm more afraid of her leaving me than her dying."

"Nobody wants to be alone."

"Why did it have to be now?"

"Now or later. Same thing."

"You really think that? She's still young ..."

"Later gets to be now soon enough. I know. The older I get the faster it goes."

"I don't feel old, Jimmy."

"No one does. What's inside me ain't old. Inside I'm still that kid from the farm, from the railway, a little mellower maybe ..."

"What about Maggie?" Ross mutters.

"Let me tell you 'bout her." Jimmy takes it calmly.

"Look, I'm sorry. I didn't mean to ..."

"Hell with that. We both gotta face things. I like an honest man. When I married Maggie"—Jimmy pauses to light up again—"she was a beauty. I mean a real beauty. I couldn't believe I could be that lucky. A few years went by and I come to know I was luckier than I thought. Her looks went. We had a hard life sometimes: me gone a lot and her tryin' to hold things together. But inside she was a hell of a woman: strong, funny, always liked a good joke and a little beer, and she loved me. Don't know why. I give her plenty of cause not to. But she did. That's still there, y'see. It's got more trouble gettin' out now but I can tell it's there. She ain't really changed. She just forgets things. But she hasn't forgot she loves me. And I haven't forgot either. Inside we're the same as always."

"But it won't be like that for me. When Emily goes part of me will go with her."

"That's what you're really afraid of, ain't it?"

"Everything will change."

"Lord, man, you told me yourself you're not sixty yet.

You got a whole part of your life in front of you. Take it from me, that's something."

"I know, Jimmy. But it's the last part."

"Don't mean it's got to be empty."

"Everything will be different," Ross reiterates softly.

"Every day's different," Jimmy says.

Simple.

∞

Returning home Ross stops to think for a moment in the dark just outside his carport door. In her nursing home thirty years before he'd visited his Aunt Louise on her ninety-ninth birthday. Surrounded by cooing relatives, she'd sat in her wheelchair and stared back defiantly every time someone had patronized her. The local MPP had given her a plaque. She'd taken it with a snarl and buried it under the rest of her gifts. She'd had spirit.

Here was a woman who had lived her life in the most dynamic of centuries. She had seen the invention of the motor car, air travel, film and television; she had lived through boom and depression, two world wars, man reaching the moon, the internet. She had lived the history he'd only read of. He thought she was remarkable.

He'd stayed till the end of the affair. He'd waited until the attendants were cleaning up and then wheeled Aunt Louise back to her room. It was cluttered with knick-knacks and old photographs. She had a story for each of them. The two talked half an hour about her life: about cooking on wood stoves and losing a son, about illness and family scandals, all personal things. Not enough for Ross, not at all what he had expected. She'd told him he was a serious young man; always had been from what she recalled. She'd smiled when she'd said it. He had asked her finally what was on his mind, his burning question: what had it been which had had the most impact upon her. She'd taken her time to reply, her old eyes sparkling. Ross was breathless for wisdom.

"Seems to me young girls don't wear white gloves anymore."

White gloves on girls.

A whole life and that was what mattered?

Someone could be that small? Think that little? Nearly a century, and that was her answer? He left her in her room with a quiet goodbye. Softly he disparaged her, muttering alone in his car on the way home. It was unbelievable. She died eight months later.

And only then, that much later, did Ross catch on.

Emancipation.

No more white gloves.

Age offers something.

Remarkable.

11

Mariner, do not ask whose tomb this may be,
but go with good fortune: I wish you a kinder sea.

—**PLATO**

Spring—The Past

On a visit to Castile, after the Higuey campaign, I went to Valladolid to receive my Knighthood from King Ferdinand. I took time to meet the two men who, though opposed in their opinions, had given us a New World. Most interesting, both were foreigners: one a Genoese, the other Florentine. Oh, we'd supplied them and given them ships but it was they who took the risks: one to discover, the other to clarify. As a result one was vilified and left to feel failure, while the other was given glory beyond even his expectation. They were unique men, needless to say, and the world has yet to find many like them.

I met the first in a monastery. He'd retired there with his youngest son, Fernando, who was writing his father's biography while battling the law to recover the rights taken from the old man. The Crown had reneged on its obligations to my mentor, Cristofero Columbus. The once

'Admiral of the Ocean Sea' was sick and wasted by then, reduced to a tortured soul embittered by what had been done him. It is difficult to write this, to tell this story of a man whom I worshipped for his vision, yet pitied his lack of practicality. In a way it is my own story as well.

One cannot say Columbus was not arrogant. It was that characteristic which, against so many odds, brought him to a new world. And that same flaw led to certain exaggerations of his discoveries in his reports to the Crown. He spoke of mountains of gold when there were but grains, of great civilizations which were mere native tribes, and, of course, he insisted he'd found the edge of the East when all know now he was wrong. Still, he was given what first had been promised him: the titles of Admiral over those waters and Viceroy in perpetuity to all his newly discovered lands; and ten percent of their revenues.

But that hubris which gave him such power made him a naive leader and others—mercenaries, courtiers and priests far more devious than he—plotted their own advancements. When Columbus insisted all men should contribute to the construction of the colony through manual labour, the nobles' sons simply refused and the priests made clear it was beneath their dignity. He fought back. Demanded their work. There was a revolt. Several peers either died or were imprisoned. The innocent Genoese thought he'd done the right thing in bringing these troubles under control. Yet he'd only succeeded in making powerful enemies at the Court in Spain. Vengeful of this commoner's treatment of their precious second sons, they acted.

A new Viceroy, Francisco de Bobadilla was named

without Columbus' knowledge and, when that fat bastard had landed with armoured troops and a writ rescinding the 'Capitulations of Santa Fe', the promise through which Columbus held power, the great man was sent in chains back to Spain. He was imprisoned, I am sure, to teach him humility and when he was released he emerged a changed man: sick, discouraged, reduced, embittered ... and forever refused his rightful remuneration.

When I met him it was at his request. He knew I had acquired the Governorships of Higuey and San Juan Bautista and, at that time, was favoured at Court. He thought I could do something for him. I recall our brief meeting quite clearly.

The monastery was a poor one, set on a rise above the ocean behind a long, sand beach. It was the very place where Columbus had housed himself and his family while he'd spent the years importuning the Portuguese and then Queen Isabella to finance his voyage of dreams. In a simple building of sandstone walls which surrounded a little courtyard, his small suite of rooms peered out through two windows. The rooms themselves were quite plain with only the roughest of furnishings, and in the second room were a rope bed and thin straw mattress. The rooms were dim; the only light coming through the narrow windows. The walls were bare but for a cross above his bed, and a well-used chart on a rough table beside him.

"You are good to see me, Don Juan," he said softly, his voice matching the arid rooms he inhabited.

"Admiral, it is I who should be grateful to once again have your hand in mine!" I spoke airily, full of myself with my new positions, as I shook his parchment-dry hand.

"I no longer own that title, my friend. I've been discharged. Fernando here fights in the courts for me and Diego has installed himself with those in power."

"I noticed him at Court. It was he who delivered me your note."

"He's a bright young man, as is Fernando." Columbus smiled as he looked toward his youngest. "Fernando here is wrapped in the law's tentacles. They seem endless. I see no way through them. I do have hopes for Diego, however. He has made certain connections, as you say, at the Royal Court. Even if I am refused my rights, he will come to be something. Just watch."

"Of course he will," I said in a voice even now I cringe at recalling. Its patronizing tone forced the intimacy of our meeting into another, more formal sphere.

"You've travelled a long way at my request. I thank you again, Don Juan," Columbus said, appropriately subdued.

"Strange, isn't it, that I should be given a title while you are relieved of yours?"

Columbus' eyes widened; his mouth was hard set; his face formed the lines of that bitter resentment which was making him sick.

"And from what I hear of this character, Vespucci, he's trying to take even my repute! He claims to be the actual founder does he not?" Columbus' whisper had pushed to a furious rasp, then rough coughing. His son rushed across the room giving him watered wine to ease his throat.

"You see what I've become," he said, the cough subsiding. "A shell, a nothing. They have reduced me, and now wish to eradicate me from the place in history I've earned."

"I don't think Vespucci is claiming anything, Admiral. He seems to be simply clarifying your discoveries with his maps."

"You've read his letters?"

"Yes. He claims what you found is a continent."

"But not the Indies!" Columbus snarled, taking a further sip of his watered wine.

"As I understand his writings, yes."

"These new charts of his, they show something huge."

"That river, just west of the Pope's 'inter caetera' line, he claims, as you did, to contain so much fresh water emptying into the sea it must mean a continent upstream."

"And that continent is the Indies! He says otherwise and so robs me of my discovery!"

"But remember, Vespucci works for the Medicis family. They control the banking which controls trade with Cathay. They want no new route to the east; thus his conclusions reflect their requirements."

"Your interpretation, Don Juan. Others believe he's found a true New World." Columbus revealed his dejection. He said little more, so crestfallen was he at the turn of events brought about by Vespucci. We talked a while longer: small things as two old friends will do. Soon after he fell asleep. I rose to depart but was halted by a word from Fernando.

"Don Juan, my father has something he asked me to give you." He produced a parchment which he presented to me as though it were the most valuable bauble in Spain. "He wants you to give this to the King. Queen Isabella is dead but surely the King will keep faith with my father."

"I have little access," I said quietly. "A simple knight amidst nobles. Why not give this to Diego? Have him deliver it. Your father said he's worked his way into their ranks."

"Alas, to feed his own mouth. I'm not so sure my brother wishes my father to regain anything, unless it comes under my brother's possession."

"Surely that cannot be true."

"Will you take the missive?"

"Of course, I will try."

"That is all I ask."

"May I read it?"

"Of course."

I untied the ribbon which held the parchment, as yet without a seal, and read, skimming the parts most dense with vitriol, finding the missive's central theme.

> It is now seventeen years since I came to serve these princes with the Enterprise of the Indies. They made me pass eight of them in discussion, and at the end rejected it as a thing of jest. Nevertheless I persisted therein ... Over there I have placed under their sovereignty more land than there is in Africa and Europe, and more than seventeen hundred islands ... In seven years I, by divine will, made that conquest. At a time when I was entitled to expect rewards and retirement I was incontinently arrested and sent home loaded with chains ... The accusation was brought out of malice on the basis of charges made by civilians who had revolted and wished to take

> possession on the land ... I beg your Graces,
> with the zeal of faithful Christians in whom
> their Highnesses have confidence, to read all
> my papers, and to consider how I, who came
> from so far to serve these princes ... now at
> the end of my days have been despoiled of
> my honour and my property without cause,
> where is neither justice nor mercy.

It was a desperate appeal. It made me aware of how much
a man might be reduced by those things he cannot comprehend. I never thought of myself at the time. It seems
I have ever been short-sighted. Instead, I promised to
deliver the letter. Later, I gave it to Diego. He accepted it
doubtfully and I made an enemy in the giving. If only I'd
listened more carefully to young Fernando and learned
more about his brother. Instead, I ignored reality and
was conquered by Diego Colon who, as his brother had
told me, was a selfish, sneaking, suckling villain.

Columbus died the next year: broken and in despair,
his life a disappointment. And the world then lost some
of its glory, and was somehow reduced.

Not long after I had presented Diego Colon with his
father's appeal, I attended a gathering in the house of
Don Pedro Nunez de Guzman, my sponsor, where I met
the man to whom Columbus had been so opposed ...
the map maker Vespucci or, as he termed himself then
at the summit of his status, 'Americus Vespucius,' which
makes quite clear in itself the nature of the man.

He had completed his exploratory voyages by
then, and received all the information and charts given
him by the Casa de la Contratacion, which controlled

everything about the New World. From these sources Vespucci had created an opus entitled "Mundus Novus". His letters were addressed to the Casa but of course they were published. The King had an ego as well. He wanted the world to know what had been accomplished during his reign.

Vespucci was celebrated by every court in Europe for he had claimed that his research had placed in the hands of Castile and Aragon a completely new territory ripe for exploitation; not Cathay, not the Indies, but an entire New World.

I spoke to the man only for a moment as he swept past me in a whirl of black scholar's robes. As I was introduced he paused an instant, stroked the long thinness of his beard and said: "Ah, de Leon. You are the man who gave me the coast of Florida, yes?"

As though I were somehow his retainer and my explorations mere footnotes in his grand work. I replied stonily in affirmation, incensed by his self-importance, and began to speak of my meeting with Columbus. Yet when he heard the old Admiral's name, Vespucci turned and swept off amidst his adherents, one of whom was Diego Colon, who appeared not to want to hear of his father any more than the great Florentine. By this time Diego had changed his name, against his father's wishes, to its Spanish version and was scheming even then to replace Nicolas de Ovando as Viceroy of the Indies; the name given it by Columbus and never altered, despite Vespucci's protestations.

A year later a German cartographer named Waldseemuller produced his epic map of the world: an incomplete map, quickly shifting to blank space in the west where the German had placed the name 'America'.

This is not an easy thing to face, nor an easy tale to tell. It is yet another reminder of what is to happen to me if I do not find the sacred fountain. Emasculation. I feel even now in the remains of my power that I, once governor of entire islands and captain-general of an army, once wealthy beyond my dreams, once worshipped at the Royal Court, would be reduced to this smattering of two small caravels in search of a promise.

Oh, this taxes my mind. I have sat up writing too late in the night. I go now to sleep with my witch.

Will I be Columbus, or Vespucci?

∞

It was after four bells when Juan Ponce closed his journal and locked it away then undressed for bed. When he extinguished the lamp the only remaining glow was the moon: blue light drifting in through the transom. He lay down beside the woman. She seemed to be asleep so he settled on his back and tried to relax his way out of his thoughts. He breathed deeply, focusing on each tense muscle, allowing it to slacken until his body was lying still and calm. It was just then when she spoke to him. She had not been sleeping at all but buried within her own thoughts which now poured out despite his protestations.

"These men, before, when you talked with your friends; this Colon, who is he?" she said.

"Let me sleep, woman."

"I heard you when I came back from the friar, I heard you say those Boriquenos were not your enemies yet you went out and warred on them. Why would you do that?"

"Orders from my leader."

"Your Chief, that King?"

"No. Another. My King's representative."

"What is that?"

"A Viceroy, the hand of the King in these parts."

"Yet he was your enemy."

"Not that one. That one was Ovando. My enemy is the new Viceroy, Colon."

"So you serve him now? Yet you hate him."

"He's stripped me of my titles and lands. I refuse to do his bidding."

"Yet he still influences things. This voyage was done with his permission."

"The voyage he *thinks* I am making. I am making another voyage, as you know."

"To reach the sacred water."

"Let me sleep."

"What voyage does he believe you make?"

"To found a colony in your land."

"If Calos allows it."

"Sleep now. It's late."

For a brief time she lay quietly, but then leaned up on one elbow, her hair tumbling down past her shoulders to fall on his chest. He could not see her face for the shadow of hair. Still, when she lay like this he knew she was puzzled. He awaited her next question and when it came, it shocked him.

"Why not just kill him, this Colon?"

"What?"

"You do it with others. Why not this one? Take him out of your way."

"I can't do that."

"Calos would. If enemies stand in his path, he sweeps them down as a surging tide."

"All this time among us and you still don't understand civilization?"

"What do you mean?"

"There are laws. There is morality."

"And this Colon, does he have morality?"

"No. Or at least no honour."

"Then kill him. He is your enemy. If he were my enemy, he would die."

"Why should you have enemies? And if you did, I think they'd be unreachable, far above and beyond your vengeance."

"There are ways, and ways," she muttered.

"Tell me of them. Your enemies. Who? Of course, friar Bartolome! You hate him, don't you? You refuse Christianity when it would make things so much simpler for you. And you won't even use the Christian name I gave you. Why would you do that? What is a name?"

"Yet this Colon is the son of a man who would not use that name," she replied. "Why would he not? And why would his son?"

"His son wishes to control part of the Spanish empire; to do that he must appear to be Spanish. Columbus came from a different nation."

"As am I, different, not Spanish. Now do you understand?"

"Tell me more. Your enemies. They must be my servants, though I haven't heard of any of them murdered in their beds." He taunted her jovially, the distraction driving his troubles away.

"But we are talking of your enemy, Colon," she replied. "You should have killed him, yet you ran away from him with these ships, on this voyage."

"And you know why. After I reach the water you speak of I will return. Diego Colon will be swept aside. And have you a plan for your enemies?"

He was too close, she realized. She should not have led him in this direction. He might get ideas, this foolish old man, with his vengeance. Mayaimi went quiet, turned over, and lay with her back to him, her eyes open to the dark.

"You don't, do you? Have a plan, I mean," the big Spaniard said, chuckling.

She said nothing.

∞

I have had no sleep this night. The witch and her questions have brought me nightmares. I drift off for a moment only to be jarred awake by another thought of another enemy from another time. I have made too many of them. She has made me think of death as well. Life can be taken so easily. I know this. I have taken enough. Each one was its own story. I was merely its end.

How will I end? Clawing and kicking in battle or suffering silently from some disease? Welcoming death or terrified of it? I cannot know.

In Toledo I attended an 'auto da fe': a burning in the public square, ordered by the Inquisition, just below the cathedral steps. I was with Archbishop Fonseca at the time and so followed along as he stood on his dais above the crowd of snarling, drunk peasants for whom this was to be an entertainment.

That day a man and two women were tied to posts awaiting their fates atop a pile of oiled sticks. I have no idea if they were unrepentant Jews, Moors, Mariscos or Gypsies or simply innocents betrayed by grasping neighbours.

Inquisition is a harsh creed. These people had been named heretics so no quarter was spared them. All three were barely conscious from their tortures. As the servitors floated about in their cassocks preparing for fire, notaries stood by ready to record any final confessions. A confession would allow the penitent strangulation; thus release from the agonies of the flames. Two of them, a man and a woman, kissed the cross, spoke the words of admission, and were garrotted. An ugly death but a quick one.

The third, a woman, would not recant. She stared out above the roiling crowd at something beyond it. When the kindling was lit and the fire began to lick upward through her clothing, burning it away along with her flesh, she never screamed, never grimaced, never even acknowledged her suffering. Whatever her god, she'd accepted her death and went willingly. Her story ended in heroism.

The crowd was disappointed. They'd come for anguish. But I was proud of that woman. Of course I could say nothing; yet I have ever revered her. I recall her now when I think of the witch. She is much like that woman. She will not succumb to our culture. She sees something beyond.

Yet she is a savage. If she has no soul, as the Church seems to think, then she is animal. Animals do not have a conscience. I wonder what she could possibly mean when she says she has enemies.

I admit, I do not understand her; this woman without a name.

12

Tomorrow, and tomorrow, and tomorrow,
Creeps in this petty pace from day to day ...
—Shakespeare

Autumn—*The Present*

The weeks pass, one into the other, unfolding gently. In the mornings Ross runs then joins Emily for breakfast in the Florida room, a windowed space which invites in the sunlight. They read the morning paper and glance up occasionally to glimpse the slow habitual stirrings of life in Happy Hills.

The first to pass their place each day is Mrs. Olive Livingstone, a spry old bird with blue hair who strides by purposefully in a pink track suit and matching sneakers accompanied by her companion of years, an ageing grey schnauzer badly misnamed with the appellation of 'King'. King's stubby limbs work furiously keeping up with the swinging strides of his mistress. He bounces along courageously thinking dog thoughts, no doubt, of the food bowl awaiting him at the end of his daily trial.

Afterward comes the gaggle of women Jimmy White calls the "shuffle demons". They have gathered gradually:

first one, then the next calling at each porch until there are five or six of them. They stroll slowly down the middle of the road gossiping; pointing out to each other things of interest on their route: new lawn ornaments, curtains in windows, garden hoses left out overnight, whose grass is not cut. They point toward Ross and Emily's home and whisper as they pass. They cannot see inside, the morning sun's glare on the windows prevents them. A car comes down the roadway. The women shuffle out of its way, averse to having their promenade interrupted by its effrontery. As it passes they give the driver hard looks then fill up the roadway again in its wake.

A little later the men appear; those who have not already left to play golf. If Ross is outside working on something, he can depend on their advice. They saunter along the sidewalk stopping often to talk in carports. They cross and re-cross the street in search of conversation. They wear straw hats and white shoes.

In the afternoons when the sun is hot the streets are empty. While their neighbours collect at the pool, Ross and Emily remain mostly at home. They sit in lawn chairs relishing the quiet, sipping iced tea, allowing the day its slow, lazy passage. Ross is well stocked now with local history. He has read more on the Calusa and found a brief biography of Juan Ponce de Leon. He wonders what kind of man the Spaniard might actually have been. Though he'd possessed a reputation and significance in his time, he is but a footnote in history, and an odd one indeed.

In search of the fountain of youth.

Myth and history are such intimates.

Jimmy White often visits. Maggie takes her afternoon nap and he casts about for something to do. He and Emily get on well. Jimmy tells her stories. They sit in the shade of the orange tree. The soft peals of Emily's laughter make Ross glance up from his book. She is so much better now. The sunshine and rest and Jimmy have each taken turns to rejuvenate her. So Ross' fears have faded. Not gone, never gone, they weigh like pebbles in his sack of hope which will never completely empty.

He recalls a time, like myth and history, both joyful and yet bewildering to him. It was when they'd brought baby Robbie home from the hospital. Emily was glowing. Ross was strangely jealous. He felt himself an intruder upon her joy with this interloper suckled to her while he ... waited ... looking over her shoulder, apart; yet a part. The baby was the foreign one yet Ross felt redundant. Then Emily had handed him the child. Suddenly, in his arms in that instant he had found enchantment. From envy to love in a breath. It had crossed to him through their son. Their son.

I was such a boy then.

If he had the chance to live his life again, he thought, he would somehow try to slow it all down, discover more of its significant moments as he had with baby Robbie. He'd hurried through life, he thought. He'd been so busy planning his future, not just his own but his son's, his students', his colleagues', his Emily's ... He had not really lived it to the full.

It comes to him now in its pieces. He remembers moments which represent years. He knows the history of mankind better than his own history. He can call upon facts, recognise movements, comprehend rises and falls of nations, and yet cannot clearly recall his life. Once he'd taught the past to the future, as a teacher to his students. Perhaps he should have concentrated on the present. He knows

Emily does that now. She gathers each day to herself as a gift. She lives every precious moment as she did once with Robbie.

And just then he sees what he is doing to her. He is the one interceding to steal away her each day. He is the one with his drawn face and patronization which must remind her of her disease. He realizes he must be more like Jimmy. He knows why she likes him. Emily says he is full of life.

∞

The days pass into evenings. They go to bed and Ross listens to the silence. Ross tries to sleep but sleep evades him; yet when he does fall asleep it turns on him. The dreaded dream slithers in, reptilian, hissing: the car, the dank track of trees with limbs that reach through the window caressing his arm, leaving scratches, the voice beside him, behind, all around.

"Don't go in there, Ross, you'll be alone don't go in there, Ross, don't go in."

Pushing through moss and into the tunnel. There are flowers amid the twisting green stems, though they seem to move, seem to disappear when they shouldn't then reappear somewhere else. Sometimes they look like melting flowers, sometimes tongues, human tongues ... then the muck. Umbrous rivulets trickle like blood. There is the flat stink of snakes.

Snakes?

His eyes snap open. Moonlight silhouettes the branches of the orange tree outside their window. A breeze moves the branches. They begin to writhe.

Enough.

"Where are you going?" Emily mumbles as he gets out of bed.

"Can't sleep."

"You're not well?"

"It's just, it's three in the morning and I can't sleep. I've been tossing and turning."

"What's wrong?"

"Nothing's wrong! I just can't sleep. I'll make some tea."

"I'll get up with you."

"Maybe I should sleep in the other bedroom for a while," he mutters.

"Tonight, you mean."

"No. Until I adjust. I don't want to keep disturbing you, Em. It's not fair."

"All the years we've been married we've never slept in separate beds."

"I just can't sleep!" Hollow, helpless voice.

The dream drifts away. He turns on the light. She does not know what writhes inside him. She is sharp with him. She knows nothing of his dreams.

"You're not active enough," she says.

"I'm running every day," he answers, dispersing shadows.

"You need something more. It's time you met some people here."

"They're old, for Chrissake!"

"Did you know there's a group that plays tennis every morning?"

"No. How could I?"

"There's a notice posted on the board in the hall. They're looking for partners."

"How did you find out?"

"I went up and looked. I asked you to come but you

were buried in your book." Her voice has gone flat; she is angry. "There's a bridge league. I'd like to join."

"You know I don't like cards."

"Alone." The retort was sharp.

"Why haven't you then?"

"Because I'm living with a martyr. Have you any idea how that makes me feel?"

"That's not fair," he says, knowing it is true.

"At home we didn't spend this much time together. For heaven's sake, Ross, if we keep this up we'll have nothing left to say to each other. I know why you're doing it. I love you for it. But you have to find time for yourself."

"Is that what you want?"

"Unless you want to keep waking up every night."

"That's not all there is to it!"

"I know that. But we have to live, Ross. If we dwell on my cancer all the time, I might as well be dead now."

"Don't say that."

"It has to be said."

"Just tell me what you want," he says.

"You make me feel selfish. I don't want to feel that way. Not now."

He can feel she is close to tears. He has done this to her. He forces some calm on himself. It is not easy. Suddenly he finds himself rigid in his attempts to answer.

"I see," he says.

"I hope so. I hope you don't think me ungrateful."

"No."

"Talk to me, Ross."

So he lies with the truth. He says she has helped him. He speaks like an automaton and knows she knows it. There is no other way to reveal his fears. He must have *no* fears in her presence. He stops talking knowing how each word affects her. He turns off the light and rolls over, eyes open, wondering what in the world he will do without her.

∞

The next day he joins the men's tennis league. They meet every weekday at nine. There are seven. Ross makes a welcomed eighth. He replaces someone named Dan whom all the men liked and who died of a stroke just a few weeks before. At first Ross is uncomfortable with this but the men seem pleased he has joined them. They speak warmly, but not often, of Dan. It is as if Dan has simply moved on.

Al Watson greets him at the court gate, a big, bluff man who smiles openly and often. He is the volunteer convenor of the group. He introduces Ross to the others, in particular to Colin Lofthouse who will be Ross' partner in doubles. Instantly Ross likes him. Colin is a soft spoken man who looks down after shaking hands. This lick of shyness attracts Ross to him. He is balding, round-faced and wears horn-rimmed glasses. His hands are thick, their backs covered with greying hair that runs like fur up his forearms disappearing into the sleeves of his T-shirt. Ross thinks of him as bear-like: stocky, taciturn and in tennis surprisingly quick on his feet.

Some of the men are actually only little older than Ross and he is pressed hard to play at their level. One particular fellow whom the others refer to as 'dad' plays with such expertise he nearly runs Ross ragged. Ross discovers later his name is Art Hedges. He is seventy-seven and he likes a beer after playing.

They play without the competitiveness which affects

younger men. At one point in their match they hear cheering when Ross makes a point. Looking over, Ross sees Darlene from the office. She wears her usual skimpy clothing and is accompanied by another, very thin girl who accentuates Darlene's voluptuousness. Colin comes to his side.

"Seems you've got a fan club," he says. "This hasn't happened before."

"What do you mean?" Ross asks quietly.

"Just watch out for that girl. Got a bit of a reputation and her father, you know, is the park manager and chief inquisitor for the committee."

"I've done nothing to encourage this," Ross says.

"It's not about you. It's her. Be careful, that's all."

When they finish they walk to the club house for lemonade and Art has a beer. They rehash their morning's game and jibe at each other with easy humour. They ask where Ross comes from, any kids, what he did in what they call 'real life' and in turn tell about themselves. Nothing remarkable. Nothing intense. Just the easy glow of men talking. Ross discovers himself relaxing within their straightforward camaraderie despite his new reservations regarding Darlene.

Ross arrives home to find Emily departing for bridge. She is bustling and cheerful and throws him a kiss as she leaves. Her hands gesture in that carefree manner he hasn't seen for a year. He takes a shower and has some lunch. He sits in the backyard under the orange tree reading a little of Juan Ponce de Leon. Strange, he thinks. Myth or history. An explorer and a professional soldier. This was a man who had given Florida its name. He had deduced the existence of the Gulf Stream, a nautical wonder. He had been a governor of colonists and a captain-general of *conquistadors*.

He was grouped with those infamous men like Pizarro, Cortez and Balboa; a list of conquerors searching out new lands then despoiling them. Ross wonders what forces gathered to create men like that?

Did they ever think of time passing?

A butterfly flutters above the book. It lands on the spine, curtailing his thoughts with its beauty. It is golden and warm like the day. A cardinal whistles a melodic song just above him. Glancing up he glimpses a scarlet flash in the foliage of the orange tree. He turns again to the book, closes it, shuts his eyes and lies back on the lawn chair.

In his mind a fireplace is crackling within their old, warm living room up home. Little Robbie sleeps on the rug by the fire and, curled up beside him, the cat is licking the boy's fingers. Candlelight brushes the room in a coppery glow. It gives Emily's face a soft radiance. It makes of Robbie and his calico friend a painting. Ross breathes the aroma of maple smoke and contentment.

All days should be like this one.

Myth and history.

13

We are not now that strength which in old days
Moved earth and heaven; that which we are, we are ...
—TENNYSON

Spring—The Past

In two days repairs were made but again the weather conspired against them. The wind lost its constancy and came now in gusts which would snap luffing sails into fullness then dissipate just as quickly. The wind was like temptation. And when the wind breathed, the decks of the ships would swarm with activity: shouted orders, running sailors, helmsmen straining to hold their course and then curses as the gusts died, the ships' prows burying themselves once again in the water; heavy now, graceless, rolling in the swells. This impetuous wind was their master. It treated them with disdain. And this weather enraged their captain-general.

Somehow, he thought, something supernatural schemed against his reaching his goal. For a brief instant the witch came to mind; then he put thoughts of her aside just as quickly. For all of her claims to sorcery, she could not control weather. But then was it fate? God? Should he even consider altering the providential flow of life by ingesting the sacred water? But God had made all things, so he was told, thus the sacred water was God's artifice. It had simply not yet been discovered as had so many novel things in this strange New World. Still, time continued, each day he became one day older. Time flowed through the sand glass and each grain meant another instant of age. He wanted so much to find the water, to restore himself and return to his former character and regain his former powers. Juan Ponce paced the deck muttering. His anger infected the crew. They grew sullen. They could only wait for the next gasp of wind. They could only worry over the storm which was rising within their captain-general.

After a while Sotil approached his superior, wary of his mood. He gestured toward the taff rail, away from the helmsman on duty. Juan Ponce reluctantly joined the pilot.

"Captain-general," Sotil said stiffly, "I am finding it difficult to work the ship ..."

"I've noticed ..."

"The crew is frightened of your displeasure and frightened men aren't efficient."

"What you are saying is I am in your way," the older man said. For a long moment they stood face to face in a dangerous silence. The frightful glare of his captain-general bore down on the pilot and in that moment Sotil recognized the peril of one who'd displeased a *conquistador*. It was a terrifying sensation. Sotil readied himself for the storm, knowing too well what that power could do. Then the tension broke. Juan Ponce looked past him at a sky puffed with billowing clouds, faces of the fickle wind, and sighed.

"Yes. You are a good pilot, Sotil. I, of all, should know better."

"You are frustrated, Don Juan," the young man said, relaxing. "It's understandable."

"I should catch up my log at any rate," Juan Ponce mumbled. "Do your best, time is wearing." Then he left the deck, climbing down out of sight of his men.

The woman was not in the cabin. Juan Ponce recalled briefly seeing her at the bow with friar Bartolome once again. He knew what she was playing at: listening to the monk's persuasions in the guise of being converted. Las Casas would be pleased to hear himself talk. She would answer occasionally and thus attain freedom of the deck. Juan Ponce chuckled softly, shaking his head. At times her intrigues amused him; their simplicity was so transparent and yet so many fell for them. Just a few moments previous he had almost convinced himself of her sorcery.

For a while he worked on the ship's log and as he did he could feel his vessel tilt each time a breeze came up and he would stiffen and will the wind on. But it would inevitably die. After a while he found himself pacing. He considered returning to the deck but discarded the notion. Sotil had been right. He must not make a show of his frustration. But the weather rankled; this interminable travel upon a recalcitrant sea. He turned again to his only solace: withdrawing the journal from his sea chest, placing it open on the narrow table, he took quill in hand and thought for a moment, then began to write.

∞

I have served the wishes of other men all my life. I served three kings in the name of Aragon, Castile and then Spain. What they asked of me, I mostly accomplished.

I attained through my service those things which so many seek: fame, wealth and power; however briefly. For each of those is like the wind, inconstant and unpredictable. In reminiscence I realise I did not ever really serve myself.

I was ambitious, I admit, but who was not? After Columbus a New World lay at our feet and we found, at first, we could do with it what we willed. I myself ruled an island larger than my homeland of Leon. Some, like las Casas, say we robbed the natives of their birthright, distorted Columbus' dream and imposed ourselves on a virgin world. But las Casas has never fought the Carib who scourged this land long before we arrived and would again if we departed. No, this was never an Eden.

Yet I cannot help thinking somehow we missed that rare opportunity to make something new. For here was a canvas, sketched though unpainted, with such latent beauty and promise that we might have taken its potential and created a new way of living much closer to God in the order he must have intended. For despite the Carib, all other people we came upon were gentle and soft, friendly in their natures. And why could not we have changed ourselves to suit them, even slightly, rather than take the other path?

Instead we imported the old ways. We brought first the disease which has killed so many natives. I have no knowledge just why they die so easily. And for those who did not die we brought next the Church to sanction our killing and the theft of their chattels, what little they had when we first arrived. And then we imported the encomiendas, partitioning their lands, taking what little remained to them for our own and making them slaves to serve us.

I did that. My greed matched the others as we plundered and murdered, bartered beauty for regulation, took softness and made it inflexible. And it turned on us as I should have expected. For with partitions and laws came the audencias, the courts run by magistrates sent from Spain who considered little more than their own status and comforts. It was they who tried to destroy me as I grew older and less like the new kind of man they'd encouraged to come here once they felt safe in this world.

They almost succeeded; almost took from me what I myself had taken. So now I possess little more than two ships and a son who despises me. He is in Spain now, far from the father who failed him. He has made a marriage for my daughter, seeking through her what I could not provide. My poor little Isabel, now the wife of a scheming bureaucrat who, ironically, will bring her back to Boriquen, San Juan de Puerto Rico, my island—which I founded and conquered and named—as the official who will rule it.

My son is that new kind of man as well.

Luis was not the son I had wished. His mother's training saw to that. I recall the last time my son turned against me. It was after the debacle of the Carib and the loss of Becerillo. I met my son a week after my return from that battle. He would not deign to discover if I was in health, or wounded or even near death. No, it was left to me to find him. And when I found him at his comida, the food piled high and immoderate on silver plates one hot afternoon on a shaded balcony, he was not pleased to see me.

"You've returned now, father," was all he said. He was eating quails in vine leaves. He wore a pointed doublet

with a gauze ruff at his neck. His meal, his attire, his genteel manner... everything about him disgusted me.

"It takes you so long to welcome your father?"

"I've had no chance. You've been closeted in your
rooms crying over a dog!"

"Jesu ..."

"That's right, father, curse like a common soldier! You
are quite good in that role. And now you've returned from
your latest war, what have you accomplished? My understanding is you were defeated by a gaggle of savages!"

"I lost good men in that battle, and Becerillo as well!"

"Your hound?"

"He was a warrior."

"This is idiotic; defending the honour of a dog. What
has happened to you?"

"Be careful, Luis. You may be my son ..."

"And what will you do to me that you haven't already
done? Your son and heir; heir to what? Diego Colon is Viceroy now and you've provoked his disfavour. You must
know he's planning your removal!"

"What do you suggest I do? I'm sure your mind has
been working its ploys."

"Go to Spain! Appeal to Don Pedro Nunez de Guzman. He is old but still has power at court. You've de-
pended on him a long time."

"And for whom should I do this? Myself? Or for you
and your mother? I know she's behind these machinations."

"We are your family! Isabel must marry well. She cannot if her father is powerless!"

"And of course it would affect your ambitions as well."

"I must have my life too!"

"And what do you seek for yourself in this life, exactly?"

"Stability."

"Not like me."

"You are a mule to those who deliver commands. Can't you see this constant warfare to put down yet another tribe is simply their way of putting you out of the way? What need was there to fight these Carib? You had everything here! You should have cultivated your reputation in Santo Domingo or at court in Spain as a man indispensable to the Crown and the Viceroy!"

"The Viceroy gave me those orders!"

"That was Ovando! The wind has changed, father. Colon is in power now."

"And how was I to know he would rise?"

"You should have kept spies at court."

"You talk like a courtier. How can it be that you are my son?"

"I am my mother's son. I thank God for that every day. I will never become like you."

He left me then. Dabbed his lips with a silk napkin to touch away the quail grease, rose from his chair, and departed without another word. As he walked away he reminded me of those young nobles I had bested years before in the training yard at Seville. Yet he reminded me too of my own fearfulness of becoming so much like my father.

I did not pursue him. I did not try to explain to him my feelings, my doubts, my fears. Instead I let him walk out of my life. Instead I sat looking at the sea as I mourned the loss of my good Becerillo, a hound who had been more familiar to me than my son.

Time passed. It constantly passes as it does now,
forcing me to sit writing this journal, unable to affect
its passage, hardly able to bear it at all. I travelled to
Spain. I went to Don Pedro and then to the Court. The
congregations of pathetic courtiers parted before me as
I approached the throne. I was a conquistador. They were
quite unaccustomed to men like me by then. The King
himself gave me audience. For a while the wind was fortunate: I was feted and humoured and given my wish to
retain my island realm. Yet when I returned my family
had become estranged from me. We lived in the same
house but shared little more than meals and occasional arguments. Leonor died soon after: drowned at sea on
her way home to Spain. Leaving me. I did not miss her.
It is strange to me now to think how I mourned Becerillo more deeply than my own wife. But then, the dog
was a loyal companion. I cannot say the same of Leonor.

So despite my efforts I began to sense those winds
of change my son had discussed. They were not in my
favour. Colon and his minions still plotted against me.
My children abandoned me for life in Spain. Those who
had once feared me seemed to fear me no more. I knew
then I had to do something extreme, something no one
would expect. I had to come about in the wind; make
a change in my life to drive it forward once more. And
that turning has brought me here on this voyage, aboard
a ship named subterfuge; for myself.

For something I missed all those years I spent serving
others.

14

Your children are not your children.
You may house their bodies but not their souls.
For their souls dwell in the house of tomorrow,
Which you cannot visit, not even in your dreams.
—GIBRAN

Winter—*The Present*

With the coming of Christmas, Happy Hills is transformed. The streets take on a festive air: coloured lights wink from mobile home awnings; wreaths are strung on lamp posts; the royal palms lining the roadways are encircled with candy stripe green and red ribbons. Emily buys an artificial tree and the two of them spend a day decorating. They had not thought to bring Christmas baubles with them so were forced to buy coloured balls and tinsel. Everything new. At home they would have cut their own tree and cloaked it with ornaments saved from a lifetime. There is one decoration Ross misses most: an old red plastic boot with a sparkled white cuff given him as a boy. That Santa boot had hung from each tree for fifty-two of his Christmases. Every Christmas morning it served as a candy cane quiver. He kept the tradition with Robert, filling the boot each Christmas Eve, being sure his son claimed it from the tree first before everything else. And after Robert it became Justin's. Yet Justin and Robert would be here this Christmas without that crimson boot.

Stupid really, he thinks, but is saddened as he peers outside at the bright, hot sunshine and remembers the kind of winter when they took the toboggan, the old wood ninefooter with leather straps, out past the houses on the edge of town to Judge's hill. It was called Judge's hill for the farmer who owned it. He allowed the town's trespassers the joy of the slope.

The sun was pale and somehow there would always be those ubiquitous flurries. Their boots crunched and squeaked in the snow. Robbie was bundled up in his snowsuit as he trundled through drifts in the toboggan's wake. Once in a while he climbed onto the toboggan and together Ross and Emily would pull him up over the drifts and he'd crash down like a winter surfer into the wells between snow drifts.

You could see a long way from that hill: off into forests and further fields. Toboggans and sleighs made tracks down the hill: straight, long tracks with occasional pits where someone had spilled. Ross would sit in front, then Robbie, then Em and they'd push off down the slope, Robbie squealing with joy and Ross shouting, "Lean left!" and "Lean right!" to stay in the tracks but inevitably they would lean too far and hit one of those pits and crash with snow spilling down his neck. He'd look past his shoulder at Emily, dusted in snow and laughing, rime in her eyebrows, eyes sparkling sapphire with the cold. She would hug Robbie but he would have none of it. "Can we go again, can we go again?" He would already be clambering up the hill.

"Ross?" Emily's voice interrupts his reverie.

"Uh?"

"I miss the snow."

She is sitting cross legged on the floor just across the room. Around her is scattered the coloured tubes, ribbons, tape and scissors of Christmas wrapping. He rises from his chair, walks over behind her, bends down and kisses her neck, then her cheek. Her lips meet his in a lingering touch.

"What was that for?" She smiles.

"I know what you mean."

"It would be nice to go home."

"Robert will be here in a few days. It'll seem more like Christmas then."

"I think I'll make Christmas cake."

"It's going to be fine, Em. We'll make it fine."

"But I still miss the snow."

"I'm going to get Justin a surfboard."

"Ross, he's only a child!"

"Well, you know what I mean, a flutter board. And we'll take him swimming in the ocean. I'll push him out over the waves, kind of like tobogganing."

"You are crazy, Ross Porter. Honestly, I never know what you'll think of next."

"Let's finish the presents. Or maybe you'd like to go to the bedroom."

"Now what's that got to do with tobogganing?" She smiles again, demurely.

"Oh, I don't know. Let's find out."

∞

At Tampa airport they await Robert, Anne and Justin. The announcement of the Delta flight takes them quickly to the Arrivals area, anticipating their family. They watch as pallid faces in winter clothing appear. Ross searches for Robert when he is struck by a pale blonde beauty descending the escalator. He is about to look away when he realizes the woman is Anne. Instantly he sees Robert behind her holding Justin in his arms. An odd sensation overcomes him. From this vantage point he can watch his son, unaware, return to him. Were it not his son he would still be impressed. The man he observes exudes confidence and sophistication in ways Ross has never or could ever hope to possess. He realises he has been surpassed.

In what moment did my son become this?

Little Robbie with tears in his eyes having wet the bed. Young Robbie smiling, holding his model plane up for his dad, curling it through the air. The adolescent, then self-named Rob smirks into his father's eyes as Ross tell him not to be late on a Friday night. Then the college man home for the weekend with that girl, what was her name, Leonara, with those legs and that heavy black hair and Ross, to his embarrassment, is envious and judgmental at the same moment. The buttoned-down Robert R. Porter unfolds himself from a too-fast sports car. He shakes his father's hand and pats his shoulder. Then the groom: steady, calm, asking his dad if he is alright, not at all nervous himself about the wedding. And then a father, breathless with his newborn son in his arms, for a fleeting moment that joyous boy once again.

Ross sees the future descending an escalator: Justin the grandson in his son Robert's arms and Ross feels suddenly caught in their past. They can visit him through nostalgia with him unable to reciprocate. Eventually he won't be there at all. Still, he is proud of his son. He has run out of things to teach him.

We hold them until they transcend us.
They move on and we are left in their wake.

"Oh, there's Robert!" Emily exclaims. "See him? Oh, doesn't he look handsome!" She is already moving toward her son leaving Ross behind in her excitement. He follows heavily.

"Mother!" Robert's face breaks into a smile. When he smiles he still looks like a boy.

"Grampa! Grampa!"

Now Justin has seen them too and his arms stretch out as he squirms for release. Robert lets him go and he scrambles across the floor and into the arms of his grandfather. Even as he is lifted he talks, nattering about the big airplane and clouds he saw from above and how come grampa's so dark and will he see a shark and he wants to go to Disney. Ross kisses the boy and says yes to everything. And then they form a tight knot, the five of them in the midst of Arrivals in Tampa airport and it could be anywhere for the only important place is inside that beautiful intimate circle.

They stroll to the luggage carousel and Justin, entranced, wants to ride it. When he is refused he pouts and turns his face into Ross' shoulder. But the commotion distracts him and soon he has forgotten the ride as he searches for his suitcase. When he sees it he shouts: "There it is! There it is!" and demands to be set down so he can pull it from the carousel. He hauls the bag over the metal lip and pitches it onto the baggage cart. He brushes his hands together to show he has done a man's work and then demands a child's ride on the dolly out to the car.

Ross takes 275 across Tampa. Robert sits beside him. He tells him they took the American flight from Detroit rather than come directly from Canada. Pearson International is jammed this time of year. They talk about the weather and then the house. Robert says it is fine; the girl living there is responsible and friendly. Ross asks how business is going and Robert says tires are tires but Anne interrupts and proudly announces her husband has made some kind of huge deal in France. Robert brushes it off, saying he was lucky but Emily says she knows that's not true and then they talk about neighbours up home. Little things. Comfortable. Important in their way. The family comes together again through this familiar prattle.

"Justin's come up with a rationale for why you now live in Florida," Robert says, smiling over his shoulder to Emily.

"Oh, and what's that?"

"He and his buddies were playing down in the rec room. He was boasting about going to Florida. So they asked him why his grandparents lived there."

"This'll be good," Ross says chuckling.

"He said: 'It's because they're old and don't have enough sweaters.'"

Everyone laughs. Justin laughs. He is pleased at the attention. Ross gives him a glance, winks, and says: "So you think I'm an old guy, huh?" He forces his own leprous thoughts away.

And finally the question hanging in the air is posed. "How are you, mom?" Quiet worry on every face in the car. It is there even in the boy.

"Oh, I'm feeling wonderful!" Emily says with that studied lightness which only Ross knows. Still, it is the truth this time. "We've been having a super vacation. The place is lovely and the weather's been fine. It's exactly what I needed. We've made some friends. Wait till you meet our neighbour, Jimmy. He's a marvellous man. He'll talk your ear off, Robert, but he's extraordinary."

And that is the end. No more questions. She has put

everyone at ease. When they arrive there is a flurry of unpacking and organising. Justin tries to climb the orange
tree, falls, scrapes his knee and cries. Ross applies antisep-
tic ointment. Emily gives him some orange juice. In a few
moments he has forgotten his pain.

Robert calls Ross into the bedroom.

"Mom's okay, huh?"

"You heard it."

"I'd like to hear it from you."

"Honestly Rob, this place really seems to agree with
her."

"How about you?"

"Oh, I'm fine!" he says. Emily is not the only one accomplished at concealment. "I'm playing tennis almost every
day and I've found some histories of Florida. I'll have to tell
you about them."

"Sounds great, dad. But now I've got something for you."

"Oh?"

"Yeah. I thought you might miss this so I decided to
bring it along. If I'm wrong don't worry. I just thought I'd
bring it."

"What the heck are you talking about?"

His son searches into his suitcase and retracts a plastic baggie. In it is the boot: the crimson boot scored and faded. He hands it to Ross and instantly Ross feels tears well-
ing. That this businessman would take time to think of this
small thing; the ache in Ross' heart is almost physical. He
looks deeply into his son's eyes, like Emily's though not so
soft, and places his hands on his shoulders. That and a
mumbled "Thank you," are all he can manage. He turns away,
hiding his tears, and walks outside to the carport. Like Justin, he cries.

In a few minutes Robert comes out. He has drinks. Ross wipes his eyes and accepts one.

"Happy days, dad."

"Merry Christmas, Robert."

And, just as with Justin, the pain goes away.

15

Two friendships in two breasts requires
The same aversions and desires.
—SWIFT

Spring—The Past

There was trouble on deck just beneath the forecastle. The breathless weather was taking effect. Some men had been gambling and, inevitably, someone had lost. There was an argument. Insults were hurled. Accusations. A sword was drawn, a Toledo rapier, its ornate silver guard enwrapping the hand which held the blade's point suspended in air. The blade weaved a dangerous, delicate dance before the face of its victim. The man with the sword advanced. The other man, surprised by the instrument threatening him, retreated. At some point the deck railing would halt his withdrawal. Then what?

Sotil had seen it happen. He knew enough not to involve himself. The swordsman was skilled despite his youth. He was also hot tempered. The younger son of a noble, he had signed on despite Don Juan's reservations about him. He dreamed of gold and glory. Now he was close to killing a man.

The man was a common sailor. The dice had fallen his way once too often. He had, perhaps, been a little too pleased in collecting his coins. Now he faced death from a thoughtless aristocrat, angered at having been humiliated. Even were he to fight back he could be executed for striking a noble. The point was moot. His opponent would not give him the chance to strike before steel had found its way through his heart.

Sotil sent a ship's boy to find the captain-general. He watched as other men subtly positioned themselves for the moment after the thrust. The sailor was the bigger man, solid and muscular from his work but the young noble was clearly the swifter, more expert fighter. He'd spent half his lifetime learning his fatal skills. He was slim and fit and wore his hair fashionably long. He had friends of similar ilk, and now they were moving to back him as the sailor's comrades did the same for their man.

Sotil began to panic. His work was to pilot the ship, work the crew; not stand in the way of a blade-wielding maniac. He shouted from the aft castle, hoping desperately to delay the altercation.

"You there! Antonio! Put down that blade!"

The young man glanced toward Sotil for an instant, then his dark eyes moved back to his victim. He was no fool to be distracted. This cheating sailor was going to die. They moved ever closer toward the railing, both men on their toes, prepared for action. The sailor's eyes were wide with disbelief. This cub was going to kill him. He thought to dodge and run down the deck but knew his opponent would be too quick. He thought to drop to his knees, beg forgiveness, yet knew as well that would be precisely the kind of confession this killer wanted before he ran him through. He thought finally, when he'd reached the rail, to grab for a belaying pin in the faint chance he might block the thrust.

"You would murder a man without a weapon?" he rasped in his fear, a final hope to appeal to the noble's integrity. He should have known better.

"I kill no man," the boy answered calmly. "I rid the world of a vermin swindler!"

"Please, your honour, I did not cheat. The bones fell my way. It happens sometimes."

"Too many times this day to be true," came the reply, the sword thrust forward, driving the sailor more quickly back. In seconds he would be finished. The young man leered at him.

"Swindler and a coward!" he said. "Will you not fight, you snivelling old man?"

The ships' railing touched the sailor's back. The rapier leapt for his heart.

And was struck aside in a clash of steel so harsh and jarring the boy's blade was driven down to the deck. The lad sought to pull it back up but as he did the other blade, which had driven his down, was suddenly beneath his sword and sent it flying into the air. It curled twice and dived into the sea, swallowed and gone forever. The young man cursed and tried to draw his dagger. Before he could, steel caressed his chin. One move and he would lose half his face.

Juan Ponce de Leon nicked the boy's chin. Blood flowed down into the lad's silk blouse, staining it crimson. The young noble sought his handkerchief to staunch the blood. He was not allowed.

"Let it bleed, youngster. Be thankful it comes from your pretty face rather than your liver," Juan Ponce uttered mercilessly. "You draw your sword against a poor sailor, then torment him before your thrust. You have much to learn Antonio de Tordesillas."

"You surprised me!" the youngster spat back. The answer given him was another quick slice of his left ear. He squealed and brought a hand up to it. The lobe was gone.

"And yet again you are surprised," his commander responded, "and foolish as well to insult a man with a blade in your face."

The boy said nothing. His face had turned pale from the shock of the wounding and the utter ruthlessness of the acts. Juan Ponce glanced past him.

"I note some of you appear ready to draw," he said carelessly. "If so, do it now. I have blood on my blade. The steel thirsts for more. Anyone of you youngsters wishing a try? What am I but an old man, eh? No? No one? What will you do when Calusa warriors surround you? Your young friend here has made an error. I shall offer a lesson to make use of this moment. When one fights a man anything might happen. A sword comes to his aid ... a shot is fired ... a dagger is thrown ... and you who would kill a man, so centred upon killing him you forget the rest of the world around you, lose the world in a breath of negligence."

"I have been taught to fix on my opponent," Antonio de Tordesillas said softly. "Was that wrong, captain-general?"

"You have been taught to fence, not to fight. In battle there are hundreds who want to kill you. You've not been in battle, have you?"

"No, sir.

"You will be. I guarantee it. The *Calusa* we met the last time in Florida came down upon us in hordes. You think I brought you along for the sailing? This sailor you threatened to kill ... he is here for sailing. He is good at his work. I brought *you* for battle. Are you as proficient as he? I think not. Look how easily you let down your guard while you faced an unarmed man. You were waylaid by the last thing you expected. This is what happens in battle. So while you fight your mind must be as agile as your body. There may be a friend to watch your back. There may be, just as easily, none. So let this be your lesson." Juan Ponce turned to the silent audience of Spanish patricians: "Tomorrow, when you practise your combative arts, remember what happened today, to Antonio, who thought himself in control until the moment he wasn't. Practise in groups. No more individual combats!"

The sermon had had its effect. There was no reply but from Tordesillas who said simply: "I am sorry, Don Juan. I thought I'd been cheated. I lost my temper."

"You have lost more than that, my young friend. You tried to kill a crew member; a man with as much right as you, indeed more, to be included among us. In my younger days I'd have had you thrown overboard, joining your blade in its swim to the bottom. As it is you have lost your rapier. It shall not be replaced. No armourer will assist you. I shall give orders that make it so."

"What am I to do, captain-general? I must have a sword to fight."

"Oh, you'll fight. I'll see to that. Once you find a weapon on the battlefield you'll use it! I don't care if it is a wooden club, or a piece of shell, or some dying friend's sword. That is how you shall restore your honour; by finding a replacement for the weapon you lost."

"You cannot do this to me," the youth said.

"Indeed I can. Indeed I do. Or would you care to challenge me now? For your honour? If that be the case, you shall have a sword!"

Antonio de Tordesillas knew very little of life, but he knew enough not to challenge a veteran *conquistador*. He backed away, silently, towards his friends who took him to the surgeon to bandage his wounds. Don Juan Ponce de Leon, his captain-general, simply turned his back and took the steps up to join his pilot, Alonzo Sotil, on the aft castle.

"No further punishment?" Sotil inquired.

"Do you think I could harm him more than I have?"

"No, Don Juan. I think not. And you've made him a better man."

"I can hope," the old man responded. "I once demolished his like when I was a lad in training. I defended myself then from my tormentors. I would *offend* myself had I done so now."

Sotil, having no idea what his leader was insinuating, left the subject alone. There are secrets to all men's lives. Some more, some less. The man beside him had more than his share. That other log, for instance, he spent so much time with. It would be useless to pry.

∞

I had a friend once, not my dog Becerillo nor my lieutenant Sotomayor, but an equal with whom I found great satisfaction. I met him out here in these Indies, for he was a man much like me. Perhaps that was why I was drawn to him. His name was Vasco Nunez de Balboa. I got to know him when he was a farmer, like me, on Hispaniola, in Higuey, where we both colonized for some years. They were good years.

We both were still relatively young, strong men then. We had settled the natives for Viceroy Ovando and then enjoyed our rewards. The land was good in Higuey. We possessed neighbouring encomiendas just outside Salvaleon, and carefully oversaw the work of building our plantations. Curiously, despite our battles, neither of us felt any animosity toward the natives. Indeed, we considered we'd done enough in taking their land and, unlike so many other, more foolish Spaniards, did not enslave them.

Instead we worked with them and in many cases paid them to work. But there was work even the natives would refuse and for that, we purchased black men shipped from Africa. Those slaves, brought by Portuguese ships, finding themselves in a world so different from the one they had known so far from this world, had no choice but to work. Our plantations out-produced other men's because of those black men. Soon enough, because so many natives died of disease, other owners began to use the blacks. I recall this was very early on, after Columbus had tried to rebuff slavery in his 'Indies'. It was under Bobadilla the practice began. The only sensible thing the fool accomplished in the year before he was arrested. Of course, Bobadilla had ensured he took a percentage from every importation and sale. He was that type.

But I write of Balboa ... to look at him one would have seen a true conquistador, which he was. He was a large man, square shaped, his muscles like a blacksmith's. His face was hard set and darkened by years of sun, his eyes were dark as well. He wore an elongated beard, very full and as black as pitch at that time.

He was my kind of man. He possessed no airs of superiority yet owned a self-assurance which held him in good stead. He commanded well, not ordering men so much as suggesting their movements. Yet his detachments obeyed as quickly and surely as any good captain's. In battle he was dependable and sure to be at your flank when you needed him. I respected him, and I liked him.

I knew he liked me as well, for we would spend evenings at each other's residences, talking quietly of our plans for our farms, recalling our days as soldiers, speaking of our homelands far away and, perhaps I must admit, plotting our ambitions for the future.

He was born and raised in Jerez de Los Caballeros in the northwest not far from Leon. His training was with Don Pedro de Portocarrero, in Moguer, in the south near Seville where my studies took place. He admitted one day, over a bit too much wine, that he too had had problems with the finer arts at Court. We laughed together, sharing our embarrassments. It was the easy conversation of men who see the world in much the same way, who are comfortable finally in their own skins.

For six years we found ourselves apart from the maelstrom of political struggles while Viceroy replaced Viceroy and the courtiers in Spain fought their parchment battles for control. It was after that time I received my orders to explore and conquer Boriquen. Vasco was sent south to Darien. As a result I became Governor of Boriquen, San Juan Bautista (as Columbus had named it), San Juan de Puerto Rico as it became known. And Balboa? He went on to greater things.

I knew him later when he became famous: finding the great southern sea which he named Pacific, so proving Columbus wrong. And I knew him when he was named Governor of that Sea and all the lands which touched it. I also heard, years later, he had been accused and tried as I too had been. He was beheaded for having been too successful; put to death as I was intended to be put to pasture.

I wish that he could be with me now on this most uncommon of voyages. He would have understood founding a new colony, having been stripped of my old ones. He would have been by my side in this, ready for battle with the Calusa yet ready, as well, to build farms and villages. But he could never have thought of that which I truly seek. He lacked the imagination for that.

Perhaps I possess too much of it.

∞

Juan Ponce lay down to rest after writing. The altercation with Tordesillas had fatigued him. He no longer relished the clash of dispute as he once had. Younger men thrived upon it and he knew the only reason for Antonio de Tordesillas' apology was his fear of Juan Ponce's reputation. He would do well to fear it, the old man half smiled, for even now he, the veteran, could destroy the lad. His thoughts brought him memories of fighting tactics but he chose not to write these in his secret log for he was tired. Still, as he rested he thought of a particular day, for that day had sealed his reputation and set him upon the life he had lived.

He recalled that the squires were in the training yard having just finished prayers for Terse. For an instant he pictured that yard: yellow dust, stacks of arms, the barked commands of the trainers echoing off the stone walls. He had been only fifteen years old at the time, young but

experienced from intense combat training. His instruct-
ors had liked him for they had found and drawn out a rare
talent within him for battle. He had known he was the envy
of other boys, even those older and nearing the time they
would leave for real warfare. What he had not known was
how deep that envy lived in certain of them: those aristocrats from the best families who considered themselves
somehow superior.

These were the ones who had laughed at him in his
other, more gentle yet less productive studies. They had
mimicked him mercilessly in the dance, mincing about the
dusty yellow yard bowing and scraping like dunces ... like
him. They were the ones who played the bear, bowling over
others playing court ladies. By this time his temper had
left him, or had been trained out of him as nonsensical and
liable to get him killed. When one entered combat, he was
taught to forget offence and terminate insult; for should
either get in the way of his focus everything he'd been
taught, then trained until his body performed functions
automatically, would be for naught. He'd developed the
stratagem of avoiding the squires' slights, only to teach
them the meaning of revenge during their drills.

He had not been gentle. Even the older ones had been
thrashed, piece by piece, and left bloody in the yellow dust.
But the day he recalled so clearly was the day they had
plotted their own revenge.

Dulled weapons were used during training and padded clothing offered some protection, though each boy was
sure to wear a *morion* to protect his head. That day Juan
Ponce had toed his line after prayers, dulled sword in his
gloved hand, not yet wearing his helmet. He'd awaited his
next training partner. It mattered little to him who it was.

Yet what happened at that moment altered everything. A cry of pain had come from a squire far across the court yard. That distraction had taken the trainers away, all rushing to help the injured boy.

Juan Ponce suddenly had found himself facing two of the older aristocrats. He knew them as his most blatant tormentors. The one on his left was tall and slim with red hair and blue eyes, clearly Aragonese. The other was muscular and possessed of that darkness which came from Andalusia. Both of them he had bested in single practice, both obviously intended revenge. For each brandished a shining, razor sharp rapier and each wore his *morion*, strapped to his chin and ready for combat. Real combat. There was no chance to prepare for them. They were on him like wolves taking down their prey. Bright metal flashed in the dusty sunlight. Juan Ponce leapt back, out of reach for an instant, but in that instant he'd found time for tactics.

Two opponents. Two killing swords. Confident. Perhaps over-confident. They advanced on him backing him toward a wall. He knew should he end at that wall his life would end there as well. He required space to manoeuvre. Quickly he took it. Juan Ponce faked a move to his left, forcing the Aragonese to thrust. Using his *morion* as a shield he blocked the thrust and spun further left, leaving the second opponent behind his partner, unable to reach their victim. Thus the right-handed swordsmen had had to pivot, and the Andalusian had had to come around his partner.

For that instant Juan Ponce faced but one opponent. He used the time well. Simulating a thrust with his dull training sword he swung his helmet, sharp peaked steel crest, into the face of the Aragonese who was just then trying another thrust. The helmet missed his face but clanged with such a ringing din, helmet steel on steel, it took the squire to his knees.

No time to think, Juan Ponce's sword swept in a parry against the Andalusian's second thrust, knowing from training where it would come. But the rapier made it through his defence and ripped open his padding, slicing his chest. His opponent smiled, thinking he'd done more damage than he had. For that split second he'd let down his guard expecting Juan Ponce to crumple. Instead he watched helplessly as Juan Ponce appeared to fall, spinning down, yet low enough then to swing out his steel sword and slash the aristocrat's unprotected kneecap.

With a wail the boy collapsed, bone bruised or broken, it did not matter. Then the Aragonese was at Juan Ponce again, aiming for his face, thrusting perfectly just missing an eye, his blade carving a six inch scar on the left side of Juan Ponce's skull. Juan Ponce rolled in the dust in the direction he'd been pivoting and sprang to his feet out of range.

He arose with blood pouring from his wound. But the Andalusian was on the ground grasping his crippled knee, having forgotten all else in his pain. Still the Aragonese, who had brought blood, was more confident and once again advanced. He'd forgotten he was alone this time. His blade was parried and his elbow smashed by the steel crest of the *morion* coming up under his offensive thrust. His hand went numb. His blade flew like an arrow out of his hand. His eyes followed it as he screamed in pain.

Juan Ponce did not miss a second time. He split the boy's face as he slammed his sword's pommel into it: breaking the nose, smashing the cheekbone, dropping the boy like a stone to the dust.

In twenty seconds it was over.

The trainers returned and saw what had happened. They helped the boys to the surgeon: the Andalusian screaming epithets at the boy who had beaten and shamed him; the Aragonese prince, unconscious. He had, after that, never been seen again at Don Pedro's court. It was clear he'd been scarred for the rest of his life.

Juan Ponce had sought help from another instructor to bandage his head. He'd refused to leave the yard. He'd felt everyone's eyes upon him as he sat quietly while the dressing had been applied. When he rose, steadily, to toe the line for his next training run, only an instructor would stand against him.

No one had ever challenged Juan Ponce de Leon to combat again.

And the old man drifted off to sleep, smiling.

16

A boy's will is the wind's will,
And the thoughts of youth are long,
long thoughts.

—**LONGFELLOW**

Winter—*The Present*

Christmas morning is chaos.

Justin bounces into their bedroom announcing: "Santa's been here! Santa's been here!" He is gone before Ross attains consciousness. Then, stumbling into the living room, Ross watches his grandson being restrained by a bleary-eyed Anne. Emily starts the coffee. She spills sugar on the floor. Robert is juicing oranges, the whang of the juicer driving like sleet into Ross' brain. Ross reaches into the tree for the candy cane Santa boot. It promptly slips through his hand to the floor. The canes sprinkle down among the presents. He steps on one. It crunches merrily, shattering into a thousand shards.

"Shit!" Ross curses half under his breath.

"Grampa said the poop word!" Justin exclaims.

"Ross!" Emily says.

"Grampa said the poop word!" the child shouts with glee.

"Justin!" his mother says.

The boy begins laughing uproariously. Ross is embarrassed, flustered by the noise and confusion, unable to gain equilibrium. He mutters an apology directed at Anne only to find her stifling a laugh. Robert is grinning slyly.

"Grampa's a little under the weather this morning, I'd say," he says, chuckling.

Interesting how time changes things.

Robbie blurted out "cunt" one particular day. He was eight years old. Ross wondered where children learned such things. He had told the boy not to use that word. To his surprise his son repeated it almost disdainfully. Ross warned him again. He said it again. Ross took him quickly over his knee. Three quick whacks. The boy cried. He said the other boys said it. Ross told him he was not other boys.

Where did I learn it?

Ross vaguely recalls a cedar copse, a group of boys passing an illicit cigar and that singular, meaningless, sexless word passed along with it, steaming out of young mouths with the smoke. Ross had been older than Robbie. He had known better by then not to speak the secret words of boys to his father.

Now I give them to my grandson.

"Let's open the presents!" Emily says. She has coffee and muffins on a tray. She glances at Ross quizzically. He forces himself up and out of his weird reverie. He shoves his humiliation aside, wondering why he has overreacted.

"I meant 'poop'," he says.

Justin insists on distributing gifts. Emily helps him by reading the names on the cards. When everyone has a pile, Justin's twice the size of the others, he can no longer restrain himself. He tears off the wrappings with gleeful abandon. He is beside himself with excitement. Emily starts taking pictures, the flash from the camera punctuates every present: Justin with his new flutter board, Justin munching a candy cane, Justin hugging his teddy bear, kissing mommy, standing on his head, flash, flash, and Ross knows this is Emily grasping life. The boy offers it in abundance. He wants a close up shot of his nose. Emily takes it.

Flash.

One strange element interferes with the opening of the presents. There is one for Ross which he opens, to find a picture of Darlene, a seductive Darlene pouting out at him, in a small plastic frame. He quickly conceals the gift, looks for a card, and finds none with the wrapping. He recalls Colin's warning, then rejoins the family in their celebration ... just a touch disturbed.

Later Jimmy and Maggie come over for brunch. They bring Justin a gift, an inflatable pelican water ring. Robert blows it up. Justin is delighted. He wants to go swimming. Jimmy tells him he can see real pelicans at the beach. A brief discussion over the dishes and soon everyone piles into the car with Ross who, confused even more by this sudden change in plans, drives thirty miles to Indian Rocks Beach.

The weather is humid but a breeze from the Gulf tempers it. The sand is hot on their feet. They spread beach towels and set up folding chairs. All down the long, curving golden strand they can see other holiday revellers setting up for the afternoon, patches of people outside the hotels and condos that stretch away into the distance, lost eventually in the haze. The surf laps softly against the shore. The air smells of the sea, a faint odour of flotsam interspersed with freshness.

For Justin this is the best Christmas present. Pelicans

wing by mere inches above the waves. Justin laughs and holds up his inflatable toy. They are not attracted. They glide below clouds of seagulls as the gulls descend in search of food. Justin chases the gulls and they flock up and away from him, peeling around above his head only to land again behind him. Justin runs at the sea rushing down with the retreating surf then scampering back, chased by a new wave coming in. Ross thinks of the sandpiper on Sanibel Island.

The joy of his grandson infects him and soon he and Robert take Justin into the water. Ross pushes the boy out over the waves on his new flutter board. But it isn't the same somehow as with Robert. The sea is alien to the boy. He grasps the board with a fearful tension. The water is cold. Very soon Justin shivers and wants to go back in to shore. He wants to be carried. His face looks past his father's shoulder as Robert holds him above the water. His eyes are wide with concern. Ross asks him what is wrong.

"Too big," he says.

"What's too big? The waves?" Ross asks.

"Everything," the boy says.

On shore Anne dries him off. He is quiet. He looks out at the sea with different eyes. Ross tries to recall when he first met the sea but the memory is lost. After a while Justin joins him, climbing into his lap as he sits in a chair.

"How old is the water, grampa?" he asks. The question stuns Ross. He pauses a moment, looking out at the waves.

How does one measure timelessness?

Justin tugs his arm, demanding an answer.

"Well, in a way," Ross says, "the sea isn't old. It's new with each wave. But in another way it's very old because the waves have travelled so far. The sea kind of changes but really it doesn't ever get old. Not like us."

"It's scary."

How does one explain the sea lives in us all?

∞

Emily has brought a plastic bucket and shovel. Justin wants to build a castle. Ross helps him. They dig a moat and pack wet sand into the bucket and turn it over to make the towers and Emily shapes the walls which connect them and soon they have built their citadel. Ross is proud of it. Even when Justin loses interest, Ross continues. It has been years since he's built a sandcastle. Emily takes another picture. Justin tries to fill the moat with seawater from his bucket. The water seeps down through the sand too quickly. Justin begins throwing buckets of water down on the castle. Each gush splashes a tower and melts it. Justin laughs. Ross asks him to stop, quietly, but the boy has discovered the joy of destruction and wades in with his feet exploding walls and bridges and precious towers with every kick. The castle is reduced to ruins. Ross feels helpless. Each blow to the sand reverberates in him. He cannot comprehend why this should pierce him so deeply.

Robert picks the boy up by the wrists and makes airplane noises and swings him around to kick at any remaining towers. Ross stands aside impotent. There is a lump in his throat. He turns and walks into the sea. The sea can't be broken. He wades deeper and deeper up to his neck, tasting the brine, feeling the lift and ebb of waves, swimming now, revived by the cold womb into which he dives deep. Safe.

The sea offers freedom, Ross thinks. Each time you swim you seem to lose gravity as you float and fly in its buoyant waters. Each time a sail sets or a prow turns out toward the unbroken horizon, there is hope, not fear, in a mariner. One does not think of rip tides, storm surges, or the awful power of the deep. A sailor thinks of freedom as he leaves the land behind.

Why can't I be like the sea?

It comes to him then that Emily has been taking pictures all day, controlling the camera, not once including herself in a shot. Justin. Always Justin. Ross swims for the shore. He crosses the sand to Emily. She is sitting in a chair, the camera in her lap. He takes the camera.

"I want to take your picture, Em."

"Ross, I'm a mess!"

"It doesn't matter. I want to take your picture: you and Robert and Anne with Justin."

"I'll take it!" Jimmy says. "That way you can all be in it."

They form their family portrait on the ruins of the castle. They sit in the brown, desolate sand, the sea behind them. Jimmy takes the photo.

"Isn't this wonderful!" Maggie exclaims.

∞

The following week is a full one. At Disneyworld they chase after Justin who seems to want everything at once. In the lines he is cranky, on the rides only wanting the next one and eventually, when the boy eats two hot dogs and develops an upset stomach, Ross decides he needs a break. While Robert and Anne lead Justin off to Fantasyland, he takes Emily shopping down Main Street, U.S.A.

"That child is spoiled," he tells her.

"He's four years old. He can't help it."

"Robert never behaved like that."

"You're suffering selective memory loss, dear."

"But Justin is so ... the boy never considers anyone else!"

"You've been a bit self-absorbed yourself, Ross. I didn't want to mention it but Robert noticed. He asked me about it. I didn't know what to tell him."

So quickly the tide turns on him, forcing him to look at himself.

I should share my feelings.

Let her know how she is loved.

At their kitchen table his first year of teaching; papers, folders and notebooks cluttered the surface. He had five classes and was trying to set a direction for them, not knowing himself where he was leading them, or even where to begin.

There is no beginning in history. It seems cyclical, yet it isn't. History is a Mobius strip always repeating yet never precisely the same. Ross was compelled to select a moment in the chronicle, remove it arbitrarily for study, and then bring it back to the fold. He had the tools but no impetus. He'd thrown his pen down in frustration.

"I can't do this!"

"You're trying too hard. Take your time," Emily said, looking up from feeding the baby.

"These kids know nothing. Really, I don't think they care. You can't teach history to people who don't want to learn it!"

"I'm sure they will."

"This is hopeless."

"It's like carving an elephant, Ross."

"What?"

"Carving an elephant," she said, smiling.

"What the hell does that mean?" he said.

"Carve away everything that doesn't look like an elephant," she said, chuckling before going back to feeding Robbie.

Ross glared down at his mess and seethed. Emily puttered about the kitchen then took Robbie up to bed. Ross muttered and mumbled a while longer, despising her dismissal of his desperate situation. It took some time until it dawned upon him that she had been right with her frivolous metaphor. He had to start somewhere. He could not put it off.

He began to carve. He looked for the root of each period, something as simple as a date, or an invention, or a school of thought. He searched for commonalities in time. He found characters who exemplified movements. He slowly thickened each folder until five hours later he had roughed out his courses of study. By the time he'd finished Emily was asleep. He went to sleep beside her happy with himself, proud of his skill.

He'd forgotten about the elephant.

He thinks he should tell her now. Thank her all these years later.

How do you carve away the inevitable?

∞

The departure is hard on Emily. Her distress goes unnoticed by all but Ross. He knows her too well. Her walk is missing its animation and there is an unsettling slope to her shoulders. He wonders what she is thinking. He hasn't the courage to ask.

When it is time to leave, when the car is packed and

Jimmie and Maggie have said their goodbyes and Ross has the car keys in hand, Emily balks. She stands at the car door looking down into the back seat at Robert and Justin and Anne. She seems to have turned to stone.

"I'm not going," she says flatly.

"What's wrong, mom?" Robert says.

From across the car roof, Ross watches her fight to maintain her composure. She has raised her face above the car window so no one will notice. In her eyes he can see hysteria. They implore him wordlessly, desperately, to help her. But he is struck by the dread within her and does nothing. Robert tries to get out of the car. Then Ross watches his wife transform her face into a smiling mask. Robert's head appears above the car roof and she grasps him on either side of his face holding him back while simultaneously receiving him. She places her lips to his in a lingering kiss and that kiss is the most loving thing Ross has ever witnessed. It is at once a lie and the truth, maternal yet passionate, intimate but distant. A gift only a mother can offer. And then Emily nudges her son back down into the car. He offers no resistance. He is a child again.

"I'm fine, Robbie. I just don't want to make a scene at the airport."

"I love you, mom," he says.

"I love you, gramma!" Justin says.

"And I love you all," Emily says. "Take care of my boys, Anne."

Anne has tears in her eyes. She says nothing.

"Anyway," Emily says, lightening her voice, "somebody's got to clean up. I don't want to face the dishes later. Ross, get in the car. It's time to go."

"See you at home, gramma!" Justin shouts.

∞

Ross turns the radio off. The tires hum beneath him. The sun sets behind him and there are long shadows reaching across the pavement. He feels hollow and strange. No one said a word on the way to the airport and now there is no one to say anything at all.

He should have known. He'd known it was coming and yet had done nothing. And then when she had needed him most, right then, in her face that anguish and panic and grief, right then, eyes shimmering, pleading for him to do something, anything, right then, right there, he'd failed her.

He drives through saffron twilight. By the time he gets home it is dark. He pulls into the driveway and notices the Christmas tree no longer stands in the front window. When he enters he sees the decorations are gone. Things have been put away.

Emily sits in a chair; small, in a chair. He breathes out, seeing she is safe, realising he has not taken a breath since he got out of the car. She smiles absently at him.

"I'm sorry, about earlier," he murmurs abjectly.

She isn't listening.

"When I was cleaning while you were gone I had the strangest feeling," she says, almost as if he were not there at all. "I felt as I picked up the decorations and put them away in their boxes, I felt I was putting myself away too, so things would be tidy. The oddest sensation ..."

"Em ..."

"Yes?"

"Emily?"

"It's alright," she says. "It's alright."

Six weeks later she is gone.

17

Friends who set forth at our side,
Falter, are lost in the storm.
We, we only, are left!
—**ARNOLD**

Spring—The Past

Juan Ponce had slept a few hours. As he awoke, quivering from a dream, he felt the witch beside him in the dark. Her hair was in his face; coiled like snakes about his face. The cabin rocked a little and he could hear the creaking of the caravel underway at last. He wanted to sleep but his mind could not settle. He knew better than to try.

There are times in life when a man feels his age: the sudden back spasm, the ache of old wounds, the need to rise in the night just to piss. What is life but the path toward death? The young never feel it unless it comes unexpectedly in a friend's or a parent's untimely demise, or a sickness which threatens to take them off. Only then do they sense their destination but, as youth will, they soon forget. It is later, with the inexorable clawing at each part of life, that having become aged, they arrive at the knowledge of their mortality. Yet even the old learn to live with it. They must. Otherwise it would drive them mad.

He arose in the dark, stumbling slightly, feeling the stiffness to which he had become accustomed. He groped for the lamp, found it, and with flint and steel made the spark to light it. The room flickered into being, unreal almost in the lamp light. The old man dressed quickly, groaning a little as he reached down to pull on his boots. He took a drink of water from the bucket kept for that purpose: cupping his hands, filling them, bringing them to his lips. Then he washed his face with his dampened hands, blinked once or twice to clear his eyes, brushed his hands together to dry them and went up on deck.

It was quiet and overcast but a light breeze had filled the sails. Except for the night watch the rest of the ship was asleep. He relieved himself over the side and thought to join the helmsman at the tiller. He could see a lamp gleaming dully up there and the lighted face of the sailor looking down to check the compass rose keeping his vessel on course. Better not to disturb him.

Something tugged at his mind.

It was not age or the sacred water. This time it was something else. The sea sang to him in whispers with the soft pound of water upon the hull below. A hypnotic, timeless song troubled by the flutter within his brain. Far off he could make out the lights of Sotomayor's caravel moving in its long, soft glide. He stood a while in the night's quiet; then remembered.

He sighed with that bitter recollection and quietly went below again to the table where his journal lay open. And when he wrote, laboriously, the quill grasped between his fingers, it seemed that pain drained down from his face through his shoulders, arms and fingers and into the ink that spilled onto the page.

∞

If, as I am told by las Casas, that Satan exists, I have met him, or at least his children. They are called Carib. Even their island, in these lovely Indies of soft shores and pleasant vistas, was a warning: a huge mountain glowering, gloomy and sulphurous, like some Lucifer rising from the sea. And the Carib, not content with their brown skins, have dyed their flesh with roucou. Their faces are painted with white and black stripes over the red. These Carib know what they are.

Man eaters.

There is irony here.

It was to have been an expedition of deliverance. For once, conquest was not the motive. The Carib were marauders known for raiding islands and carrying off the inhabitants. Ovando decided to end their tyranny. I was given two ships and two hundred men to form an expedition. And when we arrived beneath that malevolent mountain and anchored, it was a soft night with a gentle breeze that let us lie to in a cove rimmed by jungle. I met with my captains to plan our reconnaissance of the morning, everyone confident and in good cheer; even Becerillo who, full of meat scraps from the table, slept on the deck beneath my hammock.

He'd been my companion seven years; a good comrade, a veteran of war. He terrified the natives who had never seen anything like him and when set upon them he would bring them down as a wolf would a deer, one after another until called to heel. He was a massive dog, rippling with muscle and large as a calf, his coat black with tawny splashes about it. Yet for all his ferociousness he had a kind of softness to him as well. He would chase a stick when it was thrown: return it and then pretend to place it on the ground only to slip it away as my hand would reach for it. It was his game: fool the master. It was almost as if he could laugh. That night he snored beneath me. He was a comfort to me as I stroked his huge head and just before I went to sleep I listened past him to the murmur of waves lapping against a sand beach.

Gentle waves lapping. That is what has brought me to this book tonight. More irony.

In the morning I sent a small reconnaissance troop ashore to explore, under Sotomayor's command. This was standard practice. But I did not think to give him Becerillo, did not think a whole tribe would lie waiting. It was not to be the last of my miscalculations.

Sotomayor did not return that night. This had never happened before. I began to fear for his life and those of his men. I dared send no others after him; not in the dark on an island populated by hostiles. I determined to land in force the next morning. I worried myself awake through the night, listening, always listening for something to tell me what might have happened; hearing only the waves on the shore, each one lapping the shore, each wave like a ticking clock as I waited impatiently for answers.

At dawn my advance party found Sotomayor on the beach; the only one left of his squadron. Badly wounded, he had crawled down a stream bed after the ambush which had taken his men. He told me they had passed through a deserted village where around them on racks hung human limbs, pieces of men strung up

like meat in a butcher's shambles. They saw mounds of
skulls. His men were stunned by this. It brought on an
extraordinary fear among them. Many wanted to turn
back but Sotomayor, having his orders, would not think
of it. They pushed on. Not far past that village in a narrow ravine a hundred warriors came down on them.
Swarmed by the red men so suddenly, their fear from
the village broke them and they ran in panic, the worst
thing to do. Each was hunted down by the Carib. Like
animals. Like meat.

   I resolved to sweep every inch of that abominable
island to wreak massacre on the Carib tribe. We would
kill them all, kill everything; leave nothing but death in
our wake. In my passion I had no plan but vengeance.
The men were ordered into armour. We landed our
boats on the beach and formed up. Becerillo was given
the scent, let loose and soon vanished into the forest. I
knew he would find our enemies; his howl would lead
us to them. He had done the same work so often before.

   An hour passed with no sign from the dog. I'd just
considered a move inland when a horde of natives
erupted from the trees, hundreds of them in vermilion
waves howling and yelping like beasts. I ordered the
men into phalanx. Carib spears flew. A few men were
hit but mostly the bolts clattered off our armour. The
savages stopped, confused by the wall of steel con-
fronting them. Yet there were far too many for my little army to attack or even hold off. We had to get off
that beach. Still I realised not all of us could escape.
Once the better part of my force had embarked what
would become of the rear guard? I sent orders off with

the first departing boat commanding the ships' bombards to fire.

As the Carib threatened, moving ever closer, I heard a gun boom and a brace of grapeshot cut a swath through their ranks. There were screams, splashing blood and limbs flying. It stopped them. They were amazed at the sudden mangled bodies in their midst. A second gun fired and they ran. The shore was strewn with scarlet bodies. My men cheered and would have pursued the savages into the trees. I halted them. It would be too dangerous to follow those hostiles into the interior they knew so well. They had bested Sotomayor, they had fooled Becerillo; the only thing that had stopped them was cannon. I had need of a better plan. We launched the rest of our boats in retreat.

Part way out I decried the baying of Becerillo. I saw him break from the trees to the shore. He was chasing a warrior. Once on the beach the savage ran into the water, Becerillo following. I had the boat turned about and we started back for my hound, even now seeking victory in the midst of his master's defeat. He swam after the warrior. My men cheered him on. But the savage turned and raised himself part way out of the surf and, somehow keeping himself erect, shot an arrow into Becerillo's throat. The dog closed on him still, swept his great bulk upon the man and closed gaping jaws around his head. The two disappeared beneath the waves. We saw blood foam up on the water but neither surfaced. We did not see them again.

Gallant Becerillo. When he died, something in me died with him. I cannot explain it, but that death emptied me. Why it should be I do not know. I only know it changed me. After that I no longer went to war. I had tired of war and, in my weariness, had become less astute at its subtleties. My lack of a proper plan with the Carib had informed me of my flaws, and the death of my dog reinforced my failure.

I turned my ships home. I did not look back on that cursed island. I returned in disgrace to the duplicity of Diego Colon, the hollowness of a destitute marriage and the exhaustion of my defeat. I returned to the insults of my son.

And never, since then, have I fought battles not my own.

I am different after Becerillo.

∞

As she watched the big Spaniard scribbling again, Mayaimi considered how weak he'd become. Once he'd been sovereign of his realm, ruling with that same care she'd noted was so much like Calos, her father. Yet she'd watched the Spaniard over the years be reduced to a troubled, distracted leader, tied up in papers which seemed to her to have more power than his weapons. At times she found herself almost pitying him but those occasions did not last long, for with each subtraction from his powers she knew he was becoming more desperate, and in his confusion her own efforts would find success.

He began to lose his former skills and those other, significant ones taught her by her mother: that there are ways to accomplish your will if you are prudent and shrewd. Those traits the big Spaniard did not possess. And gradually he lost his self-worth, succumbed to those diminutive scribblers he'd hired who, to her, were insignificant. He should have just killed them. She would have. Calos would. Sometimes she found she did not comprehend this man; sometimes there were facets to him which escaped her. Still, he should have been on the deck this morning ruling his men, not down here scribbling like a weakling.

"You are at that scratching again," she said, disrupting him, making him look up from his work to realise it had become day. The lamp still flickered but the cabin was bright with morning light. She peered past him to the page. "What can be so important in scratches?"

She reached out to tear the page, fingers grasping the parchment. He clutched her wrist, twisting, bending her back as he rose from the chair. He might be an old man but he was still physically powerful. With his other hand he slapped her sharply across her face.

"Leave alone what you don't understand," he said evenly.

She scowled at him in defiance.

"You do not sleep. You do not lead your men! Instead you bury yourself down here and scratch and scratch! You promised my homeland in return for the sacred water."

"That will come."

"When?"

"You try my patience."

"We will never reach my land!" she said.

"The ship moves even now," he responded harshly. "Go up on deck and see for yourself. Get out of here, woman, and leave me in peace!"

She broke from his grasp and went to the door. As she opened it she looked back at him. Her eyes glimmered like hot coals, sorceress eyes, and then she was gone leaving him with an odd apprehension. He noticed then his pulse pounding and a familiar hollow feeling in his stomach. It was ever thus after an argument. A physical fight always left him calm, his enemy beaten to the dirt before him. Yet when called upon to simply dispute a point of law or some intricate contract he was left with a sense of doubt that somehow he'd never satisfied the fundamentals essential to win his point. And, it seemed, that weakness in his character was all that was left to him now: the subtle squabbles of courtiers and officials settled in *audencias*, with him always feeling he'd been outmanoeuvred, tricked by gambits of rhetoric he'd never needed before. He pulled a small cask of fortified wine from his sea chest and poured a draught for himself. The liquor was golden and dusky and burned down his throat. He knew it would settle him.

"Medicine for old men," he muttered peevishly.

His hand trembled.

∞

In Santo Domingo the conspirators plotted, hoping that I, Don Juan Hernando Ponce de Leon, Governor of Higuey and San Juan, Knight of the noble house of Leon, Captain-general of the Indies, was finished.

I was not finished.

Despite his rejection of me following my return from the Carib debacle, I had learned certain things from my son's insults. He'd told me to go to Spain to fight another fight against the new proprietors of the Indies; win my way through with subterfuge.

Putting my losses behind me, I voyaged to Spain and once there I worked to retain my lands and possessions.

But not before certain other business.

I knew even then that Colon and his minions would not be restrained. They would try me again from some other direction. And so I prepared for them. In Seville, just before I departed for home, I paid a visit to Don Pedro. He'd arranged a meeting for me with Archbishop Fonseca. I shared a flagon of rare Rhenish wine with the Archbishop. I stayed to dinner and answered his questions. He was most intrigued by the new Indies opening out before him on maps. But maps were not enough for his kind of agile mind. He wanted more. He wanted description and erudition. He asked for specifics regarding supply and communication. He did not, as I thought he might, wish to know about the Church and its place in our New World.

I told him tales of the pilot Alaminos and Vespucci the cartographer; the importance of Balboa's discovery and the danger of Cortez' mutinous path; the ruinous reign of Bobadilla and now the same thing from Colon. And in return he gave me what I asked. A patent. For a place I had come across while doing what I did best. I had, on a voyage long before, discovered a luxuriant, dangerous land and named it. It was, if I lost Boriquen, to be my future.

He gave me the patent for Florida.

Perhaps I am not, after all, so simple as my son suspects.

18

She, she is dead; she's dead; when thou know'st this,
Thou know'st how dry a cinder this world is.

—**DONNE**

Winter — *The Present*

The hospice room is impersonal beige. It is a monotonous room, semi-private, with an opaque curtain between the beds. There is a faint aroma of flowers. The flowers are withering. Ross Porter sits in a plastic tubular chair beside the bed. Emily is sleeping now. He gazes vacantly out the window at the white, bitter world that is home. Outside a blizzard howls and ice pellets rap against the window with frigid, merciless fingers.

Three weeks ago they had come home. Ten days later, here: into the pastel uniforms and the stainless steel beds and strange apparatus of sickness, into the reassuring voices whose eyes told another tale, into this room with flowers wilting and tubes in her arms and plasma bags hanging from a chrome-plated tree.

Into metastasis.

As the cancer grew it contracted their world, collapsing it into this single room, and outside was a winter so different from the warm, sunny place they had left behind. She would not go to hospital in Florida. Too far away from her family and the comfort of ending where she had begun. She did not say this but he understood. The French teacher, too, understood. She was out of the house by the time they arrived having found an apartment and, leaving their home almost as she had found it, expressed in a note her sympathy. She was a fine young woman. He was sorry he had resented her.

For a week they lived there, at home. Other than visits to the doctor, they saw no one but family. Robert and Anne came every day. Anne made dinner each evening. They would eat at the table with one empty chair. Emily took what food she could in her bed. Ross would serve her after dinner and the kids would go home to put Justin to sleep. The boy had come with them just once. Emily was so happy to see him. But she fell asleep while he visited her and he cried when she would not awaken. After that they thought it best to leave him at home.

Ross took the phone calls which started coming and thanked everyone for their concern. Eventually he used the answering machine so he would no longer have to employ his *brave* voice. And quickly, so quickly Emily was brought to the hospice. The cancer had metastasised faster than any doctor had predicted.

And now she sleeps in her own small world, in a beige room where consciousness comes and goes at a whim and agony has become her lover. She can hardly speak for the drugs. This morning she did not recognise Ross. The pain lover blocked all things out but itself. And Ross, sitting there exhausted, tormented, once again found himself impotent.

"It's me, Em," he said softly. But her eyes were glazed

and did not see him and even when he took hold of her hand there was nothing in return; just a small, dry hand lying in his own. He cried then; even while sitting at her bedside he felt already abandoned. He cried for her, for her suffering, and cried as well for his empty future. He wished death for her to end her agony yet willed her more life for himself.

And now he sits while she is asleep and looks out the window at the white world. It is silent here in this sterile room. The patient in the next bed is a stranger. She does not speak. She listens to her headphones behind the dividing wall of the curtain. The white cold pelts against the window. Despite the blizzard Ross remembers another time: he recalls Emily in their garden. Tulips bloom up to her knees as she stands in their midst, blooming as well: brown from the sun, pale yellow dress, smiling for the camera as he takes her picture.

Glimpses.

"Oh Ross, what a wonderful day!" she says laughing, and he laughs with her for on days like this which roll by long and sunny one never thinks beyond the mirage. Flowers do not die. Not really. They resurrect each spring. Emily's eyes shimmer with life. Her body is beautiful. In a yellow sun dress. Ross kisses her softly her lips pressed to his, her back warm and smooth beneath his hands with the smell of her fresh as spring flowers and she is so ... alive.

"Ross?"

The murmur snaps him back to the white world and her gaunt face gazing up at him for the first time this day in recognition. At her temple he glimpses her pulse quivering. He takes her hand once again and is thrilled to his heart by its response. She squeezes his hand in return, weakly, but still she is present and loves him and he is no longer alone.

"Emily," he whispers.

"How long was I sleeping?"

"A while."

"Have you been home? How long have you been here?"

"I won't leave you."

"Don't be foolish."

"Don't worry."

A muscle twitches below her eye. She closes her eyes, steeling herself. He can only guess at her pain.

"Should I get a nurse? Do you want something? More medicine?"

"Not yet," she says, fighting hard now against the spasm. "We have to talk ..."

"What is it? Anything, Em."

"Don't ... try not to be frightened, Ross."

"I won't ..."

"After I'm gone. Try not to give in."

"I'm alright. Really."

"Don't lie to me. Get some help. Please. If not for yourself then do it for me. I don't want to leave you so frightened."

"Emily, what am I going to do?" he answers hoarsely. He rests his head on the bed by her side and feels her frail hand run soft through his hair. Even now she comes to his aid.

"I'm not scared anymore," she says softly. "I was before but not now ..."

Her hand quivers in his hair. He looks up at her and sees someone there he has never seen. Her eyes dark now, ringed, pierce through him. She seems to look somewhere beyond him to a place he cannot follow. Her breathing has quickened. It comes in short gasps. Her eyes never waver.

"Emily?"

She does not answer. Yet she is conscious. He knows she is conscious. He should get the nurse. His wife is in pain. She needs medication. But she is with him. How can he leave? Her hand is icy. He leans over the bed, over her body putting his hands on each side of her face, his own face inches from hers.

"Emily!"

The eyes focus. He sees her recognise him.

"Water," she whispers, her voice like air.

"Yes. Right away."

He pulls away from her reaching for the thermos on the tray by the bed. His hands are shaking. He pours the water clear as diamonds, flowing like rainbows, into a tumbler. He spills some. It splashes off the tray in a minuscule fountain. He sets the thermos in the forming pool. Wavelets ring out around its base. He takes the cup in both hands and leans over her.

Her eyes are open. They are no longer blue. They are colourless.

And he is alone.

In his hands the water cup rests like an offering then slips through his fingers: tipping, spilling, sparkling, shimmering, to the floor.

∞

Dank, green chlorophyll twilight around him, on each side of the path impenetrable foliage forces him down its narrow course; tree branches reach out to scratch him. Their leaves are sharp, their bark stubbled with thorns. His arms are bleeding and a gash in his temple drips blood with the sweat that rolls down from his hair. It is oven hot in the passage; a sticky, stifling heat which makes each step arduous, each footfall more lethargic. The ground beneath him is mossy mud and his shoes sink into the earth and the earth tries to suck them from his feet. He is surprised by his shoes: dress shoes. They are wing-tipped brown leather. He cannot understand why he would wear such things here. They leave round-toed footprints in his wake, filling with water, quickly submerged.

He wants to stop, turn, heave himself back up the suffocating trail. But there is some presence in the trees and the earth and the black oily water which urges him on. For beneath its terror lies a strange promise; a pledge so nebulous he cannot comprehend it. And yet it is there, beckoning, pushing him down the narrow, wet passage bathed in emerald twilight.

He trudges on in his wing-tipped shoes.

At first he has a vague feeling of being watched. He begins to glimpse faces inside the verdure. Almost unseen, he catches them with peripheral glances but as soon as he turns they are gone. Then others appear and instantly dissolve into the leaves and snaking branches. He catches sight of them in the ground peering up through the brackish water, green like moss. He feels his shirt drenched with sweat. He is wearing a suit. Charcoal double-breasted. Why, in this hellish place, is he wearing a suit and wing-tipped shoes and a striped tie hanging like a leaf down his belly?

Ridiculous. He is ridiculous.

Then the laughter begins: the faces chuckling at first, then giggling, then building to harsh, mocking mirth. He keeps turning and turning but he cannot spot them. He sees only glimpses of tongues like pink petals rising and receding. Laughing, moving flowers. Why are they laughing?

"I have a right to be here!" he screams.

They cackle on. Yet now he thinks he knows them. He can tell from their voices. Emily. Emily is laughing at him. And he hears his father. And Robert and Anne snorting together. Jimmy White sniggering. Andy Taylor joins in and then the higher pitch of Justin. Devil Justin. Child mocking his grandfather. All of them louder. The air moving from their breath.

"Shut up!" he shouts. "I know who you are! Shut up!"

And they stop.

∞

And Ross Porter awakens. The clock radio jabbers noisily on the table by his bed. His heart hammers a painful tattoo. He is soaked in sweat. He slaps his hands over his face. Then he looks at them. They are shaking. The blue veins on the backs of his hands look like tree limbs. Peering past his hands he sees on a chair at the foot of the bed his charcoal suit, the wingtip shoes on the floor beneath it. Winter half-light seeps in through the window. It is eight o'clock, the announcer tells him. Time to get up. Time to shower the sweat from his body, dress in his suit, clear his mind. Time to shut out the laughter. There will be none of that today.

He groans as he rises. His body aches. For a moment his vision flattens and black comets cross his eyes. He can feel his pulse pounding deep down. The room is stuffy, its windows closed to a winter morning. It will be cold today at the funeral, he thinks. He must wear a T-shirt beneath his dress shirt so he will not shiver. Someone might take it the wrong way.

∞

The room in the funeral home is bone white with burgundy chairs and a carpet worn beige from the trudge of mourners. Banks of flowers ring the casket. A soft little man with wire glasses, black suit and tie and soft little shoes pads here and there through the room, preparing. He plumps up the bouquets of flowers, checks his watch, straightens a couple of chairs and joins Robert by the double doors at the entrance. He speaks in whispered condolences. Ross does not like the man. He may be a good man for all Ross knows, but right now he is the manager of the business of death, and he walks too softly.

Ross sits in a chair against the white wall. Robert joins him: Armani suit, silk shirt, rich and soft and strong. He possesses the qualities of his mother.

They are not mine. That is certain.

"We're going to go back to the lounge now. George wants to open the doors soon."

"I'll stay here."

"It's better if you come with us. George will take care of seating people. He has to close the coffin, dad."

"I know. I just, want to be alone for a couple of minutes."

"Of course. I'll tell George to hold off."

"Tell him to leave too."

"Alright. I'll come back for you shortly."

"You're a wonderful son, Robert. Thank you."

"Are you okay?"

"I just need some time here."

She lies, soft and fragile alabaster, the work of the sculptor mortician in the satin folds of the coffin. She is dressed in pale blue and her hands are clasped. The cancer ravages have been erased and so many have said how beautiful she looks, how peaceful. He has not looked at her until now.

He has been busy receiving: warm, too long handshakes, embraces, kisses and condolences until he cannot clearly remember a single moment of these past nights. The visitations have passed like shadows. He looks down at her now and does not find her beautiful. Her beauty lived in her sparkle, in the way she would cock her head or flutter her hands, in her sense of humour and the passionate flame of her living. That was her beauty. Now she is nothing.

A cinder.

He moves away from the coffin, terrified. He backs down the aisle toward the closed doors at the end of the white room. His mouth is dry. Comets slash his vision again. Something snaps in the back of his mind. He turns and opens the doors and leaves. He passes the soft padding funeral man but no longer sees him. He walks out into the cutting winter wind in a trance.

George runs to find Robert. This will not do.

After ten minutes Robert finds Ross by the garage where the hearse is waiting. His father is leaning on the hearse. He seems to be looking at wind, his face a blank slate.

"Dad?"

"Huh?"

"Dad!"

"Rob?"

"Are you alright?"

"Yes. Uh, I am now. Thanks, son."

"It's time to go in."

"I ... I know."

The two men link arms and re-enter the building. They wait with their family in the lounge. They are given the signal from George and go into the service. Ross sits through

it all very quietly. The people attending watch him carefully. He thinks they whisper to each other how strong he is,
how courageous. But he is not with them at all.

He will not accept this service, even as he hears it.

This minister speaks of an afterlife.

We all guess and hope.

It ends. It just ends.

No. It is something more.

*It comes in the final words of the dead, mystical, as it
came from Emily.*

Water.

That which gives life.

A sacred water.

In a secret place ancient and deathless.

I have read of this.

From the past comes knowledge.

I was meant to do this.

All my life.

I will find this water.

Emily told me.

I will find the water of life.

19

Then felt I like some watcher of the skies
When a new planet swims into his ken;
Or like stout Cortez when with eagle eyes
He star'd at the Pacific—and all his men
Look'd at each other with a wild surmise—
Silent, upon a peak in Darien.

—KEATS

Spring—The Past

Their sails filled; their sails big and white as the scudding clouds racing above them, the two caravels ran before the wind like thoroughbreds in full flight. The sea heaved around them and they, made for this, took each swell with grace and speed. The sea, turquoise now and muscular, tossing restlessly, seemed to help them along, carrying them sometimes on big waves as fast as the moving air, spray flying from their prows, swiftly toward their destination.

On board the ships, sailors revelled in the salt spray which would leap from the sea to lick at them affably. The sun peering out from the clouds would dry them with its glowing light and change the sea's colours before it departed once more behind some big nimbus. Across the water shadows sped into the distance checkering the liquid expanse from grey to blue to aqua and sometimes a shimmering silver. Even the helmsmen, struggling to keep their course amid the ocean's gigantic playfulness, laughed aloud from the joy of the day.

And at the prow of his ship, his preferred place at times such as this, Juan Ponce de Leon grasped the larboard rail and rode the waves as he would a warhorse. Beside him was his boatswain, Medel, the old sea dog who had been with him on other such voyages, on other such days. Medel needed no handhold. His thick legs rolled with the moving deck as though he were part of it. He was smiling.

"At this rate, your honour," Medel said, voice booming, "we'll see land by day's end!"

"Indeed," Juan Ponce responded. "But I wait to hear from Sotil of the northerly current. Until we've hit that we are not so close."

"I've seen flotsam around us this morning. A good sign."

"You're right, Medel. I am too pessimistic."

They gazed back along the caravel's deck at the humming activity all down its length. The men on watch worked the fine art of sailing, deftly going about their business, responding to Sotil's shouted orders almost before they were given. Sailors worked high up on the cross-beam of the topsail while others climbed the ratlines into the shrouds. Still others on deck clamped and held the step of the mast to its cap while more grasped the sheets, hauling and tallying sail. More men could be glimpsed clambering and chasing from one place to another through the rigging so they seemed like cats chasing through trees. The sailors sang their shanties giving rhythm to their work. Soldiers and colonists had come up on deck to avoid the grimmer conditions below: to enjoy the day, play a little dice, and feel the warm sun on their faces.

"We've shared many leagues together, Fernando," Juan Ponce said, turning to the boatswain.

"Aye, that we have, your honour."

"You've been a loyal friend, since the early days. You recall them?"

"I do, sir. Exciting days. Not like now. In them days every voyage seemed magical-like. You never knew what you'd come across."

"As Balboa finding a new ocean," Juan Ponce muttered bitterly.

"But 'twas with you, sir, we found Florida. And after that you took us southwest. There was grumblings, your honour, especially when we come across no islands those many days till we landed. I remember a good many thought we'd hit on Cathay. We know better now."

"It is a great disappointment of my life," Juan Ponce said, sighing deeply, "not to have explored inland there, found that narrow neck as Balboa did, and crossed it."

"No sense regretting the past, your honour," Medel said, "for you know now Florida can be no island. I've heard tell of some magical water up that way. There's stories, sir, among the natives ..."

"It will make a good colony," Juan Ponce said, his voice hardening, cutting the boatswain's conjecture off. "When we settle it, I'll make sure you're given good land, a place to retire. Now on with your work, boatswain, get us there quickly."

"Aye sir," Medel answered. Abruptly he moved into action, bellowing orders to the sailors aloft. He thought no more of rumours. He was not the kind of man to think deeply. Rather, he was a tool: efficient, hardened, capable. Juan

Ponce de Leon valued him and valued more his simplicity, for though he had come close to the mark, he had not known it.

The tool must not comprehend the building.

And no one must suspect the secret water.

∞

At the height of my powers, before Colon, the Carib and the anger of my son, when each endeavour brought fame and profit, I mounted a voyage of exploration. At the time there were rumours of great, rich lands to the west of the Indies; stories of enchanted islands and golden cities, of mermaids in obscure lagoons, and legends of a mystic water. The natives seemed to believe such stories enough to convince our men and so as they spread they attained a kind of veracity even among the most cynical of us.

I set off northwest. Columbus had explored to the south, followed by Velasquez and a host of others, and found good lands but little gold. It was the lack of that precious metal, promised to the Crown and unrealized by Columbus, which disappointed Spain and got him into such trouble.

I determined another way.

I have never had better sailing. It was as if destiny took a hand. We maintained a western course passing outside charted waters. We found ourselves caught in a current, running north northeast, very strong. One day when the wind was light we lost our smallest ship to that current, the water drifting her away from us, more powerful than the wind. It took days for her to rejoin us.

Since that time many have used that current, taking themselves north to catch the winds which will carry them back to Spain.

And then on a bright, flawless day in the season of Pasqua Florida, the Easter season of Resurrection, we came across the most beautiful land, in a life of looking, I have seen. This soldier's pen cannot do it justice. Across a wide, golden beach lay verdant groves speckled with rainbows of blossoms and fruits. Behind them stood lofty parks of live oak bearded with strands of that grey moss which floats from their branches. The only word I can find to describe it is soft. It was soft and fragrant and made us feel somehow at peace. It was level land, not mountainous. One of the sailors who'd farmed my plantation in Salvaleon told me it was the best land he'd seen for growing. A colonist's dream, he said.

I have not forgotten his words.

I have not forgotten the feeling as I landed to claim this marvellous realm. I felt a strange significance even then about the place. I remember as I named it recalling my mother's gardens and the flowers which grew so abundantly under her care. As the priest led us in prayer and my soldiers planted the standard, I knew that this was important for me. I named it Florida in honour of the season, of its rare beauty, and for my mother.

I named it well.

Later, we found another current running south and as we followed just offshore we began to sense the size of the place. It took us nearly a month to reach what I called the Cape of Currents where we rounded our course again to the west. As we passed the islands at its southern tip we came to a place where the ocean was filled with sea turtles. In one night we took one hundred and sixty; good, sweet meat for the men. Then we went north again and did not see the shore for two days.

When we came upon the coast once more we discovered forbidding, impenetrable mangrove for leagues along the shoreline. It seemed a fortress land protected by this mangrove wall. And just as we despaired of landing we happened upon a huge bay. It offered snug protection and room for the ships to manoeuvre. A perfect anchorage; I remember it well, for that is our destination now.

By this time our ships were in need of repair. We found a hospitable island filled with pine trees beyond its beaches and laid up there, careening our ships, scraping off barnacles, tarring the leaks. The island itself was remarkable. Its beaches were sand but with a plethora of shells washed up somehow by an ocean current. The men spent their spare time collecting the most unusual of these.

The first natives we met, those who lived on that island, seemed friendly. They called themselves Calusa, the "fierce people" in their language. They told us, through our Arawak translators, of their king called Calos, the most powerful man alive. A god, they said. They told us of his vast treasures, his sorcerer powers, his cities built deep in the mangrove. But they would not take us there. Nothing could persuade them. They said Calos would know we were here and would come to us in his own time.

The Arawak feared the Calusa warnings. They advised me to leave. But one does not win new lands through timidity. And with those reports of treasure every man was prepared to stay. I sent out ships' boats to survey the coastline. One boat found a river mouth and when its crew tried moving upstream was showered with stones from the shoreline. These Calusa were protecting something. At the time I thought it was mere territory. I know better now. For in retrospect, I do not recall having seen a single old person among them.

I should have stayed then despite the resistance. At the place I called Mantanca afterwards, the anchorage where we had careened our ships, Calos' warriors finally appeared. They had not come to parley. A swarm of them appeared from the forest and flung themselves at the men on the beach. Our gunfire did not stop them. The captain on shore formed a phalanx and it was broken by the savages throwing their atlatls with uncanny accuracy, even plunging themselves into the armoured wall of my men. These Calusa were too much like the Carib: fierce, fearless, painted: screaming their strange incantations.

Then as quickly as they had come, they departed.

Too late for my men ashore: they'd been massacred; their heads hacked off and carried away as trophies. The beach was littered with headless corpses. Volunteers went ashore to bury our dead. I paid each one in gold for his bravery. We kept firing our bombards until the burial party returned. As they did, a single canoe emerged from the mangrove. In it was a girl sent as a sacrifice to the thunder, as I was told by my Arawak translators. She murmured something about great armies gathering on the shore. We had not the strength to engage them.

We have now.

Cortez, the mutinous bastard, has shown me the way. In Darien he conquered a nation. He used horses. The Aztec feared them. He used other tribes as allies. He cracked the fragile egg of the natives with the hammer of his killing. I have done that—the killing. I am the better general. I have brought with me this time two hundred trained men, and horses and big guns, and I am ready.

The prize is so much more than gold.

Nine years have passed. In one voyage all those years ago I discovered the great northern current which led back to Spain, then I found Florida and then Darien. All great discoveries. And what have I to show for this? How often does one examine his life and find in it missed opportunities? All the should-have-dones, might-have-dones, would-have-dones gather themselves like doors unopened.

I hear shouts from above.

Land.

Sotil has brought us to Florida. It is time to set this pen down. Time to seek my destiny.

This I will be sure of.

This—is mine.

20

Were such things here as we do speak about?
Or have we eaten of the insane root
That takes the reason prisoner?

—**SHAKESPEARE**

Spring—*The Present*

The airport is cluttered with business travellers, tourists and one single-minded explorer. Ross Porter stands alone in the crowd preoccupied with his embarkation. His bags are checked but he carries two briefcases stuffed with papers. There is no one there to see him off. He has made hard choices. For in choosing this new direction he has stepped beyond the pale and in so doing has lost the comforts of friends and family. He is past them now. He is the explorer.

The boarding announcement comes over the P.A. Ross gathers his cases and, in his charcoal suit and wingtip shoes, a kind of armour he uses now to fend people away, he treads down the ramp to the waiting plane. The planning is done. The resources are gathered. This is his second expedition. The first had been accident, and fortunate discovery. His founding of a new kind of Florida enticing him through his learning of the Calusa, Juan Ponce de Leon and the still wild and untamed parts of the state became coupled with

Emily's final message. This present voyage is his return. Just like the Spaniard's return late in life. He's read little about the second voyage as very little remains of its record. The logs were lost, or might be somewhere in some dusty room, buried beneath the detritus of history. He knows a little, mostly from Herrera's third-hand account and Peter Martyr's speculations. Still, he moves like a man who knows where he is going, like a man stepping into history.

The past two months had been a tumult. A week after the funeral Ross made it clear he would sell the house. This announcement, coming as it did on the heels of Emily's passing, that he would be departing, adding loss to loss, created dismay in his family. There were conversations, cajoling, then actual confrontation. The worst was when Robert had turned on him. At first he had been patronising. He'd explained how liquefying his assets would increase Ross' taxes. He had said the house price would be reduced if Ross insisted on selling it quickly. And when Ross had refused to listen, his son had begun to attack him directly. He'd threatened to seek power of attorney over Ross' financial matters and then insisted Ross visit the doctor for a checkup, and went with him.

On the way home from that appointment, in Robert's car, the forces of father and son burst in a storm more furious than either had planned.

"Turn left here! Where are you going?" Ross muttered, irate from the doctor's probing.

"The drugstore, dad, to get your prescription."

"I told him and I'm telling you, I don't need any medicine."

"Look dad, your blood pressure is up."

"I'll start running again."

"That's not what it's about and you know it."

"So now I'm supposed to take tranquillisers?"

"Along with the counselling."

"I'm to sit in a room with some stranger and pour out my privacy! The hell with that."

"Dad," Robert said, sounding exasperated, "that's the whole point. Can't you see you're not being rational? I understand why and I'm sorry. Don't you think I feel her loss, too? But we have to get on with living."

"What do you think I'm doing?"

"You're selling the house!"

"It's mine to sell."

"You're selling everything and for what? Some whim ..."

"How would you know? Have I said anything about it?"

"I wish you would. Maybe then I'd understand. Since the funeral you've spent all your time cooped up in that house reading research! You don't go out; you don't have the family over; your friends call you and you tell them you're busy. What's going on?"

"You're spying on me! I won't have it."

"I care about you! For Chrissake, can't you see that?"

"That's not care, that's meddling!"

"I'm not going to let you sell. Something happened to you in Florida. I noticed at Christmas. I asked mom about it. She was worried over you ..."

"Well she can't worry now!" he roared.

"Jesus, look at you. You can't run away from this. You've got to face the fact that mom's dead. I remember once you could have done that. I respected you. I have all my life. Why the hell do you have to ruin it now?"

"I have my life, you have yours. I want some time for myself."

"To do what? Destroy yourself? I have a responsibility ..."

"You have no responsibility for me! Is that clear?"

Robert pulled the car over. They sat by the curb on an empty street, the engine ticking slowly, the car heater breathing out dry warmth. The street was barren and brown with early spring and along its boulevard was a line of bare trees. A boy walked by delivering papers.

"So enlighten me!" Robert said. "What happened that day in the funeral home? Something snapped, didn't it? Something altered your mind to make you come up with these plans! Come on, dad, let your ignorant son in on it! What's your secret?"

"Why do you say that?" Ross answered sharply.

He doesn't know. He can't know. I've not said a thing. I must be careful. Do I dare tell him? It's mentioned only as passing rumour in Peter Martyr's notes. Of course historians could never consider it real. The infamy of believing a myth. It would end their careers. As my son would end this if he knew. I am only beginning this voyage. Later, when I am closer, I'll tell him. But now, especially, I must be evasive. I am a man on the cusp of history, precarious, as others before me. I must be very careful.

"Listen to me," he said evenly. "When your mother and I went to Florida I started working on something there. Your mother helped me. When you were younger, I was working on that paper about Quebec, do you remember?"

"Yes," came the reply, with a note of suspicion.

"Well, this theory I have is quite revolutionary. It's about the Spanish in North America and those natives who seemed to have had no fear of them. I came up with the idea that others, I don't know who yet exactly, had been there before Columbus arrived."

"You say mom was working on this with you? Why didn't she mention it?"

"I asked her not to."

"This is bullshit. You should be ashamed of yourself."

"Your mother told me before she died that I had to have purpose to my life. I had to get on without her. I'm doing it, don't you see? I've got something important that lets me move on constructively. I'm trying, Robert. And you're trying to hold me back."

"I don't believe you." Robert looked at him, almost through him as Emily had, but he could tell his son had missed the mark.

"I don't care if you do or not."

"You've got to get help, dad."

"I'll fight you. You turn against me, I'll fight you."

"I'm going to buy the house."

"What?"

"You heard me."

"You can't afford it."

"I can easily afford it."

"What would you do with it? You've got a house."

"Keep it. Rent it. What do you expect? It's hard enough with mom gone but now you've got to add to it with your hare-brained scheme. Historical theory, my ass! I don't know what you're doing but I'm not going to let you throw your future away!"

"And if I won't sell it to you?"

"You won't have a goddamned choice! I'll match every offer. I'll have you so tied up in litigation you'll never sell the place! Do you want that? Do you?"

Robert was crying. His son was crying. He had made this happen. He wanted to hold him, try to tell him the truth but even as he considered it Robert looked at him with both scorn and anguish and he knew if he said the wrong thing this powerful man would turn on him, using his power to confine him. Instead of reaching out for his son he grasped the door handle shouldering open the door letting the cold rush in. He stepped out of the car.

"I'll sell you the house. As far as I'm concerned this business is done. And so are we. I have things planned and as long as you try to prevent me then, by God, you'd better stay out of my life!"

"Get in the car. Please."

"I'll walk home."

"I love you, dad!"

"You have an odd way of showing it."

∞

The next night Andy Taylor came by. It was evening and Ross was deep in his research. He had discarded by this time the modern historians' interpretations of the Spanish in their rough New World. They were tales told by analysts. What he sought would not be in the moderns. What he looked for he would find only in the words of the men who were there: in their diaries and log books, in letters and reports. So he was re-reading translations of Herrera, Oviedo and Peter Martyr and had found the beginnings of what he wanted.

An account by Martyr read tellingly:

> *Among the which there is an Island, about three hundred and twenty five leagues from Hispaniola, as they say which have searched the same, name Boiuca or Agnaneo, in the which is a continual*

spring of running water of such marvellous virtue,
that the water thereof being drunk, perhaps with
some diet, maketh old men young again. And here
must I make protestation to your holiness, not to
think this to be said lightly or rashly. For they have
so spread this rumour for a truth throughout all the
court, that not only all the people, but also many
of them whom wisdom or fortune hath divided
from the common sort, think it to be true.

As it happened he was contemplating this missive when Andy Taylor interrupted him. He appeared at the window outside Ross' study when Ross had ignored the door chimes. He tapped on the window, grinning foolishly, holding up a bottle of scotch. Ross could not ignore him but the effrontery rankled. He went to the kitchen door.

Andy's cold hand offered a warm grip which Ross returned perfunctorily.

"Ross," he said.

"I'm a little busy right now ..."

"The Professor in his study, huh. Jesus, you've got a pile in your office."

"Research. As I said I'm ..."

"I brought this," Andy said, quickly proffering the bottle. "We haven't talked since the funeral. I was wondering whether you'd left town or something."

"I'm planning to," Ross said, barring the way into the kitchen, hoping to end the scene quickly.

"So I've heard."

Ross said nothing.

"Damned cold out," Andy said. "So, are you gonna ask me in? We don't want this bottle going to waste."

"This isn't really a good time, Andy."

"Nonsense. Can't be working all the time," he said, pushing by Ross into the kitchen and hustling directly to the cupboard where he knew the glasses were kept. He'd poured two tumblers of scotch before Ross could stop him, handed one over, and took a stiff swallow.

"Ah, hits the spot. Now, what's all this research you're working on?" Andy moved uninvited into the study. He glanced at the papers strewn on the desk. "Spanish? When did you get interested in Spanish history?"

"Florida," Ross muttered, resignedly taking a chair and awaiting now the true cause of the visit. "I found some material when I was down there."

"You're writing a paper?"

"I've got a theory I'm working on about the natives and Spanish *conquistadors*."

"Ponce de Leon? How does he fit in?"

He was getting too close. Ross felt him probing and moved to curtail it.

"Look, why are you here? It isn't to talk about my work."

"I just thought I'd drop by; see how you were holding up. It's been a tough month."

"I miss her. I'm trying to keep busy."

"You really gonna sell the house?"

"That's the plan. I'm going to use some of the money to finance a research trip."

"So fast. After ..."

"I just don't want to live here. Too many memories."

"You'll feel different in time. Why burn your bridges?"

"Is that what this is about? You've seen Robert, haven't you?"

There was a pause as Andy tried to find the right words.

When he spoke again his voice was timid, but the words were not.

"Ross, you're hurting your son. It's bad enough he's lost his mother."

"This isn't your affair."

"I just don't like to see it happen."

Ross swallowed his drink. It was harsh and chafing on his throat. He felt its heat pass into him. He set the glass down on the desk beside him.

"What I do is my business. I'll not have you, or anyone else, interfering. Now, as I said, I'm busy. Call next time before you drop over."

"It's not what you think ..."

"Give my best to Carol. Now, if you don't mind ..."

He stood up, forcing Andy up with him.

"Sure. Uh, sure, Ross. Maybe you'd like to come for dinner Friday. We're having a few friends and you'd be welcome."

"I'll think about it."

Ross moved through the doorway into the kitchen compelling his friend to follow. In a few moments, unpleasant for both of them, filled with the clichés of distance and Emily's death, Andy was out the door. The bottle of whiskey remained on the kitchen counter, memorial of an old friendship. Ross Porter finished it, alone.

This has to do with the pure self, unencumbered by ties and constraints. Now I am alone. I have a chance to begin again, to find what I haven't had time, knowledge or inclination to seek until now; the time to learn what I was not taught.

∞

The plane thunders around him, rising into a mottled sky through the tumult of clouds, winging south like a ship under sail, buffeted by turbulence, pushing through air like some caravel carrying its explorer to his yet undiscovered destination.

In his lap are maps. Geography now. He has studied the historical tomes which had offered a path. Now he is more direct. There are thousands of freshwater springs in Florida. There are huge areas of swamp. There must still be unexplored places.

Ponce de Leon thought the land was an island. He met resistance from the Calusa when he first landed, and he'd retreated, but had not forgotten what he'd found. His career was momentous for any man: first as an explorer, then as captain-general of several fleets, and finally as the Governor of Puerto Rico. A powerful man, he knew everyone of importance in the New World at the time. But something had happened. Somehow as he'd aged he'd lost his powers. He'd been brought to trial and stripped of his titles, apparently due to corruption. It was then, for some reason, he'd gathered what remained of his wealth and outfitted a voyage. To the place he called *la Florida*. There had to be a reason. He had lost his wife, too.

In search of a water.
Into the unknown and into the future.
On the chance there might be salvation.

21

Right now is wrong, and wrong that was is right,
As all things else in time are changed quite.
—**SPENSER**

Spring—The Past

"This is a strange, peculiar land," Sotil murmured as he stared at the wall of mangrove encircling the bay they were about to enter. The pilot's voice sounded apprehensive.

"The Calusa are dangerous," Juan Ponce said. "They must learn the power of our fire and steel if we are to establish ourselves. They must learn to fear us."

"Always the *conquistador*, Don Juan?" las Casas said bitterly, "raining havoc and war upon innocent people before they can learn the mercy of Christ."

The three men stood on the aft castle as their ship ploughed slowly through aqua-tinted waters. Sand below on the bottom. Sotomayor's caravel followed. The breeze was light. They moved slowly. The crew hoped for commands to turn toward shore but their captain-general was occupied in yet another dispute with the friar.

"You forget I've been here before. There were priests with me then. One of them died; had his head cut off. The

Calusa chief is revered as a god. There will be no conversions here."

"Yet your woman listens," the friar said with a hint of mockery.

"She indulges you," Juan Ponce responded harshly.

"What begins as condescension often ends in conversion."

"Or Inquisition," the old man said flatly.

"Nonetheless"—las Casas' voice became brittle—"I prevail upon you to leave your old custom. Indeed, the Church commands such. This is a new land, untouched but for your brief incursion. Let the Church do its work, Don Juan. I will quell the savagery of these Calusa. Given time they'll welcome even you."

"You'll die in the process."

"Then I am martyred in service to Christ. What better death can there be?"

"And when you die you must be avenged. For the sake of our Lord, *fray* Bartolome, it seems the Church has ever been on the side of the strong."

"What are your plans for the landing, captain-general?" Sotil said, sensing the conversation grow dangerous. He could not comprehend his leader's predilection for conflict with the Church. It was a battle no man could win.

"We'll set up at Mantanca," Juan Ponce replied, unaware of the favour bestowed. "I know the area. It's defensible. The island's pines will provide us materials to build a stockade. Alvarez will see to its construction. He's experienced in such matters and will ensure it's done quickly. Two shifts of men. We'll build night and day. Ships' boats will patrol offshore. You and Miruelo will assume that responsibility."

"And you, sir?"

"I will take Sotomayor, the Calusa woman and a hand-picked scouting party. We'll try to determine a suitable place for the colony on the mainland. We'll go up river to where the water is fresh."

"Isn't that dangerous, Don Juan? I mean, if these Calusa are what you say, you could be placing yourself at risk."

"I've done this before, Sotil," the old man said, smiling. "Each man with me will be a veteran. At times a prepared few may venture safely where an army cannot. You are a good pilot. I've trusted you with this voyage and you've brought us to our destination. Now it is time for me to lead."

And so he had done it, quite easily, with a logical plan and the rationale to support it. Sotil had accepted it. And if he would, bright as he was, so would the others. Under Alvarez, Miruelo and Sotil, the colonists would be safe enough. And he would be free to find his dream and return to them a new man, with tidings that would change the world.

"Of course, I will accompany you," las Casas said, disturbing his brief reverie.

"Impossible!" he barked. "You stay with the ships."

"You haven't listened to what I've been saying?"

"Be reasonable, friar. This will be dangerous. Have you any idea how rigorous such a mission can be? You would hold us up. You would be a distraction."

"Nonetheless, your patents state my inclusion in all exploration. You forget that I too was once a soldier, serving under you. I am no stranger to hardship, Don Juan. You trained your men well."

"This is ridiculous. Sotil, tell this man he's being ridiculous!"

"Your woman has promised me a visit to her village," las Casas said.

"What?"

"Indeed. I will seek out this Calos she's spoken of, this chief who considers himself a god, and I will convert him before all the others."

"She's misleading you, friar. She's a native and, like all of them, she lies. Has she told you how she came to us? She was sacrificed by this Calos!"

"Exactly. And that is why I am going with her, and you."

"I'll have you placed in chains!"

"As I expected. This time your temporal powers, as you called them, have been curbed by the Viceroy. This is one decision which has already been made. Would you like me to go below and retrieve the papers? The days of Higuey and Boriquen are long gone. Why do you think you were relieved of your offices? Your methods must change as the world does."

"As Cortez did?"

"He was an aberration. You yourself call him a mutineer. You will not be given the same opportunity."

"You threaten me?"

"I do and, if you will not comply, my report to the Inquisition will be scathing, I assure you. Your patents will be revoked."

For an instant there was an awful silence. Sotil watched his captain-general seethe. He saw his hand stray toward his sword's hilt. He thought the monk very near to his death. Then Juan Ponce breathed deeply, holding himself in check, and backed away.

"When I return from my reconnaissance I'll give you the woman. Do what you wish."

"Unacceptable. The patents state clearly ..."

"God damn you, las Casas, for an interfering fool!"

"You dare curse a priest?"

"Gentlemen ..." Sotil tried once again to interrupt but the old warrior was livid, staring murderously at the friar. He shook off Sotil's warning hand. This time he did not stop himself, but his weapon was not his sword; rather he screamed into the friar's face.

"Why do you think we are in this New World? Have you no comprehension at all, las Casas? Men have come here to escape the old one, to leave the past behind them! Columbus had a vision and you are denying it! You and all the functionaries and courtiers and parasites have taken his dream and twisted it. Perhaps Cortez was right after all!"

"And your way," the friar said, "is better? The deaths of thousands, the enslavement of whole populations. This is new? You are a murderer! You are here in this new land because in the old one you'd be locked up, you and the other misfits. You are a danger to civilization!"

"I've had enough of this! Alright then. You'll accompany the reconnaissance. But you do so at your own risk. Neither I, nor any man under me, will protect you."

"I ask no more."

"And as for me, I've done what I've done. Once I was revered for it. Now I am cursed by the very people I once protected. Answer me this, *fray* Bartolome: would there be a New World at all if I, or men like me, had not paved the way?"

"That is between you and God."

With that final pretentious sanction, so judgmental, so impervious to response, Juan Ponce snorted, turned on his heel and departed. He went below deck. Sotil watched him go and wondered again what so occupied the old man with that diary in his cabin.

A tumbler of brandy trembling in his hand, Juan Ponce de Leon sat again at his table, the secret journal in front of him, pen grasped like a dart between his thick fingers. He dipped the quill into its ink well and wrote furiously.

∞

I am at this again where I no longer expected to be and this time not to unearth the past, but to quell the choler of the present. Oh, these seditious vermin who plague me at every turn! I must be calm. I must. To defend my vision from those who obstruct it.

After my return from Spain with the patents for Florida, I learned that Don Pedro Nunez de Guzman had died. Set upon by the dogs of the Inquisition, in one year a life of honour was turned into shambles by their accusations. There was no recourse. He killed himself rather than submit. His final act set him free.

And so I lost the last links with my past: my surrogate father, the mentor and arbiter who had always looked after my interests and protected me at Court, and found myself once more at war but not, this time, with Moor or Carib but against my own people. Colon's minions attacked with a campaign as vicious as any battle. Their weapons were charters, patents and registers that cut more deeply than steel. I was besieged, living lonely and outcast in my island fortress at San Juan de Puerto Rico. I saw no one but my retainers and the notaries who made up my army. I could not lead. I could merely seek their advice. And given it, only half knowing, I would proceed with my next stratagem on a battlefield made of parchment. In the end my ink bulwarks were breached. I was summoned by Viceroy Colon to his lair, to the audencia at Santo Domingo. I had no choice but to appear.

Diego Colon held audience in his great hall, built for him at massive expense to the Crown. He positioned himself on a dais, upon an intricately constructed throne, which placed him above the rest of us both figuratively and literally. The boy I had once dandled on my knee was a man now: a lolling functionary who did his best to appear uninterested in the ceremony which was to play out before him. He was a stranger to me.

After the recitation of titles, most of which were those of Colon, I was called to face the accusations. The Viceroy delivered them himself, simpering with secret pleasure.

"Don Juan Hernando Ponce de Leon, Governor of the repartimiento of San Juan, formerly Boriquen, holding the patents to said San Juan and the islands of Beniny and Florida, you are accused by the Crown and its Vice regal Deputy of fiscal irresponsibility, disobedience, and petulance in your rule as Governor. Have you anything to say in your defence?"

It rings in my ears even now.

The case had been decided in Spain. This performance was mere formality. My only alternative was submission: abject servitude to Diego Colon. Civilization, as las Casas calls it. I swallowed my pride.

An old man knows when to cut his losses.

Colon had wanted to make an example of me to flaunt his authority: strip me of everything, put the old warhorse out to pasture, take his brash powers and reduce them to curiosity, mere legend to meet young men

rising and offer advice which would never be taken; to
grow soft, malleable and expedient; to age and die grace-
fully.

But I have never been graceful.

22

Integrity without knowledge
is weak and useless,
and knowledge without integrity
is dangerous and dreadful.
—Johnson

Spring—*The Present*

St. Augustine. It is here in a town which has made history a business—excavating, researching, re-building the look of a Spanish colony five hundred years later—that Ross Porter expects some answers. There are archives here and specialists in Spanish-American history. Someone will know something. But he realizes despite his excitement that he must be careful. He knows his requests will sound strange. He must couch them in historiography. He must conceal his true search.

After multiple phone calls he connects with Professor Alice Bush. He has read her book: *The King's Treasures*, a series of articles recounting Florida's early history; nothing more than a mention of Ponce de Leon but she would have researched him at some point. No one can write about the Spanish in Florida without annotation of the founder. Ross makes an appointment for that afternoon. The genteel southern drawl has assured him he is welcome. No trouble at all.

He hangs up the phone. Almost trembling with anticipation he leaves his hotel room to go to lunch. He has a cele-
bratory meal at an expensive restaurant in the old quarter
on St. George Street. The narrow street with its weathered
stone buildings remind him of old Quebec. He takes one
glass of wine; no more, for he must be sharp this afternoon.
As he holds the glass just before he drinks, he can almost
see Emily touching her glass to his. Images of their time
together glide into his mind. The crystal glitters in restaurant candlelight. A fireplace crackles at one end and there is
a wafting of Brahms from concealed speakers. The waiter
deftly serves their braised rabbit. Emily looks enchanting.

"Here's to Quebec City," she says playfully, "and the
success of your paper. This city is so lovely."

He recalls being pleased with himself. He had spent the
day going over his paper, dealing with historians and ar-
chivists as an equal. He remembered feeling quite important. It appeared in his confident smile and the studied
scholastic fashion of his tweed suit and military tie and, of
course, in the beauty of the woman sitting across from him.
They will be seen, he'd imagined, by others as a successful,
cultured couple.

"And to you, Mrs. Porter," he'd replied suavely, "the most
stunning woman in the place."

She'd blushed.

I love her blush.

That evening, after cognac and coffee, they'd taken a
walk along the edge of the Cap aux Diamants. He'd offered
Emily his knowledge. He'd told her of 1759 when the basin
below had filled with English ships and the battlements had
thundered with French cannon. He'd told her of his day
with the scholars, of his acceptance as though he'd always

expected it. Forgotten in the moment, conveniently by both of them, was his anxiety of the morning when Emily had straightened his tie and told him things would be fine. There were lovers kissing in the shadows of the parapets as they had strolled past. Ross drew Emily inside an alcove.

∞

"There isn't much on the second voyage, I'm afraid. It ended badly, you see; a shambles really. Whatever journals there were have been lost. All we have is secondary accounts." Professor Bush speaks precisely; her dialect is melodic but the words are disappointing.

"Nothing at all?" he asks.

The historian is an attractive woman, fortyish, wearing a soft peach suit with a snowy, high collared blouse beneath. Her spectacles hang from a beaded chain round her neck and, when she reads, she places them delicately on the end of her nose.

"You say you've read Herrera's work?"

"Yes."

"You could try Davis. He analysed a great deal of Ayllon's material. Did a wonderful job. He translated the Capitulations, the patents, between the Crown and Ponce de Leon. But I recall very little of anything directly relating to the second voyage."

"I see."

"Your interest is the landing point, is it not?"

"Of the second voyage, yes. I understand the first landing was near here."

"Oh, that's another little myth we all perpetrate for the tourists. Far as anyone can tell, old Juan Ponce came ashore fifty miles south of here. That particular voyage, the first, is well documented by Herrera. There would have been mention of the St. John River if he'd come this far north. Rather an obvious landmark for explorers."

"Yet in the second voyage he didn't stop on the east coast at all. It seems such a natural location so much closer to Hispaniola. Why do you think he'd travel around the Keys and up toward the Caloosahatchee River?"

"Why that's obvious to a sailor, Mr. Porter."

"I don't understand."

"First and foremost he was a soldier but he must have known a great deal of the sea; after all, he'd travelled it often enough. Now the east coast of Florida faces the ocean but the west coast is on the Gulf. It's known for its placid waters. And the area he is thought to have landed ..."

"I surmised Sanibel Island, or thereabouts. Perhaps even Pine Island."

"That's not ascertained but it's probable he was near the mouth of the Caloosahatchee. That area has many fine harbours, deep enough for his caravels. He was planning to set up a colony, as you are aware. His people would have needed fresh water as well as access to the Gulf. He would have thought the islands offshore would provide shelter for safe anchorage. Still, we both know what happened there. He would have to have been near a Calusa settlement of some size. Just south of there are the remains of Mound Key. Theoretically, at least, that place seems the best alternative. But I'm no specialist in that field. You said you'd happened across something in your research. Are you planning a dig?"

"No. I'm retired. But I'm afraid I've become a little obsessed."

He shifts in his seat uncomfortably aware of where he

must lead the conversation. She has treated him well. She has answered his questions and tried to help. He feels for a moment suddenly foolish then quickly discards his self-doubt.

"You see, Dr. Bush," he says, "I've been studying this for some time now and I've come to the conclusion, supported by certain documentation, that Juan Ponce de Leon was not merely colonising. I believe he was searching for something else."

"Gold or silver, of course," Dr. Bush said. "He'd lost nearly everything when he was relieved of his offices. He went west as Cortez had done, to a land for which he already possessed the patents. I'm sure he expected to find his fortune as well as land suitable for a colony. Clearly he meant to begin one, then become its Governor. Regain his powers."

"Oh, no doubt. But Florida contains many freshwater springs and rivers. I know he was after gold, land, power; that's obvious. But what I'm suggesting is something a little less ..."

"You aren't actually suggesting the fountain of youth are you, Mr. Porter?"

He can hear the disdain in her voice. Her eyes glitter warily as her mouth sets itself in a tight, thin line. Her next words are curt and offer no compromise.

"I'm not in the business of romantic history, Sir. I'm afraid you've fallen under the spell of another tourist myth."

"But Peter Martyr's writings talk about ..."

"Hogwash. In those days people believed in witchcraft, relics, miracles and a great deal of other nonsense. I don't see how you could prove Ponce de Leon actually searched for a fountain of youth. It could only be conjecture and in history, as I'm sure you're aware, conjecture has little domain."

She wants to end the interview, he can tell. She rises

from her desk and walks toward the doorway. He has little choice but to follow.

"If you want to look into the fountain of youth, I suggest you take a drive just around the bay. It'll give you some idea of what I mean. Now I'm rather busy this afternoon ..."

"Yes. Thank you for your time."

"No trouble at all. You have a nice day now."

And with that he is out on the street, the afternoon sun beating down on the cobbles, the heat eddies rising in the parking lot where he retrieves his car. He adjusts the air conditioning to full. As he drives frigid air inundates the interior. But it is no help. The burning is inside him: the embarrassment, the insult, the rage; especially the rage.

Cynical bitch. Conjecture? What does she know? She is a drone in history's hive. I doubt she has had an original thought. Like me, Juan Ponce would have hidden his purpose, concealed it beneath the mundane: a new colony, a search for silver or slaves. He could never reveal his true intention.

That was my mistake.

∞

Ross has driven around the bay. There is a Catholic Mission there with a cross that stands on a point looking out at the ocean. Past the Mission's entrance he sees the first signs of what is to come, clamped to light posts:

FOUNTAIN OF YOUTH
FAMOUS FOUNTAIN OF YOUTH
NEXT RIGHT

He turns right.

Off the main road is Magnolia Avenue, a narrow street which ends at a patched parking lot. Beyond it there is a walled compound. The walls are mottled stone; at their centre is an entrance gate. The entrance is a terra cotta-coloured hut with a Spanish *conquistador*, made of plaster, which stands beside a large sign showing two ships and Juan Ponce de Leon himself on a beach with the overhead title: ***FOUNTAIN OF YOUTH***. The entrance explains the interior grounds hold an archaeological dig of what once was a native village along with some Spanish artefacts, mostly ballast and a few cannonballs. Multi-coloured pennants garland the walls. He cannot resist. He buys a ticket.

Pathways wind through floral displays and groves of trees. Several beautiful peacocks spread their tails for the few tourists there. At strategic intersections are the promised cannonballs and ballast pots and even an occasional rusted gun barrel. A path leads him out along a peninsula to a place where stands, greened bronze on a limestone block base, a statue of Juan Ponce de Leon and a plaque beneath stating that at this spot, precisely, in 1513 A.D. the great man had landed. A noble figure. Classical. Sword and flag in hand. There is pigeon shit on his nose and shoulders. His blank eyes stare blindly back up the path.

Ross studies the statue awhile, thinking of history and historical fiction, then returns to a group of buildings, old peppered walls and a bright sign saying:

TASTE THE WATERS OF THE
FAMOUS FOUNTAIN OF YOUTH!

He cannot help himself. He enters beneath another archway through timbered doors into a dimly lit grotto. Stone steps, carefully worn in the middle to seem more ancient, lead him down into an alcove and a spotlighted diorama. And there with open, welcoming, plastic arms is a native, deftly and modestly clothed in breechclout and beaded bands. He points with one hand to a dark pool of gelatinous water; with the other he beckons what Ross takes to be Juan Ponce de Leon in a silver *morion* and breastplate, a hot orange striped jacket and grey suede boots. The Spaniard wears a white ruffed collar and stares down into that plastic puddle which sits so conveniently just off the beach where three more Spaniards, holding their flag, dressed in bumblebee yellow, stand before a painted backdrop of cloudy blue with a ship in the background. Paper wavelets move from side to side to side to side back and forth like a carnival ride for fish.

Majestic music by synthesizer.

And down the antediluvian steps he wanders to the well. A middle-aged woman stands at the wellspring. She smiles at Ross. She dips a small pail on a pole down into a cavity in the stone floor. She pulls it back up, filled with water. She takes a paper cup, fills it from the little bucket, and offers the water to Ross.

Ross drinks.

"How long have you been working here," he says clumsily, needing something to pass the moment of communion.

Her smile broadens.

"I've been working hear for two hundred an' twelve years now. Hope y'all enjoy your water. Don't forget the gift shop. They got little bottles up there y'all can take home for your friends and relations."

She has done this before.

Perhaps it only feels like two hundred years.

Dr. Bush's little joke.

∞

Ross departs the place quickly, drives his car to the hotel, packs, and leaves the city going far too fast. He hardly notices the time so furious is he with embarrassment. Near Orlando he stops for the night, exhausted from the drive and his emotions. Then the dreaded dream catches up with him.

There is the road the car the trees the path and the almost unbearable heat. He wears again his ridiculous suit and again there is someone with him. He twists his head around to catch a glimpse but she is always concealed by a bend in the pathway. He calls to her. He calls the name Emily though he knows Emily is dead. No answer; just those half seen faces within the foliage tittering now, like the sound of birds, chuckling and cackling and mocking. The faces are painted. Dark, devil faces spattered with daubs of herbaceous colour. Their tongues are like flowers blooming then receding and the tongues speak words which have no meaning.

"Who are you?" he asks, his voice quavering.

When he addresses them, they disappear. He tries to chase after them. But as he steps off the path his wing-tipped foot sinks deep to his knee in the oily muck. His heart jumps to his throat as he hauls himself out. He feels a burning in his throat. It moves down his oesophagus into his chest scorching, clenching his ribs like a vice. Sweat pours from of his body. Every limb aches. Each part of him has its own agony.

He reaches for a branch to steady himself, put himself back on the path and at least have firm purchase as he

*challenges the flower tongues. But the branch breaks off and
falls, smashing into a thousand glittering pieces. And the
pain subsides, leaving numbness.*

∞

He is on the floor by his bed. A lamp lies beside him, broken,
its shards reflecting the morning sunlight which pours
through the window. Pieces of glass surround him like shrap-
nel. His legs are tied in a knot of bed sheets. The sheets are
soaked from his sweat. His body feels heavy as lead. His
right arm is numb.

He lies helpless on a hotel room floor.

Too exhausted to rise; he sobs.

And eventually sleeps, dreamlessly.

23

Who shall tempt with wandring feet
The dark unbottom'd infinite Abyss
And through the palpable obscure find out
His uncouth way ...
—**MILTON**

Spring—The Past

They had waited for the tide to rise and give them access through the passage. They had sailed slowly, sounding with the lead, carefully feeling their way forward. For the tides and time would have shifted the bottom over the years. Nothing about the sea stays the same. It is always transforming, always surprising; ever new in its antiquity. And as they passed between two points of land a cheer went up from each ship. The sight of landfall holds a special place in the heart of every mariner.

Juan Ponce de Leon stood on the aft-castle guiding Sotil. Spread before him was a lambskin chart unpacked from his sea chest, useful again after nine long years. It offered solution to the seemingly impenetrable mangrove facing them. It pointed the way to the island where anchorage would be safe and sound.

The old man could hardly contain his excitement. His grey eyes sparkled and his burnished skin glowed like the day. Overhead clouds piled one upon the other in towering pillars that seemed to support the sky. And below them wheeled flocks of gulls, circling the ships in a cacophony of screeching welcome as they swooped through the masts or skimmed the surface of the bay then soared up again like the old man's spirit. He peered out across the big bay, awed by its beauty, and found what he was looking for: a gleaming white beach on a point backed by pine trees, a shadowy forest which covered the island behind.

"There!" he shouted. "That is the place!"

Sotil grinned, nodded his head, and swung the caravel to larboard, the ship ploughing through the calm waters. Miruello followed. Just off the point they heaved to, their anchors splashing into the brink, their chains snaking down and quickly, very quickly in these shallows, becoming slack. Sailors belayed the anchors tightly so the ships would not drift. Sails dropped simultaneously and were quickly furled and bound to their spars. Shouted orders drifted across the decks as men busied themselves with the work of making safe harbour.

∞

Across the bay, far off in the distance, too small to be seen from the ships, a native stood in his dugout canoe. He was nut brown and nearly naked but for a moss breechclout. His long silver grey hair was pulled into a topknot. He was an old man. The solitude of his fishing had been disturbed by the screech of the gulls. Looking up he decried what he thought at first were moving islands with strange clouds which billowed above them, harnessed from their natural flight by trees and vines. He watched this wonder carefully.

He studied the vision more closely. Human shouts echoed across the water and the clouds fell in on themselves and men, at that distance the size of ants, climbed through the vine laden trees and the islands stopped off the big pine point and he heard the men cheer. For a moment he was confused. And then he recalled a memory of those other islands; not islands but huge canoes. Canoes possessing clouds and thunder and men with stone skins and barking sticks who stole everything they laid hands on and killed everyone who came near.

He gathered his net in quickly and propelled his dugout up a tidal canal. As he paddled, his face was grim.

∞

The ships bustled with activity, their decks swarming with colonists. The sailors continued securing the ships. Soldiers armoured themselves. Some people simply stood by the rails and stared at their new land so alien now and dreamed of what they would make it. Ships' boats were launched and soon filled with troops; the soldiers wearing their steel-grey *morions* and breastplates. Sotomayor led them to the shore where they landed and fanned out quickly in defensive positions: a wall of steel bristling with twenty foot pikes, with crossbowmen and *arquebusiers* just behind. Their flags fluttered brightly above them contrasting the dark of the forest they faced.

Then came engineers and with them four small cannon, quickly embanked on the beach, their muzzles pointing toward the forest. And after that horses, panicked and unaccustomed to open air struggling against their stays, swimming hard as the boats ran them in. On reaching the beach they bucked and whinnied and one broke loose; a grey, galloping off down the wide white strand its hooves kicking up fragments of shell. It ran half a league and then, tired and unused to activity, stopped and meandered to the trees' edge where it foraged uncertainly on sea oats.

Under Alvarez' command a huge ditch was excavated. Already he was beginning his fortifications. With parties of vigilant soldiers, he sent axmen into the forest to begin cutting trees. Cook fires were set near the shore and soon supplies came in from the ships. Tents rose on the beach inside the sandy embankment and a few men constructed open-walled huts with leaf roofs. Everyone went about his business with efficiency and not a little trepidation at the warning sight of those nine-year-old graves down the beach.

On board his ship Juan Ponce de Leon supervised the landing. There would be no mistakes this time, no under-estimations, no surprises. The experience of years culminated now in this landing. Cavalry patrols were posted down the beach and boats guarded the sea approaches. The colonists worked quickly and by afternoon had erected the genesis of a palisade. Despite his desire to place foot on soil, their captain-general deferred, remaining aboard the caravel from which he could oversee the preparations.

He was not alone in his observance. Below him on the main deck, singular amid the bustle of offloading and launching, perched on a pile of casks and bundles as if she too would soon be shipped landward, was the witch. He caught sight of her momentarily and in that instant, even from a distance, noticed her triumphant smile. She was transformed somehow, different from ever before. She seemed to sniff the offshore breeze like an animal, recalling olfactory memories which came on the wind like messengers.

He watched her raise her face to the whispering zephyrs crossing the water from the mainland. And he knew then, watching her like that, that she was indeed a sorceress and would lead him to the secret water just as she had promised. Then she happened to look up at him and her face reverted once again into that mask to which he was so accustomed; but she raised her arm and pointed her finger toward the land and held it there for him to see, and nodded her head solemnly.

She knew.

She knew where to take him.

∞

Mayaimi could smell her home; sense its presence not only in its sights and sounds, but in the feeling which filled her with joy. There was triumph too as she realized that against such colossal odds she had finally schemed her way back. She was not free yet, she knew all too well, as she sat upon stinking Spanish possessions awaiting their transport to shore. For a moment she considered stripping off her clothes and diving into the welcoming waters and swimming her way to her home. But that would not be Calos' way. Especially now she was his agent against these alien fools. She had waited years, grown old as time passed, plotting and planning for this very moment. Yet not this moment but rather the one to come when she would take the big Spaniard—she turned and saw him and pointed the way to entice him—take him into the depths and through water and end him as she would kill a roach.

And she would be free. She would be once again in Calos' arms and those of her mother, should she still be alive. And yet it would, could, never be the same. She'd been tarnished by these foreigners. Her people might thank her for her duty but would they accept what she had become?

There was still so much to design. Would the Spaniard follow when things became taxing? Would the stinking monk be fooled into letting her go? How could she lure Sotomayor, the worst man she had ever met, to his death? And what if the water had changed and she herself became lost in the labyrinth?

Her thoughts frightened her.

∞

Juan Ponce had shifted his gaze to starboard and noted with satisfaction the two pinnaces he had ordered were loaded now and the veterans who would accompany him gathered there to ensure they were fully supplied. They were a tough, fearless lot who would follow orders unquestioningly. In the lean years they had remained with him. He had confidence in their loyalty. Of all men these were unique. *Conquistadors*, he thought proudly, bold warriors like those of the past. These are the last of them, and they are mine. He turned to Sotil to find the young pilot staring down at the starboard preparations. He looked troubled.

"We'll leave before first light in the morning," Juan Ponce said simply. "That way we'll not be seen crossing to the mainland."

"But how will you find the river's mouth in the dark?"

"I know the direction from here. And she," he said, pointing down at the woman, "will know it as well."

"It's been nearly ten years, captain-general."

"I have this chart, Sotil."

"But still ..."

"She will know. She knows now. She lived here."

"But do you trust her?"

"I trust no one. But she is necessary."

"Captain-general, I don't understand why you yourself must do this. Why not simply send Sotomayor?"

"Because I command, my young friend, and a leader does not send men where he himself fears to go. You need not worry. We are prepared."

Sotil leaned back on the chart table and peered out across the bay to the mainland. He remained very still while Juan Ponce directed a messenger to shore with instructions for Alvarez. As Juan Ponce rolled up his charts for the night, the pilot turned again to his master.

"Don Juan, is there something about this you're not telling me?"

"What do you mean?" Juan Ponce said guardedly.

"Did you find something there"—the pilot pointed toward the green scowl of the mainland—"the last time?"

"As you know from the log, I explored up the coast but didn't land. Why are you asking this now?"

"Because I've never seen you like this; nor her either. I've served you with the knowledge that you would return my service with your trust and generosity. I had faith that this voyage would lead to profit. I still do. But this, you're leaving us so quickly, even before the defence is established; this is curious."

"You need have no fear for your profit," the older man said. "You will have your full share and more. I go in search of something greater than gold. I cannot tell you just now what it is. You must trust me a little longer, but when I return I will possess something so remarkable that forever you will thank me. I do not use the word lightly, Sotil. You'll share in this gift as much as I."

"I don't understand, Don Juan." The pilot looked closely at his master, baffled by his strange turn of phrase.

"Nor do I; not exactly. But there are things in this world, fabulous things which we yet know nothing of. Before Columbus there were men who thought the world was flat and sea-monsters inhabited its outer reaches. And who could have known, before Balboa and then Vespucci, of a continent here between us and Cathay? And then the stories of *El Dorado* though instead it was Cortez and his mountain of silver. In each case the reality wasn't the actual myth. But still, in each, something new and wonderful was revealed. The undiscovered lies before me, and I must go to my destiny."

To the west the descending sun bathed the sea in vermilion. As it vanished, campfires winked into existence on shore. In the balmy evening cooks served out their stews to the huddled men finished their work while others, their silhouettes cast by firelight upon the trees, paced heedfully up and down the strand as their eyes searched the depths of the forest darkness. The tension was palpable, and particularly for one man who crouched silently, thoughtfully, at the base of his caravel's mainmast and wondered at what he had heard this day. Alonzo Sotil searched the darkness for answers as he pondered the nature of men and the darkness within them.

And the man whom he contemplated sat below in his quarters alone with his thoughts, pen once more in hand.

This morning I go in search of the fountain. The woman has said it is deep in this land. She says the travel will be difficult and complains I bring too many men. We have decided as we close on our destination only Sotomayor will accompany us into the sacred ground. She says she fears the spirits there. They are powerful, she says, and will not accept easily our invasion. I do not question this. She is, after all, a simple woman. Her superstitions are her truth.

But truth is mutable. We all have our lies for each other. Sometimes our lies are prevarications and sometimes they are our truths at the time. This evening I spoke my truth to pilot Sotil. I evaded him, for candour would have set him against me. What I offered was enough. It troubled him, I could tell. He is a young man and practical. Once I too laughed at legends, considered them folk tales and superstitions, but I have lived a long time in this world. I have lived long enough to know there are realms beyond us. For Sotil nothing is so important as power and riches, so I gave him half-truth in the hope he will fear me enough to accept what I offer. Only fear is real. Fear makes truth from lies. My life is proof of that.

So I go now to face my truth, and my fear. Oh, these thoughts are too much for a simple soldier. When I took up this pen it was to journey into myself. These pages are the log of that inner voyage. And yet, after all, as I recall them, they have hardly scratched the surface.

∞

A knock ended his labour. He set his pen down and turned on his stool to face the doorway. Sotomayor entered, his armour glimmering in the candlelight. He looked fearsome, gigantic. He carried his helmet beneath one arm. At the crest of his *morion* floated an ostrich plume, its softness at odds with the steel which enclosed his body. A woollen cape was draped over his shoulders, dark like the night, rough like the man. Juan Ponce de Leon closed his book, locking it away in his sea chest.

"It's almost time," Sotomayor said quietly.

"As I thought," Juan Ponce de Leon answered. "Where is the woman?"

"Already in the boat. She has been there, just sitting, for half an hour. *La Vieja* is a peculiar creature. I still don't understand what you see in her."

"We have time to talk?"

"A little. Shall I help you with your armour?"

"Of course. You are a good friend, Cristoval."

"My thanks, Don Juan, but it's my pleasure to serve you."

"Help me dress. I have something to tell you; something unusual ..."

24

Thou Greybeard, old Wisdom, mayst boast of thy treasures;
Give me with young Folly to live:
I grant thee thy calm-blooded, time-settled pleasures;
But Folly has raptures to give.

—**BURNS**

Spring—*The Present*

Happy Hills is the shell of what was. In a way it is worse
than the house up north for here, left just as they were, are
the final artefacts of Emily. They are ornaments on the
mantle, the box of playing cards for her bridge club, or her
clothes hanging in the bedroom closet and he hasn't the
nerve to remove them. Even the mirage of her aroma remains and the chair she preferred and the Swedish biscuits
she liked before bed and the memory, each time he turns
around, of having seen her coming through a door. And the
other thing is the silence. As he eats he hears the hollow
clink of his knife and fork on the plate in front of him. Por-
tion for one.

Night is the worst. In that long hour just before bed
after he has turned off the TV, when he sits for a while, then
comes the lonely silence. Alcohol helps. A couple of bran-
dies before bed sedate him enough to ease reminiscence.
And after a while he begins to look forward to those quiet

moments with glass in hand and the silence. A few times he has a drink with Jimmy White. But Jimmy's stories and little platitudes begin to intrude and he finds more pleasure in drinking alone. He discovers it makes his thoughts somehow softer. He can examine them, particularly those most troubling, without the lump in his throat if he goes too deep or stays too long.

Heart attack.

Or the dream?

I had those symptoms. But there's been no recurrence.

Have a drink.

Better.

Why does it have to happen like this? My body breaks down like some second hand car? Do I admit to a heart attack?

Have a drink.

Yes.

As I will one day quaff the water.

Be drunk on the water of life.

∞

A knock on the door disturbs him. He looks at his watch: eleven-thirty. It can be no one he knows. He has cut his ties with the tennis group. It could not be Jimmy, for Jimmy is always in bed by now. There is no one else. No one has reason. He heaves himself up from the chair, loses balance and grasps at the chair arm, then weaves an unsteady path to the door. Knowing he is drunk, he composes himself before opening it. There will be no gossip tomorrow about the widower in number fifty nine, drinking to forget.

"How do, Mr. Porter." Darlene Skanes stands in the doorway. "I come down to pick up this month's rent check for my daddy."

He has seen her one or two times since his return. She has smiled at him. He hasn't responded, his despair and fear and unanswered dreams so deep they become the sole element in his life. He has forgotten everything else since Emily's death: the fight with Robert, Dr. Bush's joke and the night in the hotel room in Orlando. He does not want to die. He has seen Emily die and he does not want it. He is desperate to somehow be young again. Why would his heart stop now? He has always been moderate and healthy. Perhaps too much so, he thinks. How much more he could have experienced in those decades of change, the sixties and seventies. But what had he done? Got married and became a teacher. His friends had travelled to Europe or romped through rock festivals while he became stodgy and far too conservative.

Yet here, now, standing in the doorway is a budding taste of those forbidden fruits. He knows she is not here for the rent.

"Hello, Darlene," Ross says, trying to be nonchalant. "I'm not late on it, am I? I thought it was due on Monday."

"Oh, it is," she says, giggling. "I just thought I'd save y'all a little time."

"I haven't written the cheque yet. I'll just drop it off at the office."

"Oh, I kin wait. No trouble at all. You got company, Mr. Porter?"

"No, I ..."

"Well, why don't I just come on in a bit while y'all write it out."

She is past him before he can plan his next move. The alcohol has slowed his reactions. She wears her usual halter top and skimpy shorts showing plump, young flesh along with what must be at least four-inch heels. And tonight she is wearing more makeup than usual and has teased her hair. Her fingernails are painted alternate red and blue to match the halter top. It has an American flag on it with "Love It Or Leave It" in big blue letters. Her breasts swell beneath the thin material. This girl has beautiful breasts and for the first time Ross notices the sensuous pout of her mouth.

"You wouldn't have any bourbon at all?" She titters again. "I been down to Calhoon's tonight with the girls. Go every Saturday. Real good band tonight."

"That's why you're dressed up."

"You like it?" She turns in the middle of the floor trying to pose like a model. She slips a little in her high heels and Ross knows now what has brought her here. She is drunk, too.

"Yes, you look very nice, Darlene. I'll write the cheque."

She picks up his glass, swishes the remains, and holds it out to him.

"How 'bout a drink, Mr. Porter."

"I suppose it wouldn't hurt," he says.

"Better'n drinkin' alone. Y'all have another one, too."

"Alright."

She stays. He cannot help himself. She is company in the lonely hour. She is youth in his longing for youth. They share the bottle. They talk about inconsequential things. Mostly she talks. Park gossip at first, then her friends. She tells him right now she has no boyfriend. The sucker left her behind and went out to Texas last year. She tells him how bored she is here. As she says this she leans forward reaching for the bottle and her breasts swell invitingly. She crosses her legs with those heels as she sits back and the shorts ride up her thighs.

"Y'all seem kinda lonely down here, Mr. Porter."

"Call me Ross, please," he mutters distractedly. He is not accustomed to seduction.

"Ross. Yeah. I kinda like that name. Everybody says y'all a strange bird, Ross. Say you keep to yourself too much. I kinda like that in a man though. Private like."

She swims before him in the alcohol haze. He can't seem to focus on anything but her legs, her breasts, her lips. He stammers something about enjoying his privacy, the chance to contemplate, wanting her to be impressed. A woman, a young woman, is interested in him. It is almost impossible to believe.

"Goddamn, look at the time," she says a little too loud. "I'd best be goin'. I been keepin' you up."

She stands, unfolding from the chair: heels, legs, high riding shorts, peek-a-boo halter, fingernails, arms, shoulders, mouth, black-lined eyes, teased hair.

"You don't really have to go yet, do you?" He struggles out of his chair, misses his grip and falls back in a humiliating tumble. And then she is there, weaving in front of his eyes, on her knees between his legs smiling. He laughs at his own drunken folly. They laugh together. She leans forward. Her breasts push tight against the halter. Then her mouth comes to his and her tongue slips inside and his arms encircle and the kiss turns hot.

He feels her hand on his crotch.

"I thought I could see somethin' growin' down there," she says, breaking the kiss and unzipping his fly.

And soon they are on the floor and his hands are on those young breasts and his lips lick at them. They tear off their clothes heedless of buttons or zippers. The alcohol removes all inhibitions. And then he is in her, her legs around his back, heels floating somewhere above them and his hands run crazily over her and her fingernails scratch his back. He rams himself into her not trying for gentle. The sex and drink have taken him over. It is all that exists now. He has never done this; never had another woman. Then she is on top of him gyrating with him inside her. He feels himself pulsating, throbbing, amazed. When he ejaculates she screams and the release is overpowering, almost rejuvenating.

She shivers, then curls around and lies beside him telling him he is good, such a man, and he feels young again. New things. Wild things. Giving him life. *What would Emily think?*

In that awful instant Ross evokes her image at a cottage where she lies sunning herself in the mid-summer heat. There are insects humming among the flowers and once in a while a blue jay cackles languidly from the tree shade. He looks down at her from his lawn chair. He notices things he hasn't before: the slight sag of flesh in her upper arms, the grey touches in her hair. There are lines around her eyes. She shades her eyes with one hand as she looks up at him.

"Ross, do you still think I'm pretty?"

"Of course I do."

"If I died, do you think you'd find someone else?"

"You're not going to die. And no, I don't think so."

"I think you should. If it happened ..."

"Emily, what are you talking about?"

"You don't do well on your own."

"I do so!"

"You can hardly cook hamburger."

"So I'll eat TV dinners."

She closes her eyes and lies back.

∞

Ross Porter is suddenly sobbing. His despair flows from him in a flood of anguish while Darlene, astonished, picks up her clothing and quickly dresses. She cannot close her ripped halter top which exposes her breasts. Her bra has snapped too. She holds it in her hand like a broken doll. She is shocked at his tears. She is accustomed to pleasing men, not having them weeping in tearful heaps at her feet.

"What's the matter, Mr. Porter?" she asks, her voice loud enough to be heard above his sobs. He does not answer. His body is shaking with his distress. He cannot answer her. He cannot stop crying.

"Get up, Mr. Porter!" she shouts. "The windows are open. People can hear you! What's the matter with you?

She is panicked now. If her father hears of this episode there will be literal hell to pay. She does not comprehend the need and the lust and the desperation which have driven him to their act. She cannot stop a man crying when she has no idea what he's crying about. He should be satiated. Strong. She has given him her body. She is twenty-two years old. This is not at all what she had expected. She gathers her top together with the hand holding her bra, opens the door, and runs into the night. She turns into the shadows behind the mobile home. She cannot show herself in streetlight. Porch lights come on. People have heard them. People look out past their curtains for the source of the commotion. Her high heels trip her up when she steps on the grass. She falls in a heap, but she is up quickly, shoes off, in her hands then, running down the dark passage of back yards. She has accidentally dropped her bra.

When she is gone, Ross recovers slightly. He abhors himself realising what he has done: the lust, the recklessness, the unthinkable betrayal of Emily. Sweet Emily. Beautiful wife.

She is gone only a month and what has he done? Become animal. And why? And why particularly with that girl in this place at this time in this drunken state. He is disgusted. He struggles up then pulls up his pants and then the shame takes him again.

He leans over the sink and vomits.

25

Life is short, the art long,
opportunities fleeting, experience treacherous,
judgment difficult.

—HIPPOCRATES

Spring—The Past

"And you trust *la Vieja* to lead you to this water?" Sotomayor asked as he had helped Juan Ponce don his armour. He'd heard a strange and peculiar story, particularly from a man so practical and hardened as his commander. A story of a sacred water, a life giving water, a water so pure it could bring immortality. He had heard of this before, of course, in the taverns and barracks of troops, passed on through native rumour. It was said to be somewhere west in a land undiscovered. He had heard too of *El Dorado*, the city of gold, also hidden far to the west. There were those who believed it. He himself did not. He had had no reason to think on these tales beyond the cup of wine he drank as he heard them recited. Sotomayor took what came as he found it. Too often others embellished their stories through superstition or too much wine. And yet here before him was Juan Ponce de Leon speaking, a serious man speaking seriously of a magical water and a witch who would lead them to it.

"I can only share with you, Cristoval, what I know from her," Juan Ponce said softly.

"Now I understand your bond with her," Sotomayor said. "None of us considered her more than a comfort woman to you. She is beautiful, I admit, though a trifle older than the girls I enjoy. Still, I thought there was always something more: just after Leonor's death her rise in your household so quickly from slave to servant to mistress. I am glad you've told me. You've answered many questions."

"So you believe me?"

"I believe she has told you something. That thing itself I find hard to believe."

"As did I, at first. Yet as I said to Sotil today: there are countless unexplained things beyond us we have yet to witness. Who would have believed a continent between us and Cathay. Yet Balboa found another ocean and Vespucci mapped what we know of this one."

"You told Sotil about this scouting party? It's purpose?" Sotomayor asked.

"Not exactly," Juan Ponce replied. "He was curious about our advance upriver tonight. I had to give him something. I said we were going to find a suitable site."

"And the other men going with us?"

"My veterans you mean? They will follow me as I command. Yet I hold none as close as you, Cristoval. You are the only man I truly trust. As I've said before, you are the son I wish I had had. So I felt it the right thing to share with you."

"I thank you, Don Juan. I will do your bidding because you are wise and have always had my best interests at heart. If you think the woman will lead us to your destiny, I will be with you."

"And you will be the *only* one near the end. Unless we

encounter combat I intend to leave the rest behind, along
with las Casas, as we close on our goal."

"And you're sure of her?"

"She is a woman, and a native. I cannot believe she
could devise anything as complex as this tale. No, I am not
sure. But I am sure *she* believes it. Whether or not it is real
we shall discover for ourselves."

"Two boats waiting. I have command of the second?"

"Of course. I would have it no other way."

Sotomayor completed his task, slipping the final buckle
into place, tightening the leather straps just as he knew his
friend liked them.

"You'll need this," Sotomayor proffered a cape much
like his own, "to cover any glint of steel. It seems there will
be no moon tonight but just to be sure."

Juan Ponce donned the cape.

"What of these Calusa?" Sotomayor asked. "Do you
think they've seen us?"

"Oh, they will know we are here," the older man replied.
"I've little doubt of that. But we'll not see them until they
choose to show themselves. I have some hope. The woman
has told me Calos sent her to learn about us and to offer
us part of his land to colonize. It is the reason Diego Colon
thinks we are here."

"Yet that was so long ago. This Calos could have changed
his mind. There may be another tribal leader. Why not let
me take the boats upriver, scout and observe, then report
my findings? It is not necessary to expose yourself."

"Ah, my friend, this time it is. If that sacred water exists
then I will be first to drink it. If it is poisonous then you can
return with the men. You can treat with the Calusa, set up a
colony, take on the leadership of this expedition. I trust you

as no other to accomplish these things. But this is my destiny. Somehow I feel it has always been. I have erred before. My regrets are too many to count. If this is another, then I must suffer it. But you shall profit from this. Your loyalty and love shall be repaid you whatever my outcome. Something good must come of this voyage outside of myself."

"Is that why you've been so taken up writing in that peculiar book? Not the ship's log, the other."

"You know of it?"

"Everyone does, Don Juan. Some speculate it is plans for the colony, others say a list of tactics against these Calusa, a few call it your last testament. It is a mystery to us all."

"It is less than that, Cristoval," Juan Ponce said, "and perhaps more."

He sat down for a moment at his desk, withdrawing the tattered book, soft now in his gloved hand, much used and drooping. He held it up for Sotomayor to see.

"It is my thoughts mostly. My chronicle, though not in the way others think of a history. It possesses little order for it has become interludes from my life written in self appraisal. It contains no real plan other than the water, some comment on this voyage and many of my memories as well. I neither know why I began it nor why I've continued, but it has been a respite for me. Though it tells some hard truths it contains softer reminiscence as well. In this desperate voyage near the end of my life I have written my life; tried to understand what has driven me. No one will read it for if I return with a cask of immortal water then it will not matter for I will have found every human's dream. Who I am will be subsumed in my success. And if I fail... well, no one desires to read a man's book of catastrophe."

"If you have failed in any way, Don Juan," Sotomayor

said, "it has never been noticed until Colon and the *auden-cia*, and that was conspiracy; never your fault. You are not the kind of man who fails."

"You forget the Carib."

"You were not given the chance to go at them again. If you had ..."

"I had a different war by then."

"That of Colon. He fears you, Don Juan. He knows your abilities. These new arrivals, these dandies of his, fear you deeply."

"Perhaps I have lived too long," Juan Ponce whispered.

"Not at all, my captain!" Sotomayor tried to haul his friend from the dark of self doubt. We've all heard the stories. And *la Vieja* is a wonder in her own strange way. I have no doubt she will lead you to your destiny."

"Yes," Juan Ponce responded, cheering a little, "and when we have drunk of it we shall return and make a colony of immortals. The woman has said there is much, much more to this land than Florida. She says she knows little but what she does know she has told me. She said it stretches beyond imagination; that her tribe trades with others far across this sea. I have no idea what she means but can only assume there are lands to the west and north. With a colony such as we will build, we will have the time and the will and the strength to explore so much further."

"Now you speak of *El Dorado*," Sotomayor said, laughing. He was joined by his friend.

"You are right, Cristoval!" Juan Ponce responded. "I am dreaming. Scheming as I always have. I've discovered that much about myself through this journal."

He stood, walked toward the door, and opened it for his companion.

"But now it is time for another dream. One at a time, eh, my friend?"

"I look forward to this," Sotomayor said. "I look forward to what this land holds for our futures and what we will make of it. And you have not lived too long, my captain. Just long enough to become even more legendary than you are now."

"Legends are often fictions, Cristoval. It is why, just before we depart, I begin to so doubt myself. I wish not to be wrong in this."

"Only one way to know," Sotomayor said, passing through the doorway then climbing up to the deck. Juan Ponce de Leon, having been more open with his friend than any other person in his life, felt a weight lift from him. Come what may, this huge warrior would be at his side. That thought gave him comfort, and courage, in the midst of his mysterious quest.

26

What fortitude the soul contains,
That it can so endure
The accent of a coming foot,
The opening of a door.
— DICKINSON

Spring — *The Present*

It is Sunday evening. Still with a hangover Ross answers the door. It is Willis Skanes, the park manager and, more significantly, Darlene's father. He is a tall, thin man. He wears a white shirt with a black tie and trousers; strange garb for evening. Ross thinks he must have come from his church, or a meeting. His Adam's apple is so prominent it is hard for Ross not to look at it. Each time he swallows the black knot of the tie pushes down. When he speaks his voice is hard. He knows, Ross thinks immediately.

"How do, Mr, Portuh."

"Can I help you with something?"

"Mind if I come in?"

Ross remains in the doorway, filling it; thoughts of Andy Taylor and interference.

"It's late, Mr. Skanes. What do you want?"

"I unnerstan' you bin drinkin' a bit. Some folks're troubled about it. They say you bin havin' girls come by."

"That's not true. I just lost my wife, for God's sake!"

"No need t' take the name of the Lord in vain, Mr. Por-tuh. I can smell the drink on you."

"Yes, I've had a drink! But there's been no one here! It's just cheap gossip!"

"So what would you call this?" Skanes pulls his daughter's bra from his pocket brandishing it like a weapon.

"I ... I have no idea," Ross says lamely.

"It was found jus' behind your place here. This mornin'."

"That doesn't mean I had anything to do with it!" Ross says. It is a weak lie. Skanes presses his advantage.

"It's this way, Mr. Portuh. Happy Hills has got a Committee as you know. They had some sessions over you the past while. Had another one jus' an hour ago. They all'd like to see you tomorrow.

Skanes pulls out a page of foolscap typed in large letters to make it appear legal and significant.

SUMMONS

BY THE COMMITTEE
FOR THE BETTERMENT OF OUR PARK

The presence of MR. ROSS PORTER
is ordered by the Committee

MONDAY, 10 AM,

At HAPPY HILLS COMMUNITY CENTRE
LIBRARY ROOM

To answer charges of corrupt behavior
contrary to the Residents' Rules

Signed: *Willis W. Skanes*, Park Manager

GOD BLESS AMERICA

Despite the tension of the situation Ross Porter stifles a laugh. The thing is ridiculous. It was obviously written by Skanes himself and likely typed very slowly and carefully by Darlene with her father hanging over her shoulder. The paper is smudged and damp where Skanes' fingers have touched it. The situation is so absurd Ross cannot find the words to respond.

"Ten in the mornin', Mr. Portuh. The Committee's responsible to all the residents. I'm askin' you to bring your rental papers, Sir."

The threat in Skanes' words brings Ross back from the absurd. Comic or not, this is an attempt to humiliate him. He knows the decision has already been made; the rest is simply theatrics. He responds roughly to match his accuser.

"Look, Mr. Skanes, if you think I'll agree to appear in front of some kangaroo court, you're out of your mind!"

"A what?"

"Kangaroo court. Special Committee. Arrogant old farts controlled by you!"

"No need for shoutin'. It's late."

"Too damned late for you to be summoning me to your pitiful little Inquisition!"

"What?"

"Never mind. This summons is not legal. It's the work of a fool!"

"I don't like that kinda talk. If you ain't there tomorrow, I'll have you evicted."

"You don't have the right!"

"I guess you all didn't read the contract, Mr. Portuh. We got rules here. Public drunkenness'd be one of 'em."

"This is not in public! This is my place!"

"Not yours at all, Sir. Belongs t' the park. And as I said, there's been talk of girls ..."

"Another lie!"

"I got proof!" The bra.

"Of consenting adults!"

"She's on a bus home t' Tennessee. You won't be seein' her again."

"She has the right to do as she wishes! She's an adult, Skanes!"

"We don't put up with no trash here."

"You dare call me ..." Ross steps forward, fists furled.

"I wouldn't move off that stoop."

"You think your little summons can scare me?"

"That's up to the Committee. You all can have a lawyer present."

"And how would I get one by tomorrow morning? It's Sunday night!"

"Ain't my problem."

"You son of a bitch ... you timed this!"

"That langridge ain't suitable."

"Get out of here! Get out now!"

Skanes leaves quickly, frightened of Ross' show of temper. Ross knows he has made a mistake, defeated by his own desperation, this piece of paper and some inquisition he knew nothing of. The Committee, and Willis Skanes, will evict him, of that he is certain. He wonders how long they have plotted their scheme. He retrieves his rental papers and reads them but he cannot focus. The liquor has done that. He cannot defend himself because he has left himself defenceless. And so it is shame which launches him. A raging guilt empties the last of his liquor down the sink drain. He is packing his car at midnight when Jimmy White appears, his cigarette smoke curls white in the darkness. He looks worried. He picks up a box from the carport deck and hands it to Ross. It takes a moment for him to work toward words.

"What's goin' on, Ross? You goin' home?"

"No. I'm going south, back to Sanibel."

"You sure that's a good idea? Weren't you and ... Weren't you there before you came here?"

"That's right. Can you hand me that bag?"

Jimmy glances at the luggage, takes a drag on the cigarette, then does nothing.

"I just think this is wrong for you. You've changed since you came back. People can't make head nor tail of it. Then there was last night with Darlene. Don't get me wrong. I ain't makin' a judgement. I like to think of myself as your friend. A friend tells a friend the truth."

"They want to evict me. Apparently there's something in the rental contract ..."

"I noticed Willis Skanes came to visit earlier. Park Committee, right?

"That's right. Busybodies. They've set me up. Summoned for tomorrow morning."

"I seen it before. Curtain twitchers. Always lookin' but

hidin' themselves behind their rules and their drapes. I
don't think they can just throw you out though."

"What I'm looking for isn't here anyway," Ross mutters.

"Just what are you lookin' for, Ross?"

"Right now I don't know. They want me out. Fine. I'm
getting out. I won't allow them the chance to humiliate me."

"Don't think you'll find much of whatever you're lookin'
for outside yourself, Ross. Hope you don't mind my sayin'."

∞

The road of regret takes him south back to Sanibel. Filled
now with self-doubt he cannot quell the thoughts of how
close he'd come to the underside of his despair. Then he
thinks of his son and what he has done to Robert, and Justin, and Anne. They must be worried about him. He has
not called or written since he left. He resolves to phone his
son as soon as he finds a place to stay. This he must do. To
maintain any cohesion at all he must reach past the acri-
mony he has created and find a way back to his family.

He recalls Andy Taylor and how unpleasant he'd been
to the man, a friend who had simply wanted to help; then
the sharp scepticism of Alice Bush once she'd learned his
true motives; and finally Jimmy White with his sense of
companionship and his doubt. Caught up in his terrific
obsession he has not taken time to examine himself. Perhaps he has been wrong about this. Perhaps he is suffering
Emily's death by reeling from point to point, wanting an
answer, helpless to find one.

Yet there is the dream: so powerful in him; so malevolent yet so enticing. It returns and returns and there is
something in it which lures him on in his bizarre search. A

thing beyond the known world has beckoned and, just as he is powerless to know its answer, so too is he unable to stop. Not now. Not after all he has given away, given up, given in to.

What could Emily have meant about water? He tries to recall the instant of her death and finds he cannot. He cannot evoke the most significant moment in his life. The monotonous hum of the tires on pavement permeates his thoughts. And he can't think of the tune.

Perhaps I should have listened more closely.

27

*The language of truth
is simple.*
—**Seneca**

Spring—The Past

Mayaimi sat in the prow of the boat. Behind her the stinking Spanish were loading supplies and weapons. Their metal skins clanked with their motions but she knew now they wore false skins, made to protect the flesh of ordinary men. The weapons too now no longer caused her fear: the long spears they called pikes and long knives they called swords and especially the booming, smoking stick which they called *harquebus*. Deep in the forest where they were going these weapons would do them no good. If Calos decided to attack it would not be on open ground and never when the stinking Spanish were ready. No, in the forest the shark-jaw club, the swift, short spear hurled from the atl-atl and the sharpness of shell knives would seek chinks in this armour they wore and rip at the flesh beneath. She quivered with anticipation.

She knew she was right to do this: to bring these Spanish inside Calos' kingdom, to bring the two big ones far into its depths. It was her work, she knew now, to get them out of the way, make a diversion, give Calos time to gather his forces. Just before dusk she had seen whiffs of smoke drifting up with the twilight, unseen by the Spanish but clear to her. Signals. Gathering signals. Something was happening in her land.

The boat rocked as the big Spaniard stepped into it. He came forward and joined her. He was a shadow. He did not wear the thing he called a *morion* which would glimmer in the moonlight and give him away. This gave her pause. All the men were covered in dark blankets. She could tell that it would be dark this night. The stars would be covered by cloud. The moon would never appear. These stinking Spanish knew what they were about, she thought, best not underestimate them.

"What are you thinking?" the big Spaniard asked softly.

"I think on my land, its beauty and wonders," she said, lying.

"I as well," he said. He was so simple.

"You dream of the water," she said.

"And more than that, woman. I think on the things you have told me. I think of expanding our colony some day. I hope to meet these tribes you have spoken of, to trade with them, and visit their lands."

"Only to take them away from them," she muttered.

"Perhaps not. Not this time. If there is so much, as you say, beyond, then why can we not live side by side peacefully?"

"Your stinking friar would not stand for that."

"Not so loud. He might be aboard now and hear you. He is coming with us."

"No!" she exclaimed. "He will spoil every place he touches. He thinks he is god, or somehow god is in him. There is no god but Calos and Calos would never deign to inhabit such rubbish as that."

"Have you never thought in all the time you were gone that this Calos might die? Never thought he would be replaced by someone who does not know you at all, who would think you a whore and no longer Calusa?

"You think only of the things you can see, not what lies beneath. Calos mates with his sisters so Calos' seed becomes him again. Calos can never die."

"Superstition," Juan Ponce replied. He was growing tired of this witch. Once she had shown him the sacred water he would put her aside. Then he thought again. He could not afford to lose her for she, of any, would take him into the heart of the Calusa, translate his words and offer a chance of negotiation. She was significant, like it or not. She would provide the clues as to how to treat with these natives once they were defeated.

"You call me superstitious. Yet your priest tells me of how your false god was killed and returned to life. You wear that symbol, all your men do, to show your belief. Why am I so wrong then? I do not claim someone dies then returns. I tell you only of life giving water. So why is it superstition? Just because it is not your belief? I don't think you believe anything. I think you wear that cross to appease your stinking priest. You think I do not know you."

"I think you don't understand me, nor the things that make civilization. If Calos is so powerful, if he is a god, then why aren't his ships at my country's shores and his armies invading my world?"

"He chooses not to," she said. "He has enough. Lands are not owned, they are lived upon. He knows that. He knows too he can never die. That is surely enough."

"After being with me for nine years you still think that? You've not seen how *conquistadors* claim and own land for ourselves? We call it property. You've not noticed how we subjugate natives? We call them slaves and servants."

"You have broken their spirits. That much I know. You can do that to men. But the lands you live on will exist long after the last of your properties are gone. How can you not know this?"

"Then this sacred water does not exist?" Juan Ponce said, turning to her, his face very close to her face. One eyebrow rose in a quizzical manner. He is having second thoughts, she thought, now the time is at hand.

"It does exist," she said. "It is proof of never ending existence."

"Why does it exist only here?" he questioned.

"How would I know?" she replied. She had to be very careful now, anticipating this anxious Spaniard's moods. These questions were not good, his sudden doubts worse. Her plan would be a shambles. "I only know of this one. Perhaps there are more to the west."

"But why are there none in the old world?" he asked.

"For that very reason: your world is old; this is the New World as you and your friends never tire of claiming. In your old world you must have heard of sacred springs ..."

"In historical tales; nothing comes of them."

"Because those springs have been stopped up by your roads and walls and buildings and rules. The friar's church alone has dammed up all beliefs but its own. It ignores the world to believe in a world which it says comes after life and, as far as I know, doesn't even exist. Only one man has ever claimed to have been there. So your people put all their faith in his tale. What if this *Jesu* is lying?"

"Are you lying?" the Spaniard cut to the quick. His grey eyes were like the steel of his armour.

"Why do these doubts come to you now? Why would I lie?" she answered. "You think I don't want the sacred water as much as you?"

She could see him physically settle. Her words had mollified him. He *wanted* to believe in the water. He was desperate for it to heal his age and so help him quell the forces aligned against him. He had come so close with his final questions yet the overwhelming prerequisite of his life had triumphed.

He lived for revenge.

As did she.

∞

"Medel!" Juan Ponce barked. The boatswain stepped to the railing above the boats.

"Aye, your honour," he answered. His eyes found the cloak enwrapped figure of his Captain-General.

"We will depart in a few moments, just at nightfall. You will take charge of the ships. No lights. Keep men up in the cross-trees to look out for skulking canoes. Alvarez has charge of the camp. He knows what to do. If he is attacked in the night he will set an oil-soaked signal fire. It will flare suddenly. Should that happen you are to fire your bombards. Aim past the camp and into the forest. Use hot shot. Set the trees alight and so stop the Calusa advancing."

"Aye, sir."

"Good then. If it is canoes approaching fire your bombards upon them. Use every armament you have on board, even *harquebuses*. Keep them, at all costs, from boarding you."

"I will."

"We have enough food and water aboard these boats for three nights?"

"As ordered, sir."

"Of course. You are a man who knows his work, Medel."

"Thank you, your honour."

"We should be back in four days. I cannot anticipate how far upriver the water will become fresh. I assume from the flatness of the terrain it will be some way. If you don't hear from us after four days wait one more. Do not send out scouts but bring everyone back on board. Take the ships to the mouth of this bay and lie to. Three more days. If you hear or see nothing by then we are dead. Allow Sotil and Miruello to take the ships back to Santo Domingo. You command this one, Alvarez the other. Once back sell everything and pay the men."

"What of you, Don Juan?"

"I will no longer matter. If questioned by Colon's underlings, just tell them we met with overwhelming resistance and you were ordered to return. You may keep my chart of this place, Medel, for yourself. Give Sotil my second book; not the ship's log, the other. Inform Sotil to ensure that my daughter Isabella receives it and that no one else opens it."

"You fear so much danger here, your honour?"

"I anticipate it, as a commander must. But if all goes well, we will return with the most joyous of news!"

"A site for the colony?"

"More, my old friend. Much more. A thing that possesses worth far greater than gold or silver."

"Jewels?" the boatswain's eyes lit up.

"Beyond them. Beyond everything you have ever dreamed. Cast us off now. It's dark enough to cross the bay."

"I wish you good fortune, your honour."

"Mine will be yours, Medel. Be sure."

"Go with God, Don Juan ..."

The boats moved away silently, furtively, toward their destiny.

28

Strait is the gate,
And narrow is the way,
Which lead unto life,
And few there be that find it.

—MATHEW 7:14

Spring—*The Present*

He finds a motel room on Sanibel, the Parrot's Nest. It is a fine place, used and comfortable, with a window looking out over the bay. It will be his centre. Even after St. Augustine he is still sure there is something to his dream and yet, he feels simultaneously, there is something missing. He is grocery shopping when he hears a familiar voice.

"Mr. Porter?"

The soft lilt of a librarian. Another girl.

Why is this happening?

"Mr. Porter, is that you?"

He turns to face her. She has delicate features, tanned skin; he remembers her honey blonde hair and her slimness. He doesn't remember her eyes. She wore glasses in the library which somehow concealed their lustre. Unusual eyes. Sea green. Stunning eyes. She wears a crinkled cotton skirt which flows down to her ankles and an East Indian style white blouse. On her wrists are bangles. This is not the same buttoned down library girl he recalls; this one is unique.

"How are you? Oh, I'm sorry, you don't remember me," she says, blushing.

"Of course I do. Angela, from the library."

"Angela Sayer." She extends her hand, her grip soft and warm.

"Just call me Ross, Angela," he says tentatively. After Darlene he is frightened of this meeting. She notices.

"I'm a little surprised to see you here. The season's over and I'd thought you'd left when you returned the books. Well, nice meeting you again." She begins walking away.

"Yes I did leave, but I'm back," he responds. It comes to him then that this young woman might help him. She knows the history. She knows the land and shares his interest in it. She might even know waterways and places he would not think to look. "I'm following up on some of that history you gave me."

"And your wife? How's she?"

"She passed," he murmurs. "Three months now."

"I'm so sorry."

"Thank you."

"It was sudden?"

How could she know his despair?

"I'd rather not talk about it."

"Of course. Well, I'd better be going."

"Angela, have you any idea where I could find topographical maps?" he asks, taking a desperate chance. She could easily brush him off.

"Of this area?"

"Yeah. I'm, well, I'm looking for something."

"There's an outfitter just up the street."

"Could you show me?"

"Sure."

"I thought I'd look more into the Calusa, see if there are more sites."

"Really?"

"Well, I'm a history teacher, you'll recall, or I was. I just can't seem to let it go."

"That's cool!" Her eyes sparkle.

"I think you said you were interested in them, the natives," he says, smiling.

"Oh, I've been a Calusa buff a long time. I find them fascinating; kind of spiritual warriors. I just can't get over what they accomplished building their culture in the mangrove."

"Lucky for me I met you," he says.

"Have you got time for coffee?"

She invites him into her world. She is too open, too innocent. He cannot go that way again. There can be no more desperation. It must be a compact between them, or nothing.

"Actually, I've got to get groceries. Just came into town this afternoon."

"Okay, maybe some other time. I've done a bit of exploring. Actually, I have all the top-maps you'd need. I could lend them to you."

Right now he has nothing. He is cautious. She is so young. He is afraid he will look a fool. He is afraid from Darlene. Then in an instant a memory flashes. It has been forty years since he felt this way.

∞

"Don't you think you're a little young, Ross, to be considering marriage?" Emily's father in his study speaks to Ross with concern. He peers through his black horn rimmed glasses and habitually places his hands inside the pockets of his cardigan. He appears relaxed. Ross knows he is not. "After all, Emily's just finished high school; you're still in school yourself. It seems sensible to ask you to wait. Finish university, or perhaps when you've found a steady job."

"We love each other, Mr. Wilson. We'd rather not wait."

"And how do your parents feel about this?"

"They trust my judgment, sir."

"There's nothing you haven't told me, son, for wanting this marriage so quickly? You and my daughter, well, she's not ..."

"What? Oh no, sir, it's not that at all. Believe me, Mr. Wilson, Emily and I, we haven't ... I mean, we wanted to wait and ..."

"Alright, Ross. But with you in school, well, you understand. I don't want Emily getting into something she might regret. She's just a teenager."

"Yes, sir. I, uh, we, love each other. We've thought about this for more than a year."

"She's never mentioned it," he responded, seeming to feel a little betrayed.

"No, sir. Nobody knows but my parents. You were supposed to be first but you've been out of town."

"Business. Still, she could have called me."

"It's not something, sir, we thought you should hear by phone. We also thought it should come from me. She insisted I ask your permission."

"I don't like it much, Ross, but if it's what Emily wants ..."

"It is, sir. It is."

It was.

∞

"You know, I wouldn't mind coffee. Some place close?" Ross says.

"Just around the block," she says, smiling. Her smile is beautiful. Her teeth gleam. Her smile spreads to her eyes. They sparkle emerald.

The café is a funky mix of taxidermist fish on the walls, old tackle boxes and rods, rough grey tables and chairs. It perches upon a dock in an inlet. The aroma of fish and salt water wafts up to them. In the twilight they sit outside by a railing just at the water. Their server lights a candle on their table. They drink their coffee, order more, and become lost in their meeting of minds. He is surprised to discover how much she knows about the Calusa. She is excited about his theory of their fearlessness toward the Spanish. He does not reveal his true reason for being here. He does not know her well enough.

"I visited the Randell Research Center on Pine Island," he says, "and toured the Calusa Heritage Trail. And Emily and I took your advice and went into the mangrove at Ding Darling. We found a burial mound there."

For a brief moment he is surprised at himself; that he can speak his wife's name so easily to this young woman. A flash of Emily's reaction to the mound touches his mind. He pushes it aside. It is the past. He can do nothing now but what he is doing. And Angela gives him little time to reflect, she is so animated in her response.

"Have you tried the Estero River? Or the Peace? Or the Caloosahatchie? Those must have been their waterways to the interior. They must have traded inland. There are some spots that look a lot like remains to me, though they're so overgrown I don't think anyone sees sense excavating them."

"You've seen them?"

"Yeah. I'm a bit of a camping nut. Comes from my parents. When I get the chance, I get out there. I love it, just being in nature. There are so many quiet, beautiful places here but they're not that easy to find. Florida needs more environmentalists to keep development down. Did you know our water table shrinks every year? The swamps are drying up. It makes me so mad just to think of it."

"Angela, you surprise me ..."

"Call me Ange. Everyone does. Angela just seems so formal."

"I know the feeling. My full name is Rossiter. Scottish background. What can I say?"

"My dad wanted to call me 'Angel'. My mom stepped on that one. They compromised."

"These places, Ange, could you show me on the maps?"

"I'd love to. In fact, I've got a bit of a secret, Ross. I've always wanted to be a guide, work for some outfitting company. I just haven't taken the time."

"Are you saying ..."

"What if I took you myself?"

"What about the library?"

"Temp job. I'm just standing in for Josie. Contract's up in a week. I was thinking I might try an outfitter when it's done. But this could give me more experience. Maybe, if it works out, you'd write me a reference?"

"I'd pay you, of course."

"Just expenses. After all, I'm not really a guide. I've got money saved from the library job. I don't need much anyway; live sort of hand to mouth. That's from my parents, too. Back to nature types. I think people in the sixties would have called them hippies. They're up in Oregon now."

"You looked so conservative in the library."

"The Board insists on old-school clothes."

"So you're a hippie like your parents?"

"Hippie? Ancient history. Even for them. They're even younger than you."

"No, I just meant ..."

"I'm sorry. I didn't mean to insult you."

"Believe me, you haven't!" He laughs for the first time in a very long time. "What's the terminology now?"

"I don't bother with that. If I had to come up with something, I guess you'd call me a spiritualist. I was pagan once; my parents' religion. Now I'm just a free spirit!"

"Good lord! Look at the time. It's nearly ten."

"This has been fun."

"But I've kept you too long. I'm sorry ..."

"So about the guiding? I know I'm not experienced but I wouldn't waste your time. I've explored a lot of this area."

"You don't know me, Ange," he says, arresting her eagerness with reality.

"I'm not often wrong about people," she says, smiling.

"There's a bit more to this than just the Calusa."

"I thought as much. So tell me."

"It's not what you think."

"You mean do I think you're trying to hit on me? I'm the one who asked you for coffee. Somehow I don't think you're like that."

"It's complicated," he mutters lamely. She doesn't know his obsession.

"Aren't we all?" she says, laughing.

"I'm going to be honest with you. This might take some time to tell you."

"I've got work until four, tomorrow. You can tell me then. Why don't you come by my place after four? It's a walkup on Periwinkle. I'll write the address. At least you can pick up the maps. But I'd really like you to think about me help-ing you. See you tomorrow?"

"After four ..."

"Think about the guiding ..."

She is gone, waving back at him, into the softness of Sanibel night.

A guide. What was missing. But will she accept it all when I tell her? I won't lie to her. I'll give her everything: the dreams, the feelings, the research, the obsession ... perhaps even Emily's final word. No. Not that. It would be too much. I will not abuse what has been bestowed. And it has been given somehow, I know, by the mystical water. It leads me on through a dream, through a need, through all my errors and terrors and even despite them.

So, here is faith.

∞

The next morning he calls his son. He can hear the relief in Robert's voice. He tells him he's fine and will be home soon. He says not to worry about the house; thanking Robert for caring. He tells him how beautiful Florida is in late spring and he wants to stay on to see it bloom, see all its natural places. He tells Robert he has a guide who knows the land and will keep him safe. Robert accepts it. He has such a warm, resonant voice; like his character. Ross is proud of him and relieved as well. They are no longer enemies.

That afternoon he finds Angela's place. It is up a stair-way which climbs the outside of a clapboard shop. She is there to greet him. Her apartment is extraordinary. There are beads in the doorways; brightly painted, fierce wooden masks on the walls; the living room is alight with crystals and stained glass ornaments. She makes tea as he studies the maps she provides. She brings the tea on a driftwood tray. Flute music swells from concealed speakers.

"It's chai, I hope you don't mind," she says, smiling.

"Not at all. My wife was a bit of a tea connoisseur."

"I wish I'd met her."

"You'd have got along well."

"Did you think about the guiding?"

He is not ready yet to lay his truth before her: be rejected, be mocked. He fears *that* most of all from this young woman who seems so free and so generous. He changes the subject.

"These masks: they're Calusa? I've seen pictures ..."

"Oh, they're just my little reconstructions. My hobby is woodwork. I like to carve, paint. I lived in a commune for seven years. You tend to pick up some skills."

"They're beautiful."

"You think so? My friends think they're too ferocious. But to me they represent spirits. Warrior spirits. Did you know *caloos* meant fierce? Their chiefs wore the masks in their ceremonies. I think they somehow symbolized their gods."

"That's very pagan. Maybe you haven't left your parents behind after all?"

"Maybe not," she says, laughing. "I just think there's more than what we perceive."

A voice from the present mirrors a voice from the past. He decides.

"Ange, what do you know of the fountain of youth?"

29

This is the forest primeval.
—LONGFELLOW

Spring—The Past

In the utter dark of a moonless night they groped toward the river mouth. The coastline was a tenebrous murk forbidding against the sky. Their oars, silent, damped in padded oarlocks, dipped efficiently to the muffled grunts of the tiller men, hauling the pinnaces forward against the current as it emptied into the sea.

The river was wide here and except for the current they would not have recognised it. Eventually the sounds of scores of frogs and hooting owls told them they had moved inland. They kept to the middle away from the shoreline and worked their way cautiously upstream. Soon the river began to narrow and, as it did, a dusky daybreak foreshadowed the sunrise making the water slate grey. Mist appeared from the water to rise and conceal them. They could see with the growing light the tops of trees above the haze but down in the river all was a ghostly, thick fog. And as the morning began to burn off the mist, the mist dissipating in tenuous strands, they saw on the shoreline a black bird perched with its wings outspread to the air. As the vapours dispersed and revealed it, the boats slowed to observe.

"Diving bird," the woman said, smiling in recognition.

"What is it doing?" Juan Ponce whispered.

"It dries its wings in the air as you dry your clothes."

"A strange bird," Juan Ponce replied.

The humidity of the day came on fast and the men began to sweat at their oars. The riverbanks were overhung with huge trees shading the shoreline in dark, glassy pools. Beneath the trees was a tangle of foliage. The boatmen could see nothing of the land beyond them. The riverbanks concealed everything. They followed a bend in the river and, as they did, saw a gleaming, unexpected whiteness punctuating the interminable green. They moved closer, wary of this weird monolith which caught the sun and reflected its rays as though it were somehow alive.

"Burial mound," the woman said. "Very big. For a chief."

"It's a tomb?" las Casas said, genuflecting fearfully as he did.

"There are many. I told you my people build with shells. This is nothing compared to the city of Calos."

"This is a civilized culture," las Casas murmured. "They build. These are not savages."

"You make your point, *fray* Bartolome," Juan Ponce said. "But their organization makes them more dangerous. If they can build such as this, they can make an army."

"*Jesu* ... Mother of God, look at that!" the tiller man cried, his eyes wide with fear.

"What?" Juan Ponce turned to him. "What do you see?"

"Dragons!" His shaking hand pointed upriver and quickly he tried to turn the boat about. A threatening order pre-vented him.

Lying on a pebbled beach just below the burial mound, and then across the river on the muddy bank, lay hundreds of antediluvian forms. Their bodies were as large as those of horses and covered with horny plates like armour, their long low bodies a mottled grey-green, their heads three feet long, all jaw, with huge protruding teeth and promin-ent nostrils at the end. Some of them floated in the water and would, to the unsuspecting, seem like drifting logs. They were huge, the size of a pinnace from their snouts to their tapering tails. A few of them moved from water to shore lazily, lizard-like; primordial.

Then, for whatever reptilian reason, one of them began to hiss, opening its jaws to reveal huge incisors, each a knife of bone. Then it slammed its jaws shut and slithered into the water by the beach. And just as suddenly another of the creatures, already in the water, undulated toward the first. Their bodies seemed to swell and their plaited tails brandished high as they closed on each other and in that few moments Juan Ponce de Leon witnessed a violence he had never, in a life of war and massacre, could possibly have imagined.

Their roaring was like a thunder and from their dilated nostrils poured vapour. The surface seethed as they writhed together, intertwined as they sank below the waves they had made. Mud boiled up from the bottom like a cauldron. They re-surfaced, their gigantic jaws clapping together and echoing into the forest. Their enormous tails swung in great cutting arcs. Then they sank again beneath the tur-bulence. And finally only one re-appeared making a dread-ful grunt that resounded up and down the river.

"They are dragons!" the tiller man shrieked. "This place is unholy. We must leave!"

"Nonsense." Juan Ponce glared down at the man.

"These are truly the devil's work," las Casas remarked.

"To go on we must pass through them," the woman said.

"Will they attack us?" Juan Ponce asked.

"It is possible."

Sotomayor's boat had come alongside.

"The men are fearful, Don Juan," he said. "Some of them think we approach the gateway to hell. I assume, however, we're going ahead."

"We are."

"Then my boat volunteers to take the lead!" He glanced back at the cowering soldiers behind him, their love for Sotomayor somewhat allayed by his foolish bravado. Then he laughed. "If we must we will fight our way through! Christians against devil serpents!"

"But no gunfire," Juan Ponce said. "We don't want it known we are here."

"Take the right fork," the woman instructed. "The left is too shallow for these boats."

"You remember this?" Juan Ponce said.

"I have travelled this river many times on my way to the sacred country."

The alligators allowed their passage, glinting at them like Satan's spawn.

∞

In the afternoon the sky lowered and rain came in a downpour. They heard it in the distance as it moved through the forest toward them. Like drums, like ten thousand drums marching closer, and when it reached them the sky seemed to empty. Grey teeming rain. Its intensity veiled them. The rain flowed in rivers from the brims of their *morions* and clattered against their armour and settled in ponds in the bottoms of the boats. Finally Juan Ponce signalled to make for the shore.

They found a pebbled beach at a bend in the river and landed there, overturning the boats to serve as shelters. And as soon as they had, the rain stopped. In its wake, in the clearing air, Juan Ponce walked to the tip of the gravel peninsula and gazed upstream. Here the river narrowed even more. It seemed as though the air itself was green, tinged by the emerald dark of the forest. The stillness awed him.

He motioned for the woman to join him. He noticed she wore the ornaments he'd seen when she first came to him, after *Mantanca*. On her breast lay a large, carved medallion of shell and more beaded shells encircled her neck. In civilization she would appear savage. Here, in this primal place, she fit.

"How much further?" he asked.

"The river grows shallow after this," she responded, "good only for canoes."

"We have no canoes."

"Then we walk."

"Through that?" He pointed at the tangled bank.

"The spirits make their sacred land difficult. Only the brave can go there."

"Sotomayor!" Juan Ponce turned away from the woman. "This is as good a place as any to make the base camp. The water approaches are easily guarded; the boats can make a landward wall. You agree?"

"Of course. It's suitable. And what of us?"

"In the morning we set off as planned. The men will remain here with friar Bartolome."

"He'll insist on coming."

"And he will be refused. I'll explain to him if the Calusa appear it will be here where the men will make noise and attract them. He can barter his Christ with them then."

"And you, you will lead us?" Sotomayor turned to the woman.

"A short journey from here, but a hard one," she said, and she smiled strangely.

∞

I use this scrap of parchment in the half light of a green, scowling world. My old eyes can barely discern these scratchings but now, on the cusp of discovery, I must end my journal.

Here in the heart of the wild I discard all worldly things. I have quelled las Casas. Even the zealot is afraid of this place and seems only too willing to remain with the men while I and the witch and my friend journey on.

In the morning we will march into the morass of what she calls 'the sacred'. I anticipate the way will be hard, but hard has never stopped me. I will take this as I have other places. I will own it. I will again own my life. My new life. From the water. So close.

∞

That night mosquitoes descended in clouds making the camp a perdition of sleepless torment. Nearby the grunts of alligators added fear to the men's tribulation. And noises from the trees would set them staring fitfully into the dark. Their camp was an inky blackness unmitigated by fire; for fear of discovery they dared not expose themselves with light. So they ate cold dried tongue with biscuit and slapped interminably at insects while all around them forest creatures peering through the dark observed the intruders.

And some of those creatures were human.

30

None would live past years again,
Yet all hope pleasure in what yet remain;
And from the dregs of life think to receive
What the first sprightly running could not give.

—**DRYDEN**

Spring—*The Present*

"So, do you think I'm crazy?"

Ross Porter ends his story. Angela has not moved for an hour as she listened to his convoluted account. At this moment Ross cannot fathom how she feels. Her face is a mask, her eyes green and depthless as the sea. She sits with her back to the apartment window. Afternoon sunlight streams in to illumine her. She almost becomes the light for an instant.

"All because of that dream I've had," he says, struggling to continue. "It's why I came back. I know it's not logical but I think there's a connection. At first I didn't recognise it, then I fought it and now, well, now I'm resolved. I've found no answers in the research but I never really expected to. And I can't talk to anyone about this. You're the first person I've actually told the whole thing to."

For a moment the girl does not respond. She stares out through the apartment window into the light. Ross knows it has been an intense, disturbing hour for her. His quixotic tale has frightened yet fascinated her; those jade eyes clouding over with each new revelation until they have become opaque. Yet when he'd tried to stop, fearful of yet another rejection, she had beckoned him on.

"You really believe in this, don't you?" she murmurs.

"You'd like me to leave?" Ross responds, ready for ridicule.

"No. I ... It's just so overwhelming."

"I'll give you that," he says, laughing hoarsely.

"I mean, I know there are things we can't explain, things we aren't conscious of or can't grasp, even other dimensions. Everyone's heard the fountain legend but no one ever gave it credence."

"No one does, that's true."

"But if it is true, if it does exist, why haven't we heard of it? Surely in all this time ..."

"The Calusa died from disease, Angela: smallpox mainly, like so many other tribes. A plague that killed most of them, I imagine. And with them went their culture. So no one knows much about it. Perhaps this water has healing properties, or maybe it simply prolongs the lives of the healthy. There was mention of a sacred water in Spanish chronicles. That's what I've got to go on."

"So you have no idea where this might be?"

"None. But it must be somewhere here. Why would Ponce de Leon come back to a place where he knew he'd meet resistance?"

"That historian ..."

"Bush."

"Yeah. She told you it was about better harbours?"

"Yes, but why, later on, did the Spanish build their

capitol at St. Augustine? The Atlantic side: to protect the Gulf Stream."

"And you know he landed here?"

"Not exactly. Even she admitted his second voyage isn't clearly documented. But it had to be near a large concentration of Calusa; otherwise, how could he and his troops have been defeated? They were *conquistadors*, armed and trained and experienced, the best fighters in the world at that time, quite capable of victory; unless there were so many against them they didn't stand a chance."

"So this, you think, is the logical choice?"

"There's not a lot of logic. I know so little of this area ..."

"That's why you wanted the top-maps?"

"Well, they're something."

"The maps can't show you what you're looking for."

"It could be anywhere," Ross mutters despairingly.

She is quiet again, studying his face. It is the drawn, lined face of a man who has felt too much, lost too much, given too much to this obsessive search. He no longer looks like the man who came into the library. He is older now, somehow, though so little time has passed since then. His face is filled with the trepidation that she might ridicule him, send him packing, call him a desperate old man. She would never do that.

"Have you thought any more about my guiding you?" she asks again.

"Are you certain you want to?" He almost cannot believe her.

"I've got three more days at the library. While I'm doing that you could get what we'll need, maybe plot a search grid on the maps."

"You're sure?"

"This is just the thing for me. Whatever happens I'll have lots of experience when we're done. Or, perhaps I'll have no need of a job in the end." She smiles wryly. "Oh, it might seem a bit mad ..."

"You're telling me?" He laughs again. She hears relief and fixation at the same time. It does not trouble her. She is accustomed to the years of her parents and their friends. They could be manic about things yet still, they were kind and loving. She craves this adventure.

"I've got time," she replies. "So why not? I can't even imagine the fountain exists but why not give you the chance to look? We can search for places where nobody goes and I might find some great routes for eco-tourists. It wouldn't hurt my chances with outfitters."

"I'll pay for everything; whatever we need. Just give me a list. Ange, I can't thank you enough."

They have tea to toast their new partnership, then Ross leaves with a list Angela has given him. He will spend the next few days shopping. He walks east, down Periwinkle toward his hotel. The sun is setting behind him.

∞

He is calm within the dream now, having grown accustomed to it. The horrors of before: the heat, the black water, the brambles and grasping vines, those faces and their laughter are now simply part of the passage he must endure to find an end. We humans somehow adapt to things, even the most dreadful. He ignores his clothing, even shucks off his jacket as he struggles along in his wingtip shoes. For there is hope beckoning him. Now, as never before. There is faith in reaching the unknowable terminus of this claustrophobic path.

Even the voice: "Don't go in there, Ross, don't go in ..." has soft-
ened to mere suggestion.
And he knows that voice now.

∞

Their search begins. Angela is a wonder. She falls into the
spirit with youthful vigour. For the next two weeks they drive,
boat, and hike the area as far south as Bonita Springs to as
far north as North Port. They do not travel known roads.
Instead they search in such places as Myakka River State
Park, or Cecil M. Webb Wildlife preserve. They visit Pine
Island often, hoping for some clue from the Randell Centre, some Calusa titbit they might discover where others
would not suspect. Ange selects obscure markings on the
maps, old trails leading nowhere specific. And each time
they come upon some possibility they stop and search.
They wander through late spring in Florida and Ross marvels at the blooming flowers and thickening foliage as the
hot weather and the rains arrive. Sprays of poinsettia blos-
som crimson among the deep greens of vines. Wildflowers
speckle the roadsides and riverbanks with a host of colour
and life. The abundance of rebirth encourages him. He
takes it as a sign, a metaphor of his vision. It is a law of nature. Regeneration. And if it is so common then there must
be hope.

Angela takes him places he could never have found on
his own. She works hard, searching her memory to recall
cloaked lanes and pathways. They come upon hidden places
so feral Ross hardly believes they are real. It is a primordial world at once forbidding and seductive: a world of crystal ponds and meadows abundant with flowers and trees

stretching skyward, of clear pools shaded beneath cool ferns and blossoming orchids. They glimpse rare birds like the hot pink of roseate spoonbills, or green herons perched motionless on branches by streams, or the sudden beauty of snowy egrets stalking their prey with patient wading steps.

Often they camp in the wild. Angela, hiking boots and long, slim legs, prepares campfire dinners. She is good at this, having done it so often. As they spend time together, he comes to think of her as a kind of daughter. He will not go beyond this. Not after Darlene. Not even in his tent at night, fleeting visions of that healthy, robust young body so active and full of life passing through his mind; he will not abuse this gift. In the evenings they talk across their campfires. Angela believes in natural spirits, animism. She knows all things have souls. Trees, stones, even water.

"It's not the way we think of a soul," she explains, "but a life force. You can feel it around us, can't you? My parents believed in it. My dad would take us, mom and me and some other friends, out into the bush for what he called spiritual regeneration. Oh, there were drugs back then but he used only natural ones: marijuana, peyote, that kind of thing. He'd read a lot of Carlos Castenada. He still thinks of himself as a medicine man."

"He thought beyond logic," Ross says, feeling a bond with a man he has never met. "In a way, Ange, you're far ahead of me. It's taken me so long to realize. I kind of wish I'd had your childhood."

∞

It is all so simple really as he recalls what he once was and how he has changed. He remembers a woman named Ilsa

Pendereki who shook his hand, and his world as well, at a meet and greet teachers' staff meeting. She'd been hired to teach Theatre Arts. Ross had argued against this. He simply could not see the sense in a theatre course. It would take students' time away from more scholarly pursuits. It would take them away from the real world.

To Ross the school musical was one thing: bringing kids out to enjoy themselves; a solid promotion of the institute. He'd even helped with a few, building sets and props. But Ilsa would have none of that. Not for her *Oklahoma* or *Bye Bye Birdie* or even Gilbert and Sullivan. She said she wanted kids to explore themselves. Ross thought this was dangerous ground.

She was dark-haired and dark-eyed and looked far too avant-garde to be a teacher. She wore black clothing and left town each weekend for Toronto or Montreal. Ross found her suspicious. And then he saw her first productions. They were strange and alien to him, involving writhing body movements and ghostly voices. The sets and the lighting made the plays seem like dreams. Ross hated them and could not comprehend her success; for she was successful. More students enrolled in her classes each year. She won prestigious drama awards. Others on staff said she was an artist. Ross gave it no credence. She had bamboozled them with the arcane. In Department Heads' meetings he began to wonder aloud what was happening when students relinquished the basics in favour of the esoteric. And to the woman herself he became aloof. She had asked him several times for help. Ross had refused. He thought her efforts worthless. But Emily didn't.

"I happen to like her work, Ross."

"But you know how I feel about what she's doing."

"Yes, and now you know how I feel."

"There's no place in school for that kind of self-indulgence. She manipulates them."

"And are your students, when they come to you, when you explain things, are they being manipulated?"

"Of course not; it's different."

"I don't think so. You give them history that lives. You let them see the humanity in it."

"That's what history is."

"Not the way I was taught. All I remember is wars, politics and memorisation."

"No wonder you don't like it."

"I like it when it's human, when it touches me, when I know those were people like you and me who struggled to make better lives for themselves. Why do you think I prefer historical novels?"

"You think I do that? Teach like that?"

"I know you do. You have a gift, but so does Ilsa. You can't close down new ways of thinking, Ross. History has to have taught you that much."

"And I am, therefore, the old," he said, suddenly hurt by her words.

"You'll have to think that one out for yourself, Ross."

Now Ross Porter finds himself a changed man. He is no longer the obstinate conservative. He has opened himself to the cryptic.

I wish Emily could see me now.

∞

Still, as the search proceeds through weeks, nothing strikes him as familiar. He works on the premise of the dream, no matter how raw, to bring some recognition. This does not seem at all strange to him. He has discarded the old ways: the research, the studied hypothesis, the objective viewpoint, the things he has valued since he can remember. Nothing at all he has done before aids him in this. He finds himself on a quixotic journey within the primordial forests and swamps which recognise nothing more than themselves. They have lived for epochs, their secrets beyond human comprehension. And to gain those secrets one must, Ross thinks, return to the mystic. There is wisdom in the arcane, unrecognised by those who have lost touch with the source. And that wisdom of visions and dreams and signs may be the only true knowledge of man.

But the search begins to seem hopeless. So much of the land has been subsumed by development. The secret water could now lie beneath some shopping mall or condominium, its precious liquid lost underground, seeping into sewage systems or simply stopped up completely. And there is so much to search. As day after day passes with no progress, Ross feels a growing discouragement. He had hoped for a kind of ethereal guidance, some direction that would bring him to his goal. It had all seemed so fixed before, all fallen into place: the feelings, the dreams, Emily, Angela, all of it leading him to his destiny.

Yet slowly it has become less clear.

Still Angela pushes where he would have glided. The young woman offers him urgent purpose because she possesses it in abundance. She is in her element, discovering more and more of herself with each day as they trek through those subtle, hidden places. She becomes more confident and commanding, assuming leadership but leading now in an altered direction. Somehow as they have travelled, their visions have grown apart. She has something else now, removed from Ross' fixation; dreams of her own.

"I keep remembering places we've been," she tells him, "but they never seem right to you. Can you describe this dream path any clearer?"

"I'm sorry; intuition is all I've got."

"I'm sorry I haven't got you what you want, Ross. I have to thank you though. You've given me such a chance to explore."

"So how do you feel about me now?" He tries bantering, but she will not take his bait. Her mind is elsewhere: caught up in the real.

"I've been thinking, with all this exploration, eventually I might even start my own business. I just need a business plan."

So there it is. Youth and future. Peering into the distance where he cannot go.

She plots and plans their every day. But now it is more about eco-tourist routes than searching for an obscure spring. Now it has function for her beyond his nefarious dream. For her dream, despite her spirituality, is more actual and attainable than his. She arranges meetings with guides, naturalists, fishermen. She wants to know their secret places, the ones the maps cannot show: pools of beauty, orchid plots, places where people might revel in nature's perfection. There is never a mention of sacred water. What they had shared becomes depleted, overwhelmed by Angela's new agenda. The search for the fountain is too much like crawling, and the young have ever wanted to run.

He finds more and more he is helping *her* rather than the reverse. He is envious of her energy, jealous of her vision, or perhaps just hopelessly lost in his age. If the water will bring him youth again, it will give him the wisdom to govern that youth. For the water will not erase his experience. He admits to himself ageing does have its benefits: patience, a calmer demeanour, the knowledge one gains, the mind that grows as the body falters.

And there is the rub.

Angela begins to notice his irritability. She tries to assuage him. She is loyal but he knows very well she could leave any time. If their separate visions grow further apart, she will realize she has made a mistake and, as youth does, find a way out: perhaps with sensitivity, hopefully that, but more likely with brutal youthful decision.

And he must abide by it.

It comes to him then why the search has been empty. He has begun to follow the path of a youth. That track leads nowhere but toward the obvious. His track is the numinous. The road has not yet been made which leads to the mystical fountain. He must make his own.

I've done this the wrong way. I've been searching others' routes, trying to find the unknown through the known.

The unknown will only be found within. Deep.

Where youth fears to go.

Their search ends one day by mutual agreement. She cannot find what he is seeking and he can no longer follow her. They pack up their gear and return to the town, each to their own places, brief goodbyes as he drops her off. Her green eyes are dreary like a turgid sea; they no longer sparkle.

And be these juggling fiends no more believed,
That palter with us in a double sense;
That keep the word of promise to our ear,
And break it to our hope.

—**Shakespeare**

Spring—The Past

The woman had not exaggerated. The going was hard. After the riverbank they found themselves, the three of them, marching across grassy ground with pine trees interspersed. But then it had become boggy, the ground soft and wet underfoot. They moved quickly despite the heat of the morning. He was impatient. He wanted to know when they would reach the sacred place.

"There," she said, pointing toward a forest of gigantic trees in the distance. As they approached the ground became worse: soaked and acrid with sludge that would suck at their feet and make the march harder. And the forest grew into huge bearded trees reaching impossible heights. They were forced to wend their way in the narrow, dark passages between the trees. The earth not earth at all but reduced to moss.

When they entered the quagmire, there seemed to be no ground. Black water; covered with air plants and ferns and the tangle of half submerged roots of the trees. She led them into the swamp, glancing over her shoulder to discover if they were afraid. She smiled again, but the smile was merely a mask. He did not trust her. He made sure he was always directly behind her, within reach of her, with Sotomayor following at his back.

It was a strange place. Silent. Predatory. The water was cool. The sun was gone, blocked by the leafy canopy far above them, though once in a while the sun would reach through and dapple the water. They would slash at the fern growth to clear their way through. The woman said this was not necessary, that they could move around such tangles, but neither man wished to detour. They had never done so before and would not now. They barged straight ahead clearing a passage where none had ever before existed. It gave them a sense of control.

Occasionally, the woman would lead them to rises in the swamp, surprising places where the vegetation changed and there was dry land. They would rest in these places, eat a little, and question the woman.

"How far now?" Juan Ponce demanded.

"A little more. Deeper in. I told you it would not be easy."

"We've been wading for hours!"

"You can turn back."

"You know better than that. Let's push on."

"Rest a while."

"We'll rest when we find it! Move on!"

The serpent struck without warning. Sotomayor slashed at a clump of ferns and then screamed. When she heard it, the woman froze. Juan Ponce caught sight of the monster slithering into the water: long, black, quick and then gone.

He turned to his companion. The big man's face had turned pale with shock. He held up his wrist. There were puncture marks, red, bruising; a trickle of blood.

"Get him to a rise," Juan Ponce said to the woman. "Quickly. Where it's dry."

It took a long time. Sotomayor was silent, lost in himself. He seemed to want no assistance, shaking off Juan Ponce's helping arm, slogging in front of him, following the woman. They came finally to a hammock. It seemed strange to Juan Ponce that this rise had taken so long to reach when the others had all seemed closer together. He suspected the woman had done this on purpose. But before he could challenge her, Sotomayor slipped as he tried to climb onto the bank. He was sweating and nauseous. His hand had swollen and Juan Ponce peeled back his shirtsleeve to see the same of the arm.

"It throbs," Sotomayor said. "I tried to suck the poison out as we walked."

"Lie down. I'll cut it and try again."

"There are leaves that will draw the poison out," the woman said. "I can make a poultice."

"Do it!"

"I must find the leaves."

"Then hurry. It's working into him."

Using his *morion* as a pillow, Sotomayor lay on his back looking up into the eternity of the trees. He was trembling now and his eyes were glassy. He complained of the cold and Juan Ponce hoped it was just his wet clothing. He tried to remove his friend's armour but the man was a giant and weighed even more in the steel which encased him. It was useless. Each time he would move him the pain would cause Sotomayor to cry out. Finally, the old man gave up. He kneeled beside his friend and, as the fever took hold, bathed his face with a dampened rag.

"I had hoped not to die like this, Don Juan," Sotomayor said softly. "It is an ignoble way to die."

"You will not die," Juan Ponce whispered. "The woman has gone to find makings for a poultice."

"The poison is already in me. As we walked I could feel it travel. Try to bury me, Don Juan. I don't want to be food for swamp creatures."

"The woman will be back soon," the old man responded. It was all he could say. Suddenly Sotomayor grasped his arm. His face was beaded in sweat and his eyes gazed out from his face in panic.

"Do you think this magical fountain has properties to restore me? Perhaps that is what the woman is doing. She said it was close now."

"It's possible," Juan Ponce said, comforting his friend, and felt the same hope rising.

"I can see her," Sotomayor's eyes widened.

"Where?"

"Over there."

Juan Ponce looked. There was nothing.

"She isn't back yet."

"I saw her! I saw her face with the faces of devils! She is a witch, Don Juan!"

"There are no devils," he said, trying to ease Sotomayor's delirium.

"Find the fountain, Don Juan. Heal me. Convince her to heal me." His voice was hoarse, yet childlike in its plea.

"Remember when we met?" Juan Ponce tried to offer distraction. "You were a boy then, do you recall? But even then you were a big fellow and I watched you in wrestling matches. You never lost. And I thought to myself this is a young man with potential, a man I would like to second me. And you have, Cristoval, more than you know. I've loved you like a son, like the son I wish I had had. And you've stayed more loyal to me than my own family. You and I have shared more together than ..."

"We were wrong." The feverish face gazed up at him, sheeted in sweat.

"What do you mean?"

"I've killed too many men. God has sent me a serpent as punishment."

"You're a soldier. God has nothing to do with it. They were savages."

"Don't you see? Don't you see? If they paint their faces, if they are not Christian, still, they are men. Las Casas was right. We were wrong." He turned his face away and stared vacantly up to the treetops, trying to peer through them to the sky beyond. Then he murmured softly: "I love you, Don Juan. I've followed you here to the end of the earth."

He lapsed into unconsciousness, his breathing becoming shallow and sharp. He fought for breath to the end, as he had always fought. But the end came. And with a long, rattling sigh the last of his breath flowed out of his body and the soldier, armoured and girded with weapons, found peace.

Juan Ponce de Leon watched him pass and when he was dead, the old man on his knees raised his head and howled like an animal, the sound of his anguish echoing into the pillars of trees and across the black waters and was lost finally in ferns that trembled with his clamour. And then he stood peering into the timeless swamp and, realizing he was alone, began to feel fear. He called out for the woman.

"Emilia!" he wailed, time and again, loud and long,

"Emilia!" using her Christian name, her slave name given her by Leonor. She had never told him her true name. He had asked and she had muttered something unpronounceable but truly, she had never told him. He knew then that she had deserted him. She had found her opening and got away. He cursed his stupidity. He had suspected somehow she would do this and yet in an instant of distraction, in the panic of wanting to help his friend, he had forgotten her cunning. "Emilia!" he cried desperately but his only answer was the echo of his voice through the forest, then silence.

"I know you are there!" he shouted. "Sotomayor has seen you!"

"I am here," she said at last, and her voice was as dark as the water around him. Black water. And her black eyes.

"Where?" He looked around, her voice had echoed. He could not find its source.

"Here, Spaniard, where you cannot touch me."

He found her. Her face was striped now with green stripes. She appeared from behind a thickness of trees, standing in a canoe flanked by devils; hard-muscled warriors with paint daubed faces, green and brown like hers. He knew he had found his hell.

"Who are they?" He croaked out the words.

"Calusa, as am I. They have been watching since we came ashore."

"I didn't see them."

"They did not wish to be seen."

"Why do they appear now?"

"To bring me back to where I belong. I am a daughter of Calos. Long ago he sent me to you, not as a sacrifice nor as a hostage, but to learn of you and your foolish people who think they can own the earth."

"Sotomayor said you were a witch!"

"He is dead now?"

"Yes."

"I am glad. I only wish I had been the serpent, to kill him myself."

"And all this ... all this time with me, you plotted to return here?"

"Had it not been you I would have found another way."

"You used me!"

"As you have used others."

"And the fountain? The sacred water?"

"You still dream of that, old man? It is all around you. Look for a moment and finally see. Here, in this place, there is never death. Here things fall and pass through water and become of the water and after a time spring up again into life. Even your Sotomayor will live again in another form. Death, as you see it, is the end of something. Yet there is no ending. There is, instead, transformation."

"If I drink this water?"

"It will become part of you and all it contains will live in you."

"You lied to me!"

"You lied to yourself. You were always a simple man."

Her words pierced him like a spear. He sank to his knees in exhaustion, his vision annihilated. He felt himself vacant, bereft of feeling, of hope. And he cried. His sobs wracked his body, wrenched at his brain as he gave way to despair. And as he cried he heard laughter and looking up saw all around him, peering out through the ferns and wild creepers as though they were part of them, faces, painted faces, surrounding him: laughing, cackling, mocking in the gibberish of their language. Each way he turned he would glimpse them appearing then reappearing in some other place. He could not escape them; as if they were a dream and he could not awaken. Finally he stood. What remained of his manhood he gathered around him and, quivering, spoke again to the woman.

"I have a right to be here!"

"Because of your foolish patents? Because of the parchments you scratch on? You think you own this land? No one owns land."

"But you call this Calos' land."

"Calos is a god."

"And now you will kill me."

"We could kill you," she said, "but your head is not fit for a warrior's trophy. It was the beast Sotomayor I wanted dead. And he is. You will return to your men by the river. We have left them and that stinking priest alone. You will go back to your camp on the shore and you will destroy it and leave. This is not your land. No one owns land. Your patents are titles for fools."

"But this swamp, it's a maze. How can I find a way out?"

"The way you came. You've defiled the forest enough to follow the same path you used to come in, just as you defile everything you touch."

"Including you, whore."

"It is a shame I must bear. Calos will forgive me. Now goodbye, old man. Take your desperate dreams elsewhere."

They melted away into the swamp. He could not follow their going. All around him was green desolation. And he was alone. He attempted to bury his friend. He dug into the earth with Sotomayor's sword, but the earth was a tangle of roots. He slashed at them as he would enemies. They would not give. Eventually the blade snapped, its Toledo steel no

match for the forest. In his rage he threw the hilt as far as
he could. He heard it clip through branches but did not hear
it land. In the end he was forced to leave Sotomayor where
he lay; his coffin his armour. And as Juan Ponce de Leon
waded into the water he looked back to see the passing sun
break through the trees and glint off of Sotomayor's steel.

And he thought of the life he had wasted.

32

... beautiful, beautiful magnificent desolation ...
—**ALDRIN**

Summer—*The Present*

It is five in the morning when he pounds on her door. It takes a few moments for her to answer. She is half asleep when she lets him in, slightly annoyed with his intrusion. He senses her displeasure yet needs her help one last time before she decides she will leave him completely.

"What's wrong?" she mutters. It has a sharp edge.

"Where haven't we been?" he says quietly, trying not to anger her further.

"Huh?"

"We've been all over the countryside, but there must be somewhere you haven't remembered."

"What time is it?" She moves to the couch, lies down, pulls a cushion over her head. He removes it softly.

"Just for a minute, indulge me, please. Last night I was thinking..."

"I thought we'd decided to stop. I'm tired. I've got that appointment today."

"I know, but just think. Where is a place where no one would go? Somewhere that no one at all would visit."

"There's no place like that," she says flatly, "except way into the Everglades."

"Too far south. Are you sure there's nothing like that around here?"

"Cypress swamps. But we can't go in. They're environmentally sensitive. Protected. I think there's one down near Naples: Corkscrew Swamp, where there's a boardwalk."

"Cypress swamp, but not one with a boardwalk; are there any others?"

"Sure. You've seen some on the map. Near here, but I told you we can't go there. And they're not safe. Park rangers might arrange a tour but that will take time to set up. I doubt they'd allow it anyway, Ross. They're dangerous places."

"Just try for me."

"I'll do it later today. Now please, let me go back to bed."

"We'll need hip waders."

"Huh?"

"These swamps, they're water, aren't they? And trees? I'll go back to the hotel to pack."

"Pack?"

"Waders."

"Ross, I've got that meeting with the outfitters in Bonita Springs. I can't miss it. Let's go tomorrow."

"I have a feeling, Ange."

"That hasn't worked so far," she says gruffly.

"This is different. I'll be back in an hour."

"We can't go in there!" she insists, but he is gone. "Crazy old man," she mutters.

But Ross doesn't feel at all crazy. He'd had a dream during the night. For the first time in a long time, it was not the dreaded nightmare but something beautiful and so very clear from his past, something which, even recalling it now, has given him the sense he will surely succeed. The dream was about his son.

∞

Little Robbie lies in his bed, his eyes wide and fearful for this night is very important to him. This night his father will turn off the nightlight. My hand goes to the switch.

"No daddy!" he cries.

"It's alright, son. We'll be right next door."

"Dark! No dark!"

He is sobbing. Emily goes to him. She embraces him and he holds her, desperately looking over her shoulder at me. I am the villain. I am the one at the light switch.

"What's really wrong, Robbie?" Emily says. She pats his back then massages it, her hands moving in circles.

"Monsters, mommy! Monsters!"

"There aren't any monsters," I say. But he won't listen to me.

"You lie down." Emily soothes him into whimpers. "I'll stay with you and daddy will turn off the light."

"No!"

"For heaven's sake," I mutter impatiently.

"Robbie," Emily whispers, "close your eyes."

"Don't want to."

"It's okay. I'm here. Now just close your eyes."

"'Kay."

She waits a moment, holding him, her arms warm and comforting, embracing him.

"What do you see?"

"Nothing."

"But what's it like?"

"Dark."

"That's right. It's dark. And no monsters, are there?"

"Nope." He opens his eyes. He is smiling.

"So when you close your eyes it's dark and there aren't any monsters. It's just like closing your eyes. Now you close your eyes again and we'll play a game."

"'Kay."

When his eyes are closed she places her palm over them.

"What you doing, mommy?"

"I'm playing a game. Now keep your eyes closed."

"'Kay."

She signals me to turn out the light. She leaves her hand over his eyes. I glimpse their silhouettes in the moonlight seeping through the window. Slowly she takes her hand away.

"Eyes still closed?"

"Yup."

He has an angelic voice.

"That's good. I'm right here beside you. I'll stay as long as you want."

"'Kay."

She sits quietly for a minute or two.

"Mommy?"

"What is it?"

"I got my eyes open," he says, giggling.

"And?"

"Dark."

"But no monsters?"

"No monsters, mommy."

She stays with him until he falls asleep. She does this each night for a couple of weeks. One night she is out playing bridge. Robbie is in bed. I come in to say goodnight. The phone rings. I leave to answer. As I reach the door he calls to me.

"Daddy?"

"I've got to get the phone."

"You forgot to turn off the light."

There are no monsters in the dark. There is only the dark and what you make of it. There are only the monsters you make.

∞

Angela complains about missing her meeting. He tells her they will have plenty of time. It is still early morning. They have followed the map toward a bald cypress swamp, unnamed, mostly blank space on the chart. He drives purposefully. Something is happening. He can feel it. He slows the car and studies the roadside. Even before he sees it he feels it.

"I don't believe it," he murmurs.

"What?" Angela mutters.

He stops the car. It is there: a half-overgrown lane with trees on each side, curling in, reaching in, to make a tunnel of branches and leaves. It is more than familiar.

"What are you doing?" Angela exclaims as he turns the car into the lane. "That's all swamp in there."

"That's where this leads?"

"Funny. This lane isn't marked on the map. That's peculiar ..."

"This is it, Emily. This is it."

"What? What did you say?"

"I know this is it."

The trees are mammoth, smothered in moss hanging over the lane like old, bearded sentinels. Their bark is grey and cracked. Their branches reach down to scrape the car. Angela is silent now, overcome by the strangeness, and Ross must concentrate on driving for the lane is rutted and narrow and he glimpses dark water on either side. And even before they come to its end he knows the end will be there. The trees tangle together. They form an apparently unbroken wall, but he knows that is not the case. He gets out of the car and steps into the heavy, shade-dappled heat. The ground is soft and giving. He searches the snarl of trees for an opening. Barely perceptible, it is there.

"Don't go in there, Ross," Angela tells him.

"I have to."

"I told you it's protected. You can't trespass."

"This is the place. I know it!"

"Ross, please. Don't go in there. You'll be alone."

"Why don't you drive to your meeting? Pick me up later."

"It isn't safe. I can't just leave you."

"I started this on my own; I'll be okay."

"You're sure?" Her priority has hold of her.

This is where we part.

"I'm sure."

"I'll be back by four. Just be careful," she says. "Do you have your compass?"

He is not listening. He is moving in the midst of his dream.

It is not the same, exactly. It is not forbidding. But it is a tunnel, a mossy pathway covered in verdure. For a minute or two he explores down its trail then realizes he is not prepared. He looks down at his shoes, hiking boots, not wing tips. That was the monster. He decides to go back for the hip waders.

"Emily!" he calls back down the passage.

The response is the car ignition. He hears its engine race, then recede. She is leaving. She has her appointment.

Perhaps she intends to report him. He has no choice now.
As though he had ever had. He turns down the path again,
moving cautiously, waiting for faces, for laughter. They do
not come. More monsters. Instead, a snake slithers across
the trail. It is long and black and in no hurry. He waits for
it to slide through the bushes and down into the brackish
water. The passage is green and shadowy umber and the
further he travels the warmer it gets. And then his path, his
dream path, his vision, surprises him.

It ends.

It opens into a grassy meadow with pines and clumps
of saw grass, sedge and spartina. Ross hears chirps from
songbirds. He glimpses a blackbird flitting low through
palmetto clumps. A red shouldered hawk wafts aggressive-
ly in the air far above him. Then a sudden breeze through
the pines sounds like sea waves as the pines rustle in the
wind. The ground beneath him is soft and springy, grey
sandy loam covered in grass. There is no obvious track but
he continues straight on, guessing the way. The ground
slowly changes to become a wet prairie. At his feet are wild-
flower swatches, chicory mostly, their little blue flowers
dotting the turf. A grey heron on its stilt legs meanders
through a wet meadow.

He arrives at the edge of the cypress. It is starkly de-
lineated. First bare, white trees standing in water and behind them the darker shade of the swamp canopied from
the sun by the trees which tower beyond. He wades in. He
is not at all afraid. He moves through dwarf cypress and
sifting green ferns which look, but are not, impenetrable.
Butterflies, golden and red and black, flutter playfully. The
wading is hard. He must push his way through the under-
growth and air plants to clear a passage. The cypress trunks

are the only things solid enough for handholds. And he must watch the roots, the cypress roots with their knees sticking up just above the water. There are more below, he can feel them rough on his boots. He might wedge a foot and get stuck.

He is wet to the waist now. In here beneath the trees there is little sun. The water is surprisingly cool. It is not what he would have expected. Black, yes, but it is not stagnant. There must be a current which keeps it fresh. He attempts to discern that mysterious current but is defeated by the stillness. After a while he chooses a direction and moves on.

Often he comes across subtle rises. He shares the high ground with raccoons and squirrels who have made their homes here on the dry. These are the places he rests a while. He is never alone. Frogs croak and tiny salamanders scamper from branch to branch. They comfort him. He knows there are far more dangerous denizens but tries not to think of them. Instead he concentrates on his slogging walk, sinking sometimes frighteningly in the muck, but mostly able to pick his way from root to root as they interlace below the surface. Around him bloom delicate orchids. Rope-like strangler figs curl up the trunks of the trees and the trees are becoming much larger now, thick and high and festooned with moss.

The water is deeper, nearly to his chest. Here the cypress are huge, ancient trees a hundred feet high surrounded by dark water choked with ferns. It feels like a temple of the primordial, its silence punctuated by the distant hollow drum of a woodpecker echoing through the pillars of trees. A white heron perches on a log. Priest of the temple.

What did I say to her? Called her Emily? What in God's

*name am I doing? I will die here in this deranged search!
How could I have let it come to this? I'll go back. Maybe it
isn't too late. She'll surely return to pick me up. If I am still in
here when it gets dark, I am lost. I will turn and turn and
never come out. Ten thirty in the morning. Okay. Settle down,
Ross. You came in. You can leave by the same way. As long as
there's sun you can follow it, and you have your compass.*

He comes into more shallow water, rising to another
hammock. The water is almost clear in this patch of sunlight. It sparkles around him. He glances down to be sure
of his footing.

*What's this? Something in the water? Looks like ... not
possible. What is this? It's stuck. No, it's coming.*

He holds it aloft for the sun to catch.

A rusted, broken off bit of blade.

A sword hilt. Silver inlay, tarnished black in a greened
bronze basket hilt.

He has been here.

33

As for man, his days are as grass;
as a flower in the field, so he flourisheth.
For the wind passeth over it, and it is gone;
and the place thereof shall know it no more.
—**Psalms 103: 15-16**

Spring— The Past

Twilight was setting in as he reached the edge of the swamp. He had found his way back, just as the witch had told him, because of his own destruction. The slashes and breaks in the vegetation had guided him. Once or twice he had lost his way. He found himself turning and slogging in circles with no sunlight to guide him so deep in under the canopy. He could not trust the light as it refracted off water or rebounded off trees. The shafts of light and depths of shadows did indeed create a strange maze. Somehow, however, he had eventually regained his way. He worried a while over the Calusa, whether their spears would wing out of the foliage at him. There were none. She had not followed him, though he was sure some of those painted devils were lurking, following him to report to her his demise, or deliverance.

He waded through the shallower water, his clothing soaked through, his chainmail vest heavy, his *morion* feeling

heavier still. He would not remove them, nor the sword by
his side. They were as much a part of him as the shells of
the tortoises he observed perched on logs as he passed.
They would plop into the water, alarmed at the huge monster labouring by them. He moved slowly and carefully, as
they did, afraid his foot would be caught in a root, or that
he would sink in some concealed hole. As he struggled on
he began to think himself little more than one of those
swamp turtles, slow and armoured and toothless, making
his way through the dingy half dark. He felt like a foolish,
purposeless beast.

 His thoughts strayed in bizarre directions. He reflected
upon his life, perhaps to feel less an animal and more a man,
but his thoughts were not ordered or logical. They were
wisps of remembrance. He recalled himself in the midst of
battles, the rage and pain and fear simultaneous. His years
of experience, and more than a little luck, had bestowed his
survival in war. In the press of clashing steel and muscled
horses, amid stabbing pikes and slashing swords, beneath
the explosions of guns with their powder-clouds thickening the dust and blindness of battle, in the spatter of blood
and the howls of the wounded, he belonged. Within all that
confusion he had ever been alert and commanding. So why
not in his life?

 He knew war far better than he knew his own life. He
comprehended the choreography of battle more surely than
he did the actions of living. He understood tactics more
than tact. He had always been the boy in the corner while
courtiers played so adeptly around him. Even much later,
even as a man with a reputation, against Diego Colon and
Bartolome de las Casas, he'd been defenceless.

 He had remained the distant father to his estranged

daughters and deceitful son. Why was his son so successful when the boy had appeared to do nothing of note? Why had his son come to hate him? He thought briefly of his own father and his differentiation from the man as he made his own way, a way as inevitable as his character. Was life simply cycles: his father, himself, his son?

Why was it, thinking of Leonor, then Emilia, why was it he could not dominate them as he did men in war? For they had both made war upon him. What forces had fashioned them to become so sly and evasive, even as they'd pretended to love him? How could they have been taught such cunning when he, destined for command and governance, never was? Why had he never understood them as he had his comrades, his soldiers, or even his animals? Leonor had twisted him with her ploys. Emilia had bewitched him with her plots. Together, they had defeated him.

Once a famed *conquistador*, then a veteran explorer, then rising in rank to governor, he'd been reduced to believing in myths, in magical waters, and new beginnings. They had done that. Or had he done it himself?

Had it all been the fantasies of an old man; of a man so desperate not to become powerless yet in the very act of trying to prevent it, becoming precisely what he had feared? He wondered who would remember him for the things he had done in the trivial length of his life.

And yet there had been good, wonderful things: Columbus and his New World, Sotomayor's loyalty, Becerillo's unconditional affection, Medel's fearless love of the sea, Nunez de Guzman's kindness and care, Ovando's nobility, Balboa's friendship. Every instance was cause to rejoice were it not for the other side to his life. Emilia, Leonor, his children, Diego Colon, las Casas, even the bureaucrats who had come to replace the true pioneers. Nothing was new, only experience, but experience was simply the loss of innocence.

There was no magical fountain.

There were only the dreams of an ageing man, feeling the aches of his plod through the swamp. This was his reality, he realized: an old man past his prime, in is dotage, not at all what he'd dreamed of becoming.

"I am too young to be old!" he muttered, for despite the physical aches and emotional pains, he still felt vitality in his soul. Old age had come upon him so stealthily. He had been too vain to accept it thinking, somehow, that he was the exception. Until now. It was all almost too much to bear ... not so much his mortality as his ageing and knowing he would be forgotten.

At the edge of the cypress he paused for a rest. He sat on a mossy tree trunk. Surrounding him was the grey mist of dusk. He ached for himself.

∞

When he saw the panther, it was by accident. It had not been there and then, suddenly, it was. At first he was shocked at the sight of a lion in this accursed place but then he recalled the dragons of the river, the herbaceous faces of the Calusa, the witch standing in a canoe on the water, and knew he must expect anything here. He cursed himself for having been careless. The panther had been hunting him and he, in his self-immersion, had missed it.

It was tawny and sleek and its baleful eyes reflected the dusk in pools of lethal light. It was motionless: not a muscle moving, not a blink of an eye. It crouched on a large, downed tree, the tree angling up, caught in other trees' branches. The panther looked down upon him like death, patiently waiting. For what was he to it but another swamp creature: slow and slogging and stupid?

As he struggled up the big cat pounced. It seemed an impossible distance and yet the panther seemed to fly. Then it was on him, knocking him backward with the power of its weight, claws catching on chainmail, screeching on the steel of his helmet. Its breath was hot and hungry. With a gauntleted hand he punched at it desperately before it could bite into his face. He grasped its muscled neck and tried to keep its teeth away. He rolled with it and as quickly as it had attacked, it leapt away from him. But it did not leave. It glowered and circled and snarled, its movements fluid though, for the moment, tentative. The panther did not understand this big tortoise proving so difficult to kill.

It tensed again, its tail twitching as it readied itself. Juan Ponce, in the few seconds provided him, drew his blade. The cat came at him again so fast he could not find the time nor space to thrust. It clawed again at his mail and bit into his thigh. Its teeth punctured his skin drawing gouts of blood. The blood seemed to drive the cat mad. It had found a vulnerability in this huge armoured tortoise and would tear him apart.

He was able to swing his arm free, shift his grasp as he held his sword like a huge knife, then thrust the blade into the panther's flank. It screamed, a yowling howl of pain, yet it would not release him. He stabbed again. Toledo steel into its heart. For an instant it looked at him. Confused and dying, it did not understand this beast which struck back. It tried to escape the deadly skewer. Blood gushed from its mouth. It convulsed, then collapsed, upon him. The twilight of its eyes went dark.

He shoved it off, wrenching the sword from its tawny body. He rolled away from it, shaking with the adrenalin rush. It took him a moment to settle himself; enough to examine his thigh. Blood surged from wounds made by the panther's incisors. He rose and hobbled to the swampy water. Removing his scarf he dipped it into the water, then brought it to his leg to clean the wounds. He spent several minutes at this, pulling bits of cloth from the gashes, then tying his scarf tightly around his thigh to staunch the bleeding.

Once finished he rose, testing his leg. It hurt like the devil. Still, of anything in his life, he was accustomed to physical pain and these wounds had awakened him. He looked once more at the panther. It was not Death Incarnate. It lay in the dirt, a mere animal now.

He looked up at the sky. With the coming dark he glimpsed the first of the stars. He was an explorer. With his experience he would navigate out of this mire and back to the river. He recalled the direction he, Sotomayor and the witch had come. He waited a while longer until he discovered the pole star. He was no longer helpless. He had killed a panther. He was no toothless swamp creature. He was a man.

Magic water or none, he had come here to conquer and colonize. He possessed the patents and, despite what the witch had said, he would own this land. He would vanquish it and govern it and grow rich from it. He was finished with brooding. He was finished with doubt. He was Juan Ponce de Leon and it was time, once again, to prove it.

With his sword he hacked a stout branch from a tree. He sheathed the sword and, using the branch as a crutch, made his way over the uneven terrain by the light of the stars, back toward the river. He did not look back at the panther. Careful to focus upon his surroundings so as not to be prey to some other beast, he thought only of what was to come.

∞

"Sotomayor is dead. The witch is gone. And every Calusa we find we will slaughter."

Las Casas heard the words as Juan Ponce de Leon stared at him with iron eyes. The captain-general had been wounded somehow. He'd staggered into the camp, limping, a branch helping him along. Yet he did not seem to feel any pain, thought las Casas. Indeed, there was something else in his mind. Something terrible.

"We will hunt them down like the animals they are. We will scourge this land, *our* land, of every one of them."

"But the Church has said ..." Las Casas tried to interrupt.

"The Church has no business in this."

"In the name of ..."

"You fool. You think Columbus risked all for your Church? You think it was on Cortez' mind while he slaughtered? You believe it the reason for any of this at all? Your Church is a parasite, las Casas! Were it not on the side of the mighty, it would be nothing!"

"And yet once," the friar said, "it was not. Indeed it was the opposite: a small band against an empire even greater than ours."

"Stop your infernal arguments, friar! That was then! Now, rather than mercy, it employs Inquisition! That is your Catholic Church. It has changed from lamb to lion!"

The blasphemy astounded las Casas. He thought the old man had gone mad.

"What happened to you out there?" he said softly, afraid of the *conquistador's* rage.

"Humiliation."

"What do you mean?"

"We are leaving."

"What of Sotomayor? Where is the woman?"

"Dead! Gone! It was a trap!"

"You must rest, Don Juan, you are wounded."

"You understand so little. The witch set a snare for me so complex I failed to foresee it. The Calusa will do the same if those colonists on the coast are not ready. We are leaving! Now! If we do not, everyone will be massacred!"

34

Our remedies oft in ourselves do lie,
Which we ascribe to heaven.

—SHAKESPEARE

Summer — *The Present*

Ross Porter has reached the nucleus.

It is a cathedral, this place, its immense black bark pilasters buttressing an emerald leafy dome; all down from that high ceiling run adornments of climbing vines and dusky flags of Spanish moss. Its windows are openings in the leaves where the sun dazzles through to light ensconced flowers. Its stations are rising hammocks set apart from the flat of the liquid floor. And it contains secretive places too, confessionals set in the darkest grottoes and below its vegetal base and black water, the crypts which contain the remains of its tenants.

Its choir consists of a flock of storks nesting high in the tops of the trees. From their lofty stalls they drone chants echoing through the temple. Accompanying them is the organ sound of croaking frogs, their vocal chords sounding like old, dry pipes opened by comical fingers playing on stiffened keys.

The pilgrim enters the nave, a huge grassy marsh in the swamp's very centre. The sky opens out above him a cyanic blue and the rushes whisper in the breeze of the open place. Dragonflies dart about him on iridescent wings. He clutches his votive offering in his left hand, a rusty relic from another time, and his right arm pushes the rushes aside as he moves to the centre of the expanse. He can see, not far off, an oasis of trees, the altar on which he must place himself, knowing it is the heart of this feral temple. He slogs toward it. He is parched. He is dirty and tired as all pilgrims are when they reach the climax of their wanderings but his faith is immaculate. He knows without doubt he has reached the source.

The laughter of running water.

At his feet now is a burbling diaphanous spring, a fountain a few inches high in the midst of grey limestone. Ferns and flowers mark its circumference. The rippling pool is clear and unclouded but the depth from which the fountain gushes he has no way of telling, for the fountain itself conceals its well in the sparkle and dance of its effluence. In the water the rocks are gilded with a pearl shimmer. A rainbow of coloured crystalline pebbles lines the sides of the pool. They appear like jewels from the greater depths thrown up by the force of the water. The pilgrim kneels beside the pool to look deeper into its mysteries.

He wonders what properties it might contain. This close the water's aroma is acrid. At first this disturbs him but he soon discerns it must constitute elements which come from the core of the earth. He inhales the pungent, subterranean fragrance. He has come here to drink of this secret water. Preparing to drink, he kneels and cups his right hand. But before he does he takes time to relish the moment of sweet culmination. Then he looks at the surface, at the point where he intends to plunge his hand and sees something which freezes that hand in the air.

He sees life in the pool.

On the skin of the water are insects: tiny, ephemeral water striders skimming almost aimlessly. But the pool itself is not smooth for them. It undulates with the waves from the surging spring. He examines the creatures closely. Their travel is not so simple: moments of brief flight where they might catch glimpses of the whole pool, and then other moments of little submersions, minuscule half-drownings. Then they struggle again to the surface, and on the surface sharp little pushes against the ripples propel them a mere few inches. These are the smallest of creatures.

He catches sight of his own reflection: imperfect, it floats on the surface distorted by the wavelets. He peers down at the grey of his temples, at the lines in the wavering face and the eyes which stare back at themselves, refracted by memories of the life behind them. He looks at the familiar face of a stranger.

In the scheme of things is he any more than these transient sprites? He has had their flights of comprehension as he raised himself fleetingly above the travel and beheld the far, far distance. And he has suffered the awful submersions, the harsh baptisms below the ripples, glimpsing the depths. But mostly he has just pushed along on the surface, moving here and there almost thoughtlessly, sometimes with purpose, sometimes without. The water sprites live fleeting lives. He does not know how long but suspects it is merely weeks. And in that time they are born, procreate and die. The ripples move them. They move with the ripples.

∞

*I am in the birth room when my son enters the world. He has
no name; he has nothing human. He is wet and bloody before
they clean him and cut his umbilical. He surfaces for the first
time. He already knows how to breathe.*

I was like that once: at the source.

I see now what I have become.

Emily is taken from me so I begin to lie to myself.

Then I take myself away from Robert. I make my boy cry.

Oh, how I wish I could cast off my armour.

I obsess in a search for the ephemeral.

Sometimes I think I have gone too deep.

The sprites swim away from the fountain. It is far too
tumultuous there. They travel out to the edge where the
water is calmer. They lose the source as they find the shore.

Is that what death is? A shore?

Yet the water escapes through gaps in the rocks and is
lost beneath the ferns. The water transforms, touched by
what it touches; still water but changed, not the same as its
source. It feeds the marsh rushes and circulates through
them to make the swamp and then flows in a soft indeter-
minate current to streams and rivers running to the sea. It
evaporates then into the vastness of sky. It becomes rain-
clouds and that rain falls and touches the ground and per-
colates down once again into the earth.

And begins again.

Cycles.

We all know the truth.

It is not profound.

At the source.

At the edge of forever.

∞

Ross Porter looks up from the water. He rises and shifts his gaze to the sky. There is daylight enough to leave safely. He knows he will find his way back. In his hand he still holds the rusted sword hilt. He studies it quizzically, turning it this way and that, the way an archaeologist would. He smiles at it: a collaborative smile. He will not keep it.

It is not his to keep.

He tosses it into the pool. The water sprites dance with the splash. It sinks: turning and turning and for one brief instant seems to gleam in its former glory. It comes to rest on a bed of pebbles. The water is a good home.

Though he is thirsty, Ross Porter rises from the edge of the pool.

He does not need to drink.

Instead, he turns and walks back to the rest of his life.

Smiling.

35

Oh as I was young and easy in the mercy of his means,
Time held me green and dying
Though I sang in my chains like the sea.
—THOMAS

Summer — The Past

I write this now as I weaken. The poison works through me, making my limbs grow cold. I lie on this bed in the bowels of my ship. Sotil commands now. He knows I am dying. He is trying to make for the nearest port. I will not reach my home. I will not see San Juan de Puerto Rico again. My friend Sotomayor has died from a serpent. He called it justice. My own serpent was a different style: it was long and straight and barbed at the end and sailed through the air like destiny to embed itself in my thigh. Poisoned spear. Precisely where the lion had wounded me. Oh, these Calusa are cruel.

I will try to tell what happened. Yet my mind wanders. I cannot govern it. My hands do not function as I wish. I write slowly and bitterly lying upon this narrow bed. I write to those who come after me now, as a warning, and as a confession.

We arrived at the beach in the morning. We had travelled down river all night, my men fearful of me. I could feel their dread. I believe they thought me a phantom, a wraith returned from the dank catacombs through which I had journeyed. Even then I was the walking dead; my mind filled with murder.

The fortifications were incomplete. I summoned Alvarez and Sotil. They seemed surprised at my abruptness and said the natives had been friendly. When they had appeared they bore gifts. They had traded. The next day they came again with food. After a welcoming feast they departed.

The construction of the defences was halted. The guard was stood down.

Thus, when the Calusa warriors came we were not prepared. A caravel fired one of its guns. The shock boomed over the water. A sailor hailed us from his lookout atop a mainmast. He pointed wildly to the east. Across the bay a hundred canoes were racing toward us filled with painted devils.

On the island they poured out of the trees in shrieking waves spreading carnage among us. They began to encircle us. Then Alvarez led a charge of nine horses along their lines. His men swept down at the savages slashing with swords and axes, scything heads as they galloped, driving them back momentarily. He died for his effort, his horse pulled from under him. And as he went down, disappearing amid a ring of Calusa, all I could see was their weapons rising and falling as they reduced Alvarez to pulp. But his action had given us time to regroup. Sotil ordered more cannon fire from the ships. Boats began to evacuate men from the beach. The wounded went first.

I went first.

My disgrace was complete, consummate, with the sting of that viper spear. No, that is not right. In this journal I swore to tell the truth. The spear felled me, true enough, but I was already mortally wounded. They carried me through the surf to a boat. They thought they carried their captain-general: Don Juan Hernando Ponce de Leon the famed conquistador, explorer, governor, legend. Instead, their freight was a wounded old man.

Even now I do not know how many died. I was carried here where I lay now, an invalid on board a ship I once commanded. Las Casas administered to me. When he wrenched out the barb it was black with poison. He crossed himself and left the cabin. Las Casas can be a gentle man. Perhaps I was wrong about him.

The ship's boy is now my physician. He is frightened of me, of my death as it hangs in the air about me, and so does not speak. He is young. He has dreams and aspirations. He watches death as it comes, quizzically, for he feels himself somehow removed from it. How could it be otherwise? He has his future before him. The end of a life must seem unreal to him: the fading away, the awful ebb. Though he watches over me as he has been ordered, though he cares for me gently and still is a little in awe of me, I can tell he sees past me, beyond; into the passionate distance.

As I did once.

I must sleep. The fever has grown. My mind wanders.

∞

I have slept, the boy tells me, a very long time. He says I spoke in my sleep. The fever delirium gave me a dream. Yet now, awake, I recall it quite clearly. I was in a soft grove in the heart of a marsh. I was kneeling beside a pool of water. In its midst a fountain bubbled. As I peered down into the water I saw myself reflected there. And in that moment of self, looking back at self, I saw what I had become.

I saw the face of a stranger.

I have tried in these pages to bring some sense, some glimmer of meaning, to the life I have lived. I thought I commanded life.

One might as well command water.

As it seeps through one's fingers.

I will ask the boy for some water to drink.

And then I will sleep again.

I am so tired.

∞

The cabin was dim. Two men peered down at the form on the bed.

"How long has he been like this?" las Casas murmured.

"The boy says all night and all today. He cannot wake him. He's dying."

"I know. He didn't ask me to hear his confession."

"He wasn't that kind of man."

"It's best to be rid of such as him."

For a moment the pilot said nothing. He reached out and with his forefinger touched the hand of Juan Ponce de Leon.

"He was courageous. I'm glad I knew him."

"You admire him?"

"Look at what he's accomplished!"

"Look elsewhere for heroes, Sotil."

"I have his journal."

"The ship's log you mean?"

"No, another. I read some of it. I think you are wrong about him."

"Give it to me."

"When I've finished it. There is something to learn from these pages."

"Don't be a fool! No one will read it."

"I will."

"Give it to me. I command in the name of our Holy Church! Submit, or face the consequences!"

For a moment the young man tightened his grasp on the book. His glare met the friar's eyes and he saw in them a familiar danger. He was young. He had a bright future. He held the book out. Las Casas snatched it.

"What will you do with it?"

"Burn it. Burn it now, and scatter its ashes."

∞

Alone on the after deck by the stern rail, the dun coloured silhouette of the friar was framed by the dying rays of sunset. A gentle ruby light shot with streaks of amethyst shone around him and Sotil, looking up at him, could not help but think how the priest blocked the light. Then a smaller, harsh glow appeared in his hand: a torch flickering, reflected in his face. It burned like a minuscule *auto da fe* as he ripped each page from the journal and consigned it to his holy flame. And as they burned, down to his fingers, he would drop them one by one into the sea. And the ashes floated a moment on the surface, then disappeared; dissolving into the immortal water.

Acknowledgements

Ed Carson, retired Director of the Corkscrew Bald Cypress
Swamp, Audubon Sanctuary

Michael Mirolla, an inspiration, as well as my editor

David Moratto, a designer who listens, then delivers

Mervat Haddad, technical and creative advisor

Archivo General de Indias, Seville, Spain
Archivo Fundación Luis Muñoz Marín
Archivo General de Puerto Rico
Archivo Histórico Arquidiocesano de San Juan (ARQSJ)
Columbus: The Four Voyages by Laurence Bergreen, Viking,
2011
*Spain's Men of the Sea: Daily Life on the Indies Fleets in the
Sixteenth Century* by Pablo E. Parez-Mallaina, Johns
Hopkins University Press, 2005
The Spanish Seaborne Empire by John H. Parry, University
of California Press, 1990
Randell Research Centre: Florida Museum of Natural History
Waterloo Region District School Board

Cancer Medicine by Waun Ki Hong, MD, DMSc (Hon), Robert C. Bast, Jr, MD, William N. Hait, MD, PhD, Donald W. Kufe, MD, Raphael E. Pollock, MD, PhD, Ralph R. Weichselbaum, MD, James F. Holland, MD, Emil Frei III, MD

About the Author

Once a teacher, theatre director and adjudicator, Brian Van Norman left those worlds to travel with his wife, Susan, and take up writing as a full time pursuit. He has journeyed to every continent and sailed nearly every sea on the planet. His base is Waterloo, Ontario, Canada though he is seldom found there. This is his second novel.